CRIMSON

CRIMSON

LAURA FOSTER

Copyright © 2016 by Laura Foster.

Library of Congress Control Number:		2016902197
ISBN:	Hardcover	978-1-5144-4704-8
	Softcover	978-1-5144-4703-1
	eBook	978-1-5144-4702-4

All rights reserved. No part of this book may be reproduced or transmitted in any form or by any means, electronic or mechanical, including photocopying, recording, or by any information storage and retrieval system, without permission in writing from the copyright owner.

This is a work of fiction. Names, characters, places and incidents either are the product of the author's imagination or are used fictitiously, and any resemblance to any actual persons, living or dead, events, or locales is entirely coincidental.

Print information available on the last page.

Rev. date: 03/08/2016

To order additional copies of this book, contact:
Xlibris
800-056-3182
www.Xlibrispublishing.co.uk
Orders@Xlibrispublishing.co.uk
724355

To Jordan,

Thank you for all of your support. Happy Reading!

[signature]
x

CHAPTER 1

It was the early hours of the morning. The night sky was without a single star to shine, and the wind was frighteningly bitter. A right-minded person would shelter from the frost and the unforgiving weather, and yet a young girl was walking. She couldn't shelter. Her skin was pale; her eyes closed. She'd shut them to rest a while ago, and now they refused to open. Her hands were stuffed in her pockets, her fingertips turned blue, and her blonde hair lashing against her numb skin. She took small, agonising steps; her feet raw with blisters and bruises. Her dainty eyes opened for a brief moment, only for a moment, to see she was walking into an alleyway.

In her mind, she would rest just for a moment. It wasn't safe to linger. Her senses had become dull; the terrain was getting the better of her. Her body cried for water, for warmth, for food. She had none to take. She had been running for days, putting her body through torture. Her head began to lower, and her knees buckled beneath her. She couldn't sleep; if she did, she may never wake up. There was no strength left though as she slumped forward, and her body fell to the floor. The winter air continued to bellow as the darkness closed in on her conscious. She couldn't sleep. She could hear someone calling, but her mind could no longer translate. She must not sleep. Her eyes opened. Shadows moved. The cast of a silver gleam came briefly into view from the corner of her eye. She needed to move, but the cold pressed down on her. Exhaustion got the better of her; her eyes closed and sleep she did.

She was disturbed by a nightmare—one she'd had on and off for the past few weeks. She wanted to wake up, to escape the terrors that would occur again. The atmosphere had a sinister feel to it as though an ungodly action was taking place. A long and narrow corridor stretched for miles before her eyes. The walls seemingly encroached around her, but they were made of steel that was still. She had never been here in person before; she was sure of it. Or at least she thought she was sure. But the vivid dream continued to haunt her, and each time, more detail was added.

A stench overwhelmed her, making her gag as it drifted into her nostrils. It was a strange smell similar to meat. She began to cry silently, knowing what was going to happen. It was always the same. She desperately wanted to wake up now and not face what was to occur.

Ahead of her were the shadows of people. She could hear them whimpering and whining from afar. She started running towards them. Forever and ever, her feet raced towards them. The figures sat up, some sobbing. They turned their backs to her. Their attention was set on a dangerous and demonic silhouette. Its outline was larger than any creature she had seen before. Her feet struck the ground in loud steps as she desperately tried to reach them. She knew what was going to happen and frantically wanted it to stop. The sound of machinery racketed from elsewhere. She could hear gears turning from far away. The figures moved down the corridor and towards the fiend. All of them disappeared from view except one person, who remained, staring back at the girl as she tried desperately to reach them. The sound of screaming emitted from far away, the machinery louder.

Losing her footing, she tripped over. Her head hit the cold floor with a dull thud. She lay on the ground, pain seething in her head. The sound of whirring blades and ripping echoed around the corridors as the walls seemed to get closer together. The flow of blood from somewhere far away could be heard. She lifted her head. Everyone was gone. Everyone was gone but that one girl only metres away. And as the dreamer watched, the walls behind that girl began to produce strange patterns . . . patterns that became trails . . . trails that traced their way toward the other girl, reaching for her like dark red fingers.

That girl was in danger. In terror, the dreamer pulled herself up from the floor and onto her knees. The other girl turned her back to her, staring at the dangerous being. She screamed out for her to run away from the monster, but no sound left her throat. The seeping fingers moved quicker. They peeled off from the walls, darting towards the other girl. The victim's eyes were closed tightly. The bloody fingers coiled around the body forcefully. The dreamer pulled herself from the floor and grabbed the child's hand, trying to pull her free. The fiend emerged from the darkness. Its pair of large crimson eyes, the only visible portion of its being, was staring in their direction as the red ropes tightened and pulled harder. It began to lift the girl from her feet. The dreamer was crying out loudly, gripping the victim's hand as tightly as possible. She was struggling to hold onto the damsel, but her grasp was weakening.

'Flee from him. Flee from the Crimson!' The other girl pleaded with her, opening her eyes to look upon the girl, her face distorting into one the dreamer recognised. In shock, she let her go, and the child from the dream was launched down the corridor towards the monster.

The girl had been watching herself being taken by the devil.

It hadn't been a simple nightmare. The vision had tortured her for weeks on end the many times she had slept. The voices and sounds; the colours and images; the stench and the fear within the dream were now gone. The only thing that remained on her mind was the shattered sentence. The people that were in her dream didn't have faces before. For one of them, to cry out to her was perplexing. For one of them, to be her was terrifying.

She stirred from her position after it had awoken her. Her head was too foggy, for her to open her eyes. She shifted through the grey in her mind, trying to make sense. The relentless cold that seeped into her bones made it difficult to think rationally. She knew she had to keep moving, and falling had been a bad idea. But as she tried to move her numb body, she realised there was a pressure on her shoulders.

'She's coming to', a stranger's voice came from behind her. It wasn't a voice she recognised; at least she didn't think she recognised it. Her shoulders and arms were beginning to warm; the rest of her body still felt unbelievably frozen.

'Keep an eye on her then, won't you?' Another voice spoke out. The sound of footsteps moved away from her. She realised the pressure she felt was a friction running up and down the length of her arms and shoulder, now seized.

'Wait, Ricky; don't just leave me with...'

'I'm getting her some water. Don't let her freeze!' She assumed the other voice was Ricky as she heard footsteps walking away. The pressure on her shoulders came back. Slowly, her eyes opened. It was still extremely dark, but her eyes slowly began to adjust to the faint light coming from the main street. She noticed a jacket was round her shoulders and the movement of a hand going up and down, trying to bring feeling back into her body. She glanced over her shoulder to meet a young man. His hands stopped moving; his eyes widening as he looked at her.

'Thank you,' she whispered to him. As she spoke, her throat felt dry and rough. A shy smile crept onto his face.

'Don't worry about it,' he spoke quietly; his hands resting against the jacket. 'Do you want anything to drink?' A tangle of dark brunette hair mopped over his face. His cheeks were dirty as though he hadn't washed in a good while.

'Please.' She heard her own voice come out. She felt fingers grasp her arms as her body was pulled up into a standing position. Every part of her body protested against being moved, but she couldn't stop it from happening. She slumped backwards, her back resting against a brick wall, her legs trembling as she tried to steady herself. It wasn't the boy that had lifted her but a man with a crooked smile.

'What drugs are you on kid?' He spoke coldly to her. His clothes didn't fit properly, showing off sturdy muscles and tough skin, visible even in the dark.

'Ricky, don't.' The boy protested but was cut short by a quick glare from his friend.

'You don't know anything about her, Mike,' Ricky scolded him angrily. Ricky turned back to face her, his head pressed close to hers, and their foreheads almost touching. He pulled a torch from his back pocket and held it up. A light shone brightly in her eyes as she closed them sharply. Ricky placed his fingers over her eyelids and pried them open. The bright light highlighted deep bags under her green eyes. A single black pupil shrunk as the light touched her eye.

'Well your eyes aren't blood shot,' Ricky commented as he turned the flashlight off. 'So who are you and why are you collapsed in the street?'

'Dawn Pearson', she managed to speak up a little more, 'I was travelling and—' It was hurting her to talk. Mike pressed towards her and she felt the end of a bottle touching her lips. Without hesitation, she took his hand into her own and forced the tip of the bottleneck to push against her lips, water rushing into her dry mouth and down her throat. The water had never tasted as wonderful to her as she drank it as quickly as she could, scared as if it would be taken from her in an instant.

'You're too bloody kind, Mike. You know that, right?' Ricky said as he stepped back.

'Thank you for the water,' Dawn gasped in relief when she finally let go of Mike's hand, bowing her head slightly in courtesy. She rested her hand against the wall and looked towards the opening of the alleyway. She vaguely remembered walking into this alleyway. It had been unwise to stop travelling. She had to keep moving.

'I have to go,' she mumbled, prying herself away from the wall. Before the two could respond, she removed the jacket from her shoulders, placed it in Mike's hands, and unsteadily walked out of the alleyway. As she stepped onto the path, she gazed up at the street light that illuminated the roads. It was still deathly cold; the alleyway no longer shielded her from the winter's cruel wind. She placed her hand against the streetlight, taking in a deep breath, and the cold air rushing into her lungs and biting at her insides. Footsteps approached from behind.

'It's dangerous to be out here on your own,' Mike called out, walking to her side. 'Where are you from? Your parents must be worried sick!' For a while, she stood still. Her mind was having a tantrum, demanding she ate and drank and slept until she was satisfied. She couldn't think straight. Her mind kept jumping to the demand that she keep moving. It was the only true thought she had.

'If she wants to go, let her go,' Ricky told his friend as he tried to pull Mike away. Dawn's legs were shaking as she attempted to walk. Her mind was unclear, and she still felt a pang from hunger. There was only one thing on her mind. She had to move. She couldn't stop; she must keep moving.

'You're trembling. Please let us help,' Mike insisted, resting his jacket over her again. She stared at him; her mind still numb. She was in conflict. She needed to leave. She needed help. She hadn't eaten or drank or slept properly in days.

'We'll sort you out kid,' Ricky let out a strained sigh, pushed into helping her from the insistence of his friend.

'I . . . I need to get going,' Dawn protested. Ricky approached her from the front. He bent his knees slightly, so their eyes met at equal height.

'You need energy then. We're squatting at the moment. There's food and shelter there. Get your energy back, else Mike's going to worry himself sick about you.'

'I know they say to not trust strangers, and I know Ricky is a bit rough looking, but it's only to keep ourselves safe,' Mike added.

'I know neither of you are going to hurt me,' Dawn muttered under her breath. 'I don't want to be a burden, but . . . I could really do with some food and warmth.' With that, Ricky placed his arm under hers and helped her to stand up right. The awkward trio walked along the pathway, making their journey through the night.

'So where do you live?' She asked them politely but neither replied, simply coaxing her to follow. They bypassed through side paths, besides shops and through residential blocks. As they continued to travel, she noticed how the houses became less and less welcoming. Her head throbbed as they walked towards an industrial site. Large warehouses towered over them; their lights long since been turned off for the night.

'You doing okay?' Mike asked her. 'It's not much further now.' She nodded, but she was nervous. They diverted between tall factories. Dawn placed her free hand to her head. Mike noticed and placed his hand on her shoulder. Her mind was throbbing more and more with every step.

It was happening again. This feeling was not uncommon to her and it was starting up once more. As they took a few more steps, a strong sense kicked in. Her eyes widened as she heard distorted cries within her mind. She heard the sounds of machinery stirring. She took in sharp breaths as it began to feel hotter. So much hotter, far too hot to be a part of the real world. Her fingers trailed over her arms, finding goose bumps all over. They felt icy to the touch, yet the heat continued from within her head. Echoes of her nightmare were creeping into her mind. It was then the girl from the nightmare screamed through Dawn's soul in desperation.

'Don't go that way!' Dawn exclaimed sharply. In a panic, she pulled away from Ricky's aid, stumbling slightly backwards. The two boys stopped in their tracks and turned to face her. It was the first time she had spoken above a whisper, let alone a normal tone. Mike raised his eyebrow, uncertainty showed within his expression.

'Look Princess, I'm frozen, and I don't want to linger outside.' Ricky told her firmly.

'You don't understand,' she begged, 'I can sense . . . We can't go down there.' Ricky shook his head in disgust, shoving his hands into his pockets. In pure arrogance, he stormed down the path. The walls were closed in tightly. Bins were dotted around the place in a chaotic fashion, forcing him to twist and turn as he made his way through. At the other end was a slit of dim light coming from a streetlight.

'They didn't believe me either, and now they . . . I tried to warn them,' Dawn trailed off, her eyes watering.

'Warn who?' Mike asked her.

'Nut-job,' Ricky called out unpleasantly, nearing the end of the stretch.

'Come on, Dawn. I don't think you'd be able to take the detour. This way is much quicker,' Mike tried to persuade her as he followed his friend. Dawn stood still. He turned and made his way through the industrial site, the narrow pathway between two factories. He figured she would follow when she realised she wouldn't want to be on her own.

'Is she coming or what?' Ricky called out as he was halfway through. A flash of steel caught Dawn and Mike's sight. The smash of a crowbar echoed across the passage. Ricky smashed against a huddle of bins, sending some of the trash flying out of the alleyway. The metallic sound rang out and bounced across the walls. Mike took in a sharp breath and for that split second, noticed the three men that came towards him. He gulped, gazing back along the dark walls he had passed, looking in Dawn's direction. Had she known?

'I've got nothing on me!' Mike cried out in defence, trying to back away from them. He felt his back touch the wall as one of them laughed, taking out a knife. Mike was outnumbered. Two of the men grabbed his arms and held him against the wall. He felt the knife touching his neck. There was nowhere to run to. The one with the crowbar flashed his rotten teeth as he raised his weapon high. His black grin grew as a stench filtered out from between them. Mike closed his eyes tightly, ready to embrace the blunt instrument.

Dawn watched the spectacle from the other side. Her body felt like it was on fire as the distorted cries continued loudly. Her eyes glanced down to her feet as the lid of a bin rolled from the alleyway and toppled next to her. Taking in shaky breaths, she stared down the dark alleyway. The three men were going to kill Mike. These people were strangers to her; it would have been easy to leave them and find her own safety.

'Get away from him you thugs!' A loud call came from out of the alleyway. Mike glanced over in fright, spotting Dawn standing at the entrance. The wind blew harshly against her, making her body shiver slightly. Her hair whisked harshly to one side. He trembled, begging in his head that she ran away. She was going to be beaten to death.

'Thugs?' One of the attackers snarled, lifting up the crowbar and walking towards Dawn. The other men kept Mike pinned to the wall. In the distance, Ricky was trying to pull himself back to his feet. If the knife wasn't touching Mike's Adam's apple, he'd have yelled at her to run. He was too terrified to swallow though. He could only watch as the muscular fiend approached her.

'If you know what is good for you, you should leave,' she spoke, 'Now!' The large fellow laughed hard, swinging the crowbar effortlessly in the air. The heat doubled; it felt like her insides were being burnt alive. She had to touch her arm again to make sure. Her fingertips brushed the goosebumps from the cold once more. Mike held back the tears as best he could. He prayed that Dawn fled.

He defiantly told her, 'Oh, you little bitch! You're going to pay for. . .'

She interrupted him; a wave of courage pouring into her. 'Pay for what? You're all low life scum.' His face screwed up in rage. He roared out as he charged towards her; the crowbar held high. She simply stood there as he was feet away. Rage blinded people. Her eyes widened as the world around her changed. Everything went in slow motion. As the crowbar made its decent, she simply kept her ground. It crashed downwards, a few centimetres away from her foot. His warning shot had seemingly been unacknowledged. His head turned as the girl smiled at him. Before he realised what was happening, her foot rose quickly and struck his groin. He screamed as he fell to his knees, sobbing like a child on the floor. She wasn't strong, but in that moment, she knew exactly where to strike.

As the other two men spotted the spectacle, they immediately darted towards her, letting Mike go. He stood there, trembling and gobsmacked.

He couldn't bring himself to move, frozen in shock. Her eyes studied both of them. His mind was yelling at himself to flee, leave her and save himself.

Dawn's senses had spiked in her mind. It was overwhelming, knowing that if she timed it wrong she would be in more trouble than Mike was in. Her eyes were set on the man with the knife. He was the greatest danger. She picked up the bin lid that was on the floor, running her fingers over the rim. Her eyes locked on to her target as she held the lid to her chest; her arm coiled around it. Her arms trembled, still fatigued from before. She didn't need to rely on strength, only accuracy and timing. He was only a few metres away as she turned her body slightly. The heat was building up, intense like she'd thrown herself into the heart of the sun. The sounds were now shrill and high. She was waiting for the screaming in her head to reach its peak.

She licked her lips once; she was cutting it very short. Then she knew the moment had come as her mind pounded against her skull, and a sheer screech drilled into her subconscious. She threw the lid towards him as hard as she could. She felt strength in her arm that she knew she didn't have before. The lid struck him in the head, the metal clanging as it made contact. He toppled backwards and collapsed on the floor. The third man instantly stopped his pursuit, taking a few steps back.

'Step aside', she told rather than asked. He nodded, taking a step to one side; his eyes fixated on the others, who continued to whimper on the floor. As she passed him, she sped towards Mike.

'Are you okay?' she asked him. 'Where's your friend?' He shook himself from his frozen state as he ran to the other side and knelt next to his friend. He was nursing his right hand, cursing under his breath as he slowly stood up. As Dawn approached them, Ricky lunged for her, grabbing her by the scruff of her collar and thrusting her against the wall with his left hand. She was pinned up against the factory wall; her feet no longer touching the ground. She did not squirm or struggle.

'Did you set them up?' Ricky spat at her.

'She saved us.' Mike exclaimed, trying to pull his friend from her.

'I promise you, I didn't.' Dawn expressed concern as she looked up at him.

'Are you fucking with me?' Ricky snarled at her, flipping a switchblade from his pocket and held it in front of her, allowing the dim light to catch in the metal's surface.

'I know you won't hurt me,' she replied. As she spoke, she raised her hand, touching her palm to the sharp blade. The two stared at each other for some time. Dawn seemed fairly relaxed, while Ricky glared. Mike eventually intervened, pushing his friend away from Dawn. She was dropped to the floor, looking up at the two.

'I can sense danger,' she explained, 'I can sense it right down to the seconds. I was travelling because something big was coming. I had to leave my home. I tried to warn them, and they didn't believe me like I tried to warn you.' Mike stared at her, gobsmacked that a girl who barely looked to be a teenager was coming out with this. She could sense danger? Was that even possible?

'Who the hell are you, and where the fuck did you come from?' Ricky bellowed.

CHAPTER 2

'I'm telling you the truth,' Dawn repeated herself after the trio had settled into the squat. The windows were boarded up, save for a few planks of wood that had been removed and allowed the streetlight to filter into the place. The residence was one that had been abandoned, and from the scattered cans and newspapers, she knew the two boys had turned it into a temporary home. She sat on a well-worn sofa, and the two men stood before her. Ricky had threatened her when they arrived, and Mike showed concern. She hadn't been lying though. She was telling the truth when she said she could sense danger. Ricky saw it as nothing more than smoke and mirrors.

'I come from Oak Wood house,' she told them again. She sat further back on the sofa that had seen better days. Ricky stared down at her from where he stood. Mike sat at the other side of the three-seated furniture.

'I'm not listening to your shit anymore. You're an attention seeker,' Ricky finally spoke up.

'Ricky, what's up?' Mike asked his friend directly, 'Do you know the place or something?'

'You may just burn the newspapers, but I read the articles sometimes,' Ricky turned his back to them both. 'It was all over the papers three days ago. Arson at Oakwood house. Forty-two bodies. No survivors.' The room fell silent. Dawn stared at her feet. She could feel Mike's eyes on her.

'You . . . you're sure you're from there?' Mike trembled. She nodded slowly, tears welling. All of the people she had grown up with were gone. They were dead. She sat within the dim room, a well-worn blanket around her shoulders, and a can of opened beans she had been slowly consuming still in her left hand.

'But that's hundreds of miles away! You barely look like a teenager. How on Earth . . . why . . . just why?' Mike asked her.

'I just kept running. I can sense danger. You know I can, and you witnessed it. Something much bigger than that was coming to Oak Wood House. Much bigger. I tried to warn them but . . . I—' she began the stammer out. She remembered back to the number of foster parents she had been with. She'd been passed back and forth between different children's homes and different couples. The last family she had been with was over two years ago before they realized that looking after her would cost too much to carry on. She had lived at Oak Wood House since then, the longest she had ever stayed in one place. Everyone there was supposed to be her family, but instead, they only seemed to tolerate her. Even so, she didn't want them coming to harm.

Danger was coming. She knew it was coming. She begged them to leave the old building for a while, then they would all be safe. They tried to encourage her, to convince her that it was simply her overactive imagination, that the sooner they got her to a foster family, the better. She remembered she had begged them to listen. She begged them to leave. But they locked her in her room and told her she could come out when she'd realised she was being silly. As the day had gone by, her senses became worse and worse.

She had fled from the Oak Wood house. She knew she had to leave but could not truly explain why. She'd been having the dream and episodes of heat and noises bouncing in her head, and for her, that was enough. She'd grabbed everything from her room that she could. All of the money she had saved, sweets and snacks, and an empty bottle. She'd smashed the bedroom window with a chair and had left. She ran at first, then walked and kept walking, following the sun until it was night. During the night she'd continue to walk, looking at signs, heading towards the next town. When the sun rose, she walked away from it. When it was past noon, she followed it. Her legs cramped, her throat dried, and her food soon depleted. She'd poured water into her bottle from puddles, and the contents had made her sick. She felt drained from the journey. Despite all this, she never allowed herself to sleep; it was too risky. It was too risky because every step she took, she knew danger was also taking a step towards her. The last day, she could barely remember.

Mike stared at the young girl, who he had rescued from the cold of the night, a girl who had been travelling for days. Her clothes were muddy and discoloured but not to the extent that they were well worn like his. Her features were thin but not aged, that this had been her only hardship. She must have been running non-stop. But why? Could she really sense when things were going to go wrong?

'A word Mike', Ricky broke the silence as he walked out of the room. Mike pulled himself from the sofa as Dawn watched him. He gave her a weak smile before leaving the supposed lounge, stepping into the deteriorating kitchen.

'Is it possible?' Mike asked Ricky as he took a swig of water for himself.

'It said no survivors,' Ricky commented, 'but it also said not all the bones were recovered. It is possible she'd runaway before it burnt down. Sensing it was going to happen though is bullshit.' Mike pulled a rusted garden chair from a well-used table and sat down, looking up at his friend.

'I believe her Ricky,' Mike insisted. His friend gave a grunt in response. Ricky did not trust things easily, not without exact proof. He was a hardened man that looked out only for himself and for Mike. Mike was the only person he had ever shown consideration for as far as his friend was aware.

'Let her stay here tonight,' Mike insisted. He didn't want her going back out on the streets, whether her senses were real or fake.

'She's too good for this place, and we definitely cannot support her. Can barely feed ourselves,' Ricky spoke as he sat at the other side of the table.

'She's got nowhere to go,' Mike replied.

'That's not on us. I reckon the sod burnt it down and fled the scene. Take her to the police tomorrow; they'll still put her up. There's got to be other children's homes. Seriously, could it be worse than this place?' Mike never liked confrontation. It was that reason the two seemed to work well that Ricky had a hardened expression whereas Mike was still quite sweet and able to pull off begging directly.

'For one, I'm sure she didn't burn it down,' Mike defended her as Ricky scoffed in response, 'But you are right. I best go to the police with her and ask what to do. Could I get done for kidnap?' Mike questioned, gazing down at his hand.

'You didn't kidnap her, Mike. Gosh! You're making up your own troubles. You know that? As soon as morning comes, take her to the police. They'll sort out the arsonist,' Ricky told his friend.

'I didn't know there would be a fire,' Dawn interrupted their conversation. The two men looked over at her as she stepped into the kitchen. She did not look directly as them as she placed the empty can at the side of the sink.

'I don't understand why or how, but I knew something was coming,' she insisted. Ricky shook his head, turned away from her, and snatched the bottled water from his friend. Mike looked up at her with concern.

'I've been calling it common sense,' she tried to explain directly to him. 'It's common sense when say you know it's dangerous, so you back away from it, right?' she asked.

'Not really. It means you instinctively know that . . . er . . . I really don't know how to explain it,' Mike confessed. Dawn slowly approached the table. Mike pulled out the third and final chair, and she sat herself next to him.

'I can try and explain,' she continued, 'I was standing on the edge of a cliff a week back. My mind jumped and began to scream to me that something was very wrong, so I went back to the house.'

'Not an actual scream,' Mike interrupted her.

'It sounded like a real scream in my mind. It felt real enough.' She told him in a matter-of-fact tone. 'But the screaming didn't go away.'

'Voices in her head . . . you've found a real nutcase,' Ricky sneered. Mike glared over at his friend. Ricky ignored his gaze though as he took another chug of water.

'I asked my roommate what it was, and she said it was common sense. It was telling me to get away from the cliff. She made a joke about how no one has common sense these days that it's quite uncommon. It got worse and worse as hours went by,' Dawn continued, noticing Mike was staring at her strangely, his face pulled in awkwardness. She felt upset. He was just like the others. They didn't believe.

'I knew something was going to happen, but nobody listened to me,' she accentuated.

'Do you hear the crap that is coming out of your mouth?' Ricky asked her directly.

'I tried to warn you both back there that we shouldn't have gone down that way,' she cut in, becoming frustrated with Ricky's sarcasm and stabs. 'I tried to warn them too you know. I tried, but they didn't listen.' Ricky rose from his chair sharply, glaring at the young girl. She looked up at him unflinching at his sudden stand.

'Please don't,' Mike tried to cut between them, turning to Dawn, 'I'm listening, okay?' Dawn gave a weak smile and a slight nod, turning her attention away from his friend. Ricky slowly sat back down; his fingers clenching into a fist on the table. The girl had no fear of him and that in itself unnerved him. She was either stupid or telling the truth.

'It was a few days ago that the screaming in my head became unbearable,' she continued to explain to both of them, 'I knew then . . . that . . .' her words trailed off. She couldn't bring herself to finish her sentence.

'Whatever you felt before, do you feel it now?' Ricky asked her directly. Mike looked up at him in surprise. It had been a genuine question, the first.

'No. It's so peaceful now, like someone had turned the switch off,' she told him.

'You better stay here; sleep through the rest of tonight. Sleep through the day if you have to,' Ricky finally presented his decision, 'We'll figure this out tomorrow.'

'Thank you.' Perhaps she was quick to trust the two men, but she felt she had very little options. She still felt ill from travelling nonstop with little food, water, and no sleep.

'Mike likes to drag in strays, feels sorry for people,' Ricky explained. 'Besides, I know a kid like you isn't going to be staying around for long.'

'What do you mean?' Mike asked him directly. Dawn knew what he meant. She fully understood that this would be only temporary. She intended it to be that way.

'We'll talk later mate,' Ricky pushed the topic to one side. He pulled a can of beans from one side and opened it with the blade he'd originally threatened Dawn with. Mike swallowed hard and stood up from the table, took her hand, and led her back to the sofa. There was no protesting as she fell to the sofa and immediately lay on it. For a while, Mike stared at Dawn. He could see that she was starting to drift off, still not fully over her ordeal.

'Dawn, when you were out there, you were tossing and turning in your sleep. Was that to do with your common sense?' Mike sat on the floor next to her. She stared at her fingers for a while. She didn't want to recall the nightmares that haunted her at nights and remained in her mind during the day. For a moment, she closed her eyes. He deserved to know, no matter how far-fetched it seemed.

'I'll explain, but you need to have an open mind,' she cautioned him. He paused for a moment before nodding. She started to explain. She talked in depth about her nightmares. She explained what she thought it meant, that it was a warning. A warning of something known as the Crimson. She explained how the nightmare had been haunting her for the past week. Each time she fell asleep, the dream seemed to develop more and more detail. She explained how when her common sense screamed in her mind about danger; it was the scream of the girl in her dreams.

'Who's the girl then?' Mike finally asked. Her nightmare was horrific, but Dawn had explained she'd never been there in her life.

'She's . . . I found out she's me last night.' She sighed. 'Except she's not quite me. She's like a reflection.' She recalled the girl's speech. She wondered if it really was the Crimson that had attacked her home. Was she safe now she was gone?

Her eyes drifted to Mike's hands. For a while, the two sat in silence until Mike broke the ice.

'That's a lot to take in. You know that, right?' Mike told her, closing his eyes. 'Living on the streets—it's not a picnic, but this isn't a normal situation either.' He began tapping the wooden floor, letting out a deep sigh and slowly getting to his feet.

'Well, get some sleep. We can think about it tomorrow, right?'

She nodded as he smiled and placed a heavy blanket over her. She ducked her head under the blanket. It was cold in there, but it wasn't intolerable. Her eyes closed as Mike watched her. It didn't take much encouragement for her to fall asleep. Her blonde hair fell over her face. For that moment in time, she looked peaceful and content. Ricky entered the room and looked down at the two teens. Dawn looked no older than 12 or 13, and although he had given her a hard time, he was doing it to protect his friend.

'I'm going to sleep near her tonight,' Mike told his friend. Ricky grunted in response. Mike was already becoming friendly towards her. It was a lonely life living rough on the streets.

'Don't get too attached mate,' Ricky warned him. 'Once she's recovered, she's gone.'

CHAPTER 3

The nightmare had come back. In desperation, she shook her head hard, smashing her hands against the walls, screaming. She couldn't face it again—she wouldn't. The long and narrow corridor lay before her yet again. The walls were not as dark, allowing her to see a steel mesh surrounding it. In fear, she stared at the palms of her hands; the wires had left an imprint on them. The smell of burning drifted from the crimson room down to her left. She covered her mouth, trying to block out the smell. Instead, the scent of blood wafted from her palms.

Suddenly, the place shook violently, and the machinery started to roar loudly. Dawn was hurled backwards, banging her hand against the wire mesh. The people had already walked towards their deaths. The sound of equipment racketed louder than ever before. More detail had been added like it did every time she had this nightmare. She couldn't bear it; it was becoming too realistic.

Then a brilliant light flashed from the right, forcing her to cover her eyes. She peered slowly, staring towards the defiant glow. A large gate way was open; the light pouring out of it. It was an escape. In fear of the nightmare, she ran towards the new path, away from the clashing blades and the screaming that ensued afterwards. She sprinted down the corridor as fast as she could. She wasn't going to let the nightmare win.

'Don't go through there,' Dawn heard a voice call out. Her own voice. Dawn peeked over her shoulder. Stood there was her clone. Dawn bit down on her lip hard, now close to crying. She wasn't going to face it again. The light continued to shine brightly. The borders surrounded in a washed out pink. A gentle breeze came from it, enticing her. Dawn took a step towards it.

'Please believe me. Don't go in there!' The girl cried out. Why couldn't she get away from this scene that occurred over and over? The crimson fingers slipped from the walls and made a beeline not for the girl but for the exit. It planned to seal it, to stop her from leaving. In desperation, she threw herself into the light to escape.

The skies were blue and dotted with smooth white clouds. She was in a large city, where skyscrapers were almost as high as the clouds. The sun was shining bright, and groups of people were walking by. The skies filled with snowflakes, drifting downwards but not settling. Dawn peered behind her to look back at the corridor. The gateway had disappeared. Staring down at her hand, she realised she was holding a burger. Hesitantly, she took a bite from it. The taste was incredible—the best she'd ever had! The gentle snow, the smiling people, the amazing food—she felt so happy she never wanted to wake up.

'You never want to wake?' a voice called out softly to her. Dawn turned, her eyes meeting with a tall man with blonde hair and dark shades. He stood there with a sincere grin on his face. She took a small step back, nervous of him.

'Oh, I . . . it's so lovely here.' Dawn smiled at him, not knowing who he was.

'Do not be afraid. What else do you enjoy, sunshine?' the stranger asked, smiling back. He pressed his finger to his dark shades and pushed them further up his nose. She couldn't see his eyes behind the thick black lenses.

'Are you saying I can have anything I like in this dream?' she asked, getting giddy at the thought. He nodded. Before she had been stuck in a horrible nightmare, and now she was in paradise.

'Anything you like while you are asleep, this is your dream after all,' he told her in a sweet voice.

'I don't know what to ask for,' Dawn replied. He clicked his fingers. The sky was filled with a vast amount of colour. A million butterflies flew before her; their bright colours shining in the sun and at a fast pace. She burst out laughing, holding out her hand to touch one. They flew around her, filling her vision with a beautiful burst of colour. Their wings were large, covered in intricate patterns. Despite the snow that was falling, she felt very warm. Dawn glanced over at the man through the stream of colours the butterflies were casting. He was looking over his shoulder, staring at the alleyway, where Dawn had come from.

Suddenly, a spark of pain struck her head. She fell to her knees and clutched her head as the butterflies flew slightly back. She was being hit with an overwhelming headache. She didn't know what had suddenly brought it on.

'Ignore it, mind over matter. This is your dream,' the guy said, coming close to her. She took in a deep breath as the pain left like an echo. She couldn't make head or tail of it. The headache had drifted away, but she still felt very hot. The insects landed on her skin and began to flap their wings hard. She felt the gush of wind hit her skin, and her temperature began to drop.

'This is just a dream. Nothing can harm you here.' He knelt beside her. She rubbed her eyes and looked up at him. His blonde hair mopped over his shades. She felt lost and confused, as though a thick fog had coasted into her mind and her train of thought. His voice was hypnotic, sending her into a dreary trance.

'Nothing can harm me.' Dawn heard her own words drift out from her lips. His smile grew as he clicked his fingers again. This time, the butterflies flew away, and the colour vanished. What was left was the sight of the setting sun shining through the buildings. The scenery was dazzling as she smiled at the scene. Her body began to feel hot again, as if somebody had started a fire within her heart.

Then she knew. How could have she been so foolish? She brought herself to her feet as quickly as she could. Her head began to hurt, muffled echoes wafting in and out of her mind. They were being muted, and the heat was being diverted, but she knew what it was. Common sense. Not just any danger was approaching; the danger that had burned Oak Wood was coming for her in real life. In a panic, she shook her head hard. He was coming, and she was stuck in the dream world.

'I have to wake up!' She yelled out, unsure how to. The man's expression changed.

'Ignore it, sunshine.' Each word came out like a threat. Her eyes widened. His teeth grinded together; he knew she wasn't going to be persuaded. She ran past him in a hurry, heading towards the alleyway where the nightmare had been. The sound of cracking could be heard underfoot. The tiles of the pavement were giving way. She continued to run as fast as she could, but she tripped on one of the broken shards. The pavement shattered and fell through the ground as though it were made of glass. She felt her body being thrown downwards. Lashing out, she grabbed onto the side with her hand, but she was slipping.

'Help me!' she called out in fear. Her fingers slowly slid away from the secure tiles. She desperately tried to haul herself up. She looked directly upwards. He stared at her. His face was emotionless. His tongue trailed over his teeth as she tried to reach a hand out to him. He stood tall as he placed his fingers to the rim of his shades. He slowly took them off; his eyes staring directly at her. She gasped sharply, feeling nauseous at the sight of them. Without another thought entering her mind, he lifted his foot up high and smashed it against her hand. She screamed as she fell into the dark abyss before landing on a foamy substance. The light could no longer be seen. Everything was gone. She was standing in darkness. There was nothing but a sweeping and continuous black. Unsure what to make of it, she took a step forward in her dream. What she stepped on didn't feel solid.

'I . . . I have to wake up,' she said out loud. It didn't feel like a dream anymore. She knew she was still asleep, but it wasn't like any dream she'd had before. She bit her lip hard, willing in her mind to wake up, but her mind still felt groggy. Her mind had been tampered with; she knew it had been.

The thought of the room being empty was soon distant as she felt something slither across her foot. In shock, she peeked down at the once dark and cloudy floor. A crimson stream rushed over her feet and ankles. She lifted her foot, the red liquid sticking to the bottoms of her feet before dripping back into the pool. The liquid rose slowly, parts of it forming into chains. She stared in horror at the unnatural occurrence. The chains shifted and rose further. They began to take on a metallic form, dropping slightly. They bowed towards her like snakes, glaring at her with no eyes and no face.

Let's talk. A dark voice echoed across the strange world. The chains rose higher and surrounded her, as though they were being lifted by someone. She turned from left to right, but there was no gap in the formation. There was nowhere to run to. The chains lashed towards her, tightening around her body, her legs, her arms, her torso, and her neck. She couldn't move from the spot. She couldn't break free. She pulled as hard as she could, but nothing was working. Everything was out of her control. She began to panic. That was when common sense started building up. Danger was coming in the real world. Danger was coming at a fast and menacing rate. Common sense had only built up to such intensity once before. The same one that made her run for three days straight. She had to wake up.

There is no need to wake. I'll be there soon. The voice called out to her, sending chills up and down her entire body.

'Leave me alone!' she cried out, trying her hardest to pull against the chains that continued to tighten around her like a serpent. It was crushing her as she gasped out, tossing and turning. She wanted to wake up, now! She struggled harder, but the crushing sensation persisted. Eventually, she could no longer struggle, exhausted from her efforts. She pleaded one last time, but it was in vain.

Don't cry little sunshine. I'm coming to collect you. I can't allow you to flee again. The unwelcoming voice told her. She tossed her head left to right. Nothing but the crimson chains and the continuous darkness surrounded her.

'No! W-where are you?' she begged, unable to move at all. There was nothing but a low rumble of laughter. The way it echoed around the dark world reminded her of thunder.

It grows tiresome chasing you. I was trying to be nice about it, but it won't suffice. You had to act like one of them, didn't you?

She needed to wake up, to get away from this madman. Common sense had suddenly jerked. Danger was getting far too close. He was getting far too close. The girl was screaming in her mind already. The machinery went loud, fast, and brutal.

'Why?' she asked in a trembling voice. 'Why me!' She felt her cheek prickle a little. She felt the chains loosen slightly. She waited for an answer from the danger. Another sensation hit her, stronger than the last time. The chains rattled, untangling around her a little. The chains were becoming thicker and larger as they tried to tighten around her again. A sharp pain erupted from her right cheek. Another harsh sting and she heard her own voice yelp from the outside. He was losing his grip on her. She tugged back as hard as she could from the supernatural chains. She felt the chains snapping as a larger sting hit her face.

She opened her eyes harshly—trembling and shaking. Mike was holding her by the collar of her shirt; his right hand raised in front of her. She was back in the real world, her hands on the sofa in the abandoned building. She could feel the sweat staining her shirt and the tears on her cheeks.

'Dawn!' he exclaimed, hugging her tightly and sobbing. 'I'm sorry, but you were screaming in your sleep. You wouldn't wake up.' She felt as though she couldn't breathe. She placed her hand on her cheek. They were sore and bruised. In desperation, Mike had been striking her cheeks to bring her back. It had worked and never had she been so relieved.

Common sense hammered in her mind and the screams occurred, reminding her that it was not over. They were worse than they had been before. The girl's screaming was hysterical, as though it was near the end of her life. The fire within her body intensified into an inferno.

'I have to leave!' She yelled out. Common sense was suddenly very strong. The danger, the Crimson, was very close, much closer than he had been last time. She tore herself from Mike's arms before he could say a word and ran for the door. She dashed across the squeaking floorboards and through the hallway. She heard Mike's footsteps following her at the same speed. In her state of shock, she collided into Ricky, knocking him to the floor. She didn't apologize as she threw herself to the door.

'Stop!' Mike grabbed her by her jacket and pulled her back. The door swung open; the winter morning greeted her. She frantically tried to fight him off, and panic was overwhelming her. Danger was extremely close, every second counted. The Crimson was going to get her; it was inevitable.

'I can't,' she cried. The screaming was rattling in her mind. The shrieks were no longer humane as they bounced against her conscious. Mike clung to the young girl that was panicking, taking in a deep breath. In those few seconds, he made a decision that would change his life completely.

'Go right, and keep going straight. There's a train station. Wait for me there,' he told her. Mike didn't understand what was worrying her but he did have a plan for her. They could hop onto any train and clear tens of miles away from whatever it was, perhaps even hundreds. He didn't truly understand what was going on, but he wasn't going to question her. She had so far been right about her instincts.

'Y-you don't understand.' Dawn wept in fear.

'Trust me. Wait for me there,' Mike insisted. She pulled herself free as she bolted down the road without giving him an answer.

'Keep going. Get to the station,' he called out to her. He watched her run to the right. She was taking his advice. He turned back into the squat and entered the lounge. Mike felt something being thrust into his hand. In confusion, he looked up to see Ricky glancing at him. His expression was anxious.

'I can't stop you from believing her shit,' Ricky told him, taking his hand and pulling Mike up from his stoop. 'Just come back safe, promise?'

Mike gave an awkward smile, nodding as he turned and grabbed Dawn's bag from the sofa. He ran up the stairs and staggered into his own room, grabbing a rucksack from the side. He took her small bag and rummaged through his own, hauling into it notes and coins. He took a moment to stare at what Ricky had given him. A wad of notes were scrunched into his left hand. He put those into the bag too, making a note to himself to repay his best friend later.

The front door was slammed from downstairs.

'Hey, who the fuck do you think you are, barging into someone's home. Scram!' Ricky's voice boomed from the stairs. Mike gazed over at the door that was ajar. He took a few hesitant steps forward and looked out of the gap. Ricky was halfway up the stairs, his back to Mike, his arms out wide, staring downwards. In front of him was a tall figure with his head low. Mike couldn't fully see the stranger's face besides the blonde hair and sneer. Slowly, the intruder tilted his head upwards. His eyes stared directly at Ricky.

The intruder's eyes were crimson in colour. Not blood shot or ill. Those eyes were naturally coloured—dark red and white pupils. It was obvious this stranger was not blind as the white pupils flickered slightly, always staring at Ricky.

'Where is the girl?' the man asked calmly. Mike's eyes widened, feeling a chill run down his spine. Ricky pulled the switchblade from his pocket, pointing it in the stranger's direction.

'You had better fuck off right now. I'll do you in. You hear?' Ricky stood his ground. The man simply grinned at the boy blocking his path. Ricky pointed the blade towards the trespassers throat, refusing to let him further up the stairs.

The sinister man never made a sound as his smile widened. Ricky's grip tightened as he lunged forward. What came next was too fast to see. There had been no movement from the stranger, yet he was past Ricky's left hand side. His eyes seemed to shine in delight as a horrified groan filled the silence. Ricky tilted backwards. His eyes rolled back, and he fell. His body slumped awkwardly on the stairs; his neck had a clean fresh deep slit across of it, from left to right.

The crimson eyes stared directly at Mike.

Mike kicked the bedroom door shut. He grabbed the chest of drawers and toppled it in the way, hoping it would barricade him from the killer. He pulled Dawn's bag over his neck and grabbed the boards that were nailed over the window. The murderer's footsteps were making their way up the stairs. Mike kicked the boards and desperately tried to smash them off the glassless window. He grabbed a second board and pulled it hard, but it wouldn't budge. He turned back to face the door. He crept forward, wondering if he could barge past the killer and get out of there.

He leapt out of his skin when he heard the shattering of wood echoing behind him. He spun round and stared at the open pane. The boards had been torn off. The wood had shattered inwards. Somebody outside had ripped through the wood as though it were paper. Engraved in the windowsill were deep claw marks. They were large enough to be a lion's. For a moment, he trembled on the spot. Two monsters? A loud thud bounced behind him, feeling the floor beneath him tremble slightly.

He darted towards the opening and peered down, staring at the unattended garden. The trees covered the jagged pathway in dark shadows, unable to see what was beneath him. This was high, very high. He heard the door smash open behind him, and the chest of drawers clattered to the other side of the room. It didn't matter how high it was. He threw himself out the window, landing awkwardly and smashing his arm against something hard in the garden. He cried at the pain. He knew he couldn't stop though as he hobbled to his feet, gasping hard. He forced himself to run. Tears were welling as his side cried out in pain.

He kept glancing behind him, certain that the killer would come chasing after him at any moment. He couldn't see anyone though. He forced himself to the train station, his eyes darting from left to right in panic. He stared up at the train times. One was leaving in three minutes. Underneath that sign, curled up in the corner was Dawn trembling violently. She had waited for him. Her face was horribly white. For a moment, he hesitated. She looked up at him with unease. That intruder had come after her, had specifically asked for the girl.

'Dawn, we have to go,' he told her as he grabbed her arm. She couldn't hear him. The screaming in her head had become too much. He gripped onto her tightly, pulling her up, wincing as waves of pain shot through him. She blinked and realised what was going on as she stared at Mike. They stood before the ticket machine, as he fed the notes into it.

'Where's Ricky?' she asked shakily. Mike closed his eyes for a moment, remembering Ricky's lifeless body. He had been his closest friend. Now he was dead. He swallowed back tears. He couldn't show weakness in front of Dawn.

He forced a smile, grabbing the two single tickets. He shoved them into the other machine and darted towards the train. He saw the doors beginning to close. He hurled them both towards, slipping into the carriage before the doors closed. A few seconds later, they both felt the wheels turning and the train moving.

CHAPTER 4

Dawn paced back and forth along the carriage. Her head still hurt, but she knew they were getting away. She kept glancing out the window of the speeding train, expecting to see the man in her dream with the crimson eyes. She would then shake her head and continue to pace. Passengers, at first, were curious why she was so stressed. Her cheeks were a deep red from the slaps Mike had dealt to them, and her eyes still had deep bags underneath them. Eventually, they went back to their own thoughts.

But how could she settle? Dawn was exhausted, realising she had only managed to sleep until the morning. She blamed the intense dream that she couldn't wake from before. She blamed the sudden sprint she had to make to the station and the severe terror she was put through as she waited for Mike to return. Her body was begging for more rest. She was still unwell. The lack of food and sleep from the previous days had made her body twitch. She hadn't left herself enough time to recover, and because of it, she now felt worse than ever from the mad dash.

She walked over to the public toilet and knocked on the door lightly. 'Are you okay, Mike?' As soon as they had entered the train, he made an excuse to use the bathroom, but it had been twenty minutes.

'Yup,' an answer came. She paused for a moment, almost pressing her ears against the door to make sure, before telling herself he was fine. He was not. He listened out as he heard her walk off again before closing his eyes. Tears were running down his cheeks. He had to get it all out of his system, before Dawn saw and questioned what had happened. He swallowed hard, wiped his eyes, and stared into the small mirror. His eyes were sore and red from the crying. He would have to wait a few more minutes for the marks to fade away. The memories kept shooting back as he desperately tried to force them behind a wall in his head.

Ricky was dead—murdered. The image of his friend's eyes, unseeing as his body fell against the stairs, couldn't be wiped from his mind. Nothing was going to bring his best friend back. And what had he done? He'd fled and left him there. He should have been stronger. He should have ran out the door and charged at the fiend that had killed his friend. He should have knocked him down the stairs, broken his back. A life for a life. But he hadn't. He'd jolted out the window and fled for his life.

No, it wasn't strictly true. He must have done the right thing. Ricky was definitely dead; nobody would have survived that. If he'd barged through that door, he'd probably have been killed too.

Everything was out of touch. What he had seen, was it possible? The crimson eyed man hadn't drawn a weapon. The movement had been too quick. He gazed over at the door where Dawn had been. Why was he after her? He could see a small reason why. She could predict things or at least sense when dangerous things could happen. If the wrong kind of person had her, they could abuse her powers. He didn't really know what he was going to do from this point. The killer had seen him. The killer somehow knew that Dawn had been there.

He couldn't hide forever. He let out a deep sigh and opened the door. Taking in a deep breath, he forced a smile and walked towards the carriage Dawn was striding around in. He had to be emotionally stable for her.

'Running that hard made me sick,' Mike made his excuse to Dawn who was staring out the window. Her sight left the rolling factories and faced him instead.

'Were you crying?' she asked. Mike panicked. He hadn't waited long enough; his eyes must have still been bloodshot, and his eyes shiny from recent tears.

'Err . . . throwing up hurts like a bitch,' he muttered, rubbing his neck. She gave a sympathetic smile, unzipping her bag and taking out her bottle. It was still half-full of water. She offered it to him, but he shook his head.

'What do we do now?' she asked him as she placed the bottle back into the bag. Her eyes strained as she struggled to stay alert. The crimson had invaded her dream, taken control, trapped her within the confinements, and left her more exhausted than she had been before she'd slept. She was worried he could do it again, only next time she may not escape.

Mike stared out the window, avoiding her gaze. Was it really us at this point? He had known Dawn for less than a day. This was beyond his understanding. She was such a sweet girl though and the first time he had felt human in a long time.

'Plan is to catch as many trains as we can afford. It'll put a big distance between us and him,' he started to explain.

'I never mentioned it was a guy.' Dawn focused on him. Mike gulped hard. This was why Ricky was the hustler on the street and not him. He couldn't keep a secret and was a terrible liar.

'Thought you did,' he mumbled under his breath quickly.

'Did I?' Dawn questioned. She was so tired she couldn't fully comprehend if she had or not.

'Yeah, so we'll put a big distance between us and him,' he stuck to his story, glad he got away with it before noticing her eyes droop. 'Dawn, you look awful.'

'I can't rest. I mustn't.' She whined shaking her head hard. What if Mike couldn't wake her up again? What if she was trapped within the other world until he came to collect her? Whimpering, she stood from the seat and frantically paced back and forth once more.

'Promise you will on the second train? If your sense doesn't kick off that is,' he begged her, seeing how unwell she was. She continued to storm left and right. He grabbed her jacket sleeve, seeking her attention. She glared at him; he had no idea what she was going through. She closed her eyes. She was acting like a spoilt brat. Mike didn't have to stick by her. As far as she was concerned, he could easily go back to his best friend and the squat.

'I promise,' she whispered softly to him. The two stood side by side. They had a plan, which was all that mattered. They were going to outsmart danger. But even then, it didn't seem real.

Hours went by before the final stop was declared by the announcer. By this stage, Dawn was twitching and rubbing her eyes continuously. She was struggling to stay alert and worse. She felt a subtle warmth from behind her eyes. Mike took her hand and half dragged her off the carriage. His eyes looked up at the notice boards. There were two trains about to leave, one went further north, and the other headed back in the direction they had come from. The north was the way to go. It would be a while before the train came though. It gave more time for that man to find them. Mike pushed his anxiety as far back into his mind as he could.

'Mike?' she began to question as they paid for their single tickets. Her voice was weak. Her hand rubbed harshly against her eyes.

'What is it, Dawn?' he asked her sincerely as they walked towards platform three. He could feel her body trembling. He reached out his hand to comfort her but thought better of it.

'Do you believe me?' she asked quietly as they sat down on a bench. The question was abstract, and for a moment, he had to consider what she meant. The sun was starting to set. The clouds above them were white and completely covered the sky. She struggled to keep her eyes open.

'Yeah, I believe everything you say. Honest,' he told her. She stared at him for a while, seeing if his expression would falter. He was telling the truth after what happened in the run-down house. How could he not believe her?

'I don't know why he is chasing me. I'm scared,' she confessed to him, 'Is it possible he's not . . . well, human?'

Perhaps she wasn't human either, he thought to himself, unable to give an answer. He felt her head fall and rest against his shoulder, succumbing to an awkward daze. He stared at her for some time. It was the first time in his life a young lady had touched him. He looked across the rails. It would be hours before their train came. He wondered who else knew of this or if it were only that man hunting her.

He couldn't deal with all of this. He couldn't act a hero. He was a coward at best. His eyes gazed back over at her. If he leaves now and abandon her, at least, he'd be safe. Heck, why should he worry about a girl he'd only known in less than a day? He'd lost his best friend because of her.

He took her bag and placed it next to her. He slowly rose to his feet, trying to ease her head onto the side of the bench. He stood there for a while, staring at her chest slowly rising and lowering through shallow breaths of slumber. He turned and began to leave a handful of notes in his pocket. He'd catch the train back to where he lived. He clenched his fingers tightly. If she always knew when he was coming, then she could flee. Why was he trying to help her when this psychopath was willing to slaughter anyone in his path? If the streets taught him anything, it was to look out for number one, himself.

'Why am I crying again?' he whispered as he wiped his eyes with the back of his hand. The tears felt heavy on his skin as his head began to pound. If he left now and went back, sure he'd be alive, but what for? There was no family to fall on, not even his adoptive one in the form of Ricky. There would be no career for him, no ambitions to chase. He had been depressed already, a numbness in his day-to-day life. But when he saw Dawn, unconscious in the alleyway, it had reminded him of when he had run from his stepfather, been beaten senseless and left with nothing and no one. If Ricky hadn't found him and taken him under his wing back then, he was not sure if he would have survived.

Dawn was trembling on the bench. Her nightmare had returned. Mike pulled her towards him; his arm around her shoulder, tilting her head onto his shoulder.

'I'm here. That bastard won't get you, not while I'm around,' he whispered to her, holding back his crying as he did so. She trembled in his arms as she slowly began to calm down. He held onto her tightly. In that moment, he realised he cared about her more than he cared about anyone else. The girl he had found alone. He was never going to abandon her, never.

'You listen good, you hear?' he spoke under his breath, 'You're not touching a hair on her head. I'm making sure of that!' He made his vow on deaf ears, but he felt more content. He bit his lip hard, looking down at Dawn. He wasn't going to allow anyone to hurt her; he'd make sure of it. They'd run; get as far away as possible. Catch a dozen trains or more and then keep heading in that direction, perhaps take a few turns to throw him off the trail.

When they got on the train, they knew the journey was going to be long. Mike could feel his own eyes drifting as the night swept into full motion. Dawn was awake, watching out the windows although the outside was black. He fell asleep as she had done on the bench. She checked the items they had in the bag. There was a packet of crisps and money. She was ravenous. Her hunger kept her awake, but she wouldn't eat them. The salt would make her thirstier than she already felt.

Her mind felt dull and cloudy as she rested her head against the glass and closed her eyes. The wheels clattered against the rails, but they seemed to be louder. Disorientated. She peered out the window to see if a train was passing, but she could see no lights to indicate it. She leant forward and listened more intently. It was almost like heavy boots sprinting against stones, a constant thud and clicking sound combined. A glint of silver caught her eye, and her attention focused. Something had been out there. For a moment, it seemed as though the noise had subsided.

The carriage surged backwards, sending its passengers off their seats. The sound of screeching, like nails on a chalkboard, erupted from the train. Mike was woken with a start. The train had done an emergency stop or so it seemed.

'What's happening?' he cried out in shock. She scrambled to her feet awkwardly, trying to regain her balance. The lights were barely glowing above them, and they could feel the cold snap of the outside touch their skins. Fog and dust made it difficult to see as it drifted into the carriage. Mike stood up, blinking hard several times as he stared straight ahead. Something was glowing within the fog. Two circular silver objects were seeping through the thickness. Those spheres were followed by a dark silhouette. For a moment, he couldn't understand what he was seeing. As the dust swept downwards, a large paw thudded against the floor. Mike's heart skipped a beat. They were the eyes of a beast.

'Mike!' Dawn yelled out. Her eyes also witnessing the same monster before them. An ear-splitting howl rattled from the other side of the carriage. He stared down the corridor, eyes wide. He couldn't comprehend what he was seeing. The carriage had been torn open, the roof partially missing. Mike's eyes met with those of the large canine. It was staring directly at them.

The dust began to settle, and soon the other people noticed the beast. They screamed in panic, running away from the creature. Their hands smashed against the button to open the train doors. Its silver eyes seemed to be set on Dawn with fierce concentration. Its claws dug into the train floor like those of a large cat's, tearing through the steel beneath it, leaving deep claw marks like the ones left on the windows ledge. Its large eyes turned to him as it licked its lips, pulling them back to display its long canines. Its fur was long and seemed darker than the night itself.

Mike was terrified of dogs. Normal dogs, big and small, were bad enough, but this thing was unnaturally large and bulky. He couldn't take his eyes away from the beasts' silver ones. The animal's jaw opened, howling loudly for a second time. Its tail rose high and bold. Its entire body seemed to double in bulk as the light's shine grew so weak they were nothing more but distant glows. Passengers continued to scream and flee from the train. Mike had frozen in fear.

He felt his hand being grabbed and his body being pulled. He shook his head hard, realising Dawn was dragging him away. As they got off the train, they saw other people were panicking around them. All of them were running along the tracks. The train had come to a halt a mere few metres away from the next station. They all heard the dog snarling loudly behind them. Suddenly, Dawn heard the girl screaming within her mind, louder than it ever had been. It came abruptly, as though someone had clicked a switch. Why had it delayed so much? Why was it warning her only now that a monster was after her?

The two of them ran towards the exit as fast as they could, desperately trying not to be split up. They could both hear the creature barking and snarling behind them, getting closer and closer. A man barged between them, knocking Mike to the floor. Their hands separated as his arms smacked against the concrete floor. He screamed in pain as a woman trod on the back of his leg with her high heels. It felt as though it had stabbed through his skin. He thought he heard Dawn calling out to him, but he couldn't make it out.

This was all too much. First, a maniac was hunting down Dawn and killing anything in his path. Now, a feral creature had appeared before them, and its intention was very clear. He couldn't get over the shock of seeing his greatest fear come towards him tenfold. He stumbled onto his feet, trembling violently. He could feel a wet patch trickling down the back of his leg. The station was practically empty. The barking and snarling was outside.

Bang!

The ricochet of a gunshot bellowed. The beast's noises seized immediately. Had somebody killed it? He was still crying loudly as he hobbled towards the exit. He could hear nothing but a buzzing sensation in his ears as he collapsed a second time just outside the station. He stared around, his mind unfocused. A few police officers stood at the entrance. One of the officers held a gun, a small pillow of smoke coming from it, presumably the one that had shot at the monster. All three officers were ignorant to Mike, two of them staring at the tracks at a dark silhouette that was still. The officer with the gun walked away and headed towards the station.

The man seemed familiar. He watched the man walk casually into the building; his blonde hair was long enough that it covered his facial features. He had a sneer on his face as he walked past Mike, not paying any attention to him. The way his bangs flopped over his shades and the curve of his grin made Mike panic.

It was him, the one with the crimson eyes! Where was Dawn? Was she still in the station? He made to run but felt a harsh tug pull him back. *No, not now, no!*

'Now you just wait up! The station is closed off,' a stranger spoke to him sternly.

'My little sister is in there!' He lied, trying to pull free from the guys grip.

'Don't worry. I just saw a police officer checking . . .'

'No! Not him!' He screamed out hysterically before he could finish his sentence. In irritation, he turned and punched the man across his face. He keeled back, and blood was dripping from his lips. Before he could regain his balance, Mike had fled into the building.

The station looked eerie without people standing there. The lights beamed across the empty stairways, yet they seemed dull. In terror, he hobbled behind a pillar, staring out from behind it. He watched in horror as the man ran his fingers through his blonde hair. His red eyes shone from underneath, staring towards the halted train. Mike couldn't help but look across to it as well. Three carriages had trailing claw marks coming from them, dragging downwards. Mike covered his mouth, desperately trying not to let a sound out. The beast had done that; the beast had stopped the train. It must have been the man's pet, stopping the train, so the killer could get to Dawn.

'Where are you, sunshine?' His deep voice called out, walking further into the station. Mike felt his heart sink, and his knees attempt to buckle underneath him. How had he managed to get to them so quickly? Was there no way they could ever outrun him? He felt helpless.

The right, Mike heard a voice call out in his head. Startled, Mike tossed his head left to right, trying to find the source of the sound. The killer had started walking down the stairs towards the lower tracks. Nobody else was in sight. He stepped out from behind the pillar, turning and following the instructions that had called out in his head. He walked towards the right. There were stairs leading upwards, towards the café.

A deep growl rumbled behind him. Mike's eyes widened, too frightened to look back. It wasn't dead. He bolted up the stairs. He fell through the doors, slamming them shut behind him. Dawn was sat on a cafeteria table, trembling violently, and tears stricken across her cheeks. She took in a sharp breath. Mike was smiling as he rushed forward and grabbed her hand. All he could think about was that she was safe. Her mind was throbbing from the overwhelming adrenaline that coursed through her. Mike had just slammed the doors. The sound of the metal smacking into the frame now echoed around the empty station.

Through the glass panes of the cafeteria doors, a pair of large silver eyes glared at them. The canine's head was pressed against the door; its attention was on them. Dawn looked back at the monster, feeling incredibly sick. The sheer amount of danger they were in was causing her common sense to reach a level she had never felt before. And it was tearing her apart from the inside. The hound snarled as its teeth snapped at the handles, breaking them, metal chunks crashing to the ground. Nothing but blind terror filled Mike as he turned and ran towards the window. He could hear Dawn whimpering as Mike picked up a chair and threw it into the cafe's window. The glass shattered. He pushed the rest of the broken shards through the opened window and glanced downwards. Directly underneath was a small roof. It was the squat all over again. He was going to have to jump down from a height. They could lower themselves down from the window, and from there flee into the night.

The beast barked loudly behind them, a deep and intimidating sound that echoed through the building. The two flung themselves out the window, landing awkwardly on the roof and sliding down. From behind them, they could hear steel being crunched into and fierce barks echoing through the buildings walls.

That beast is letting his master know where she is, Mike thought to himself.

Dawn and Mike ran as fast as they could, the adrenaline coursing through their bodies. They could hear gunshots ricocheting from behind them. The sky filled with the sound of yelps from the demonic dog and the shouting of other men. They fled as far as they could until their bodies caved in. He fell onto a bench, wheezing hard. Dawn collapsed beside him, taking in sharp breaths.

He began to feel sick. He sat himself up awkwardly, staring at his leg. His jeans were stained in blood. The woman's heel had broken skin, but it didn't appear too bad. His body shivered as he closed his eyes. He knew they had to keep running. They mustn't stop. In desperation, Mike grabbed Dawn's sleeve and tried to pull her up. She shook violently, tears forming in her eyes. He could feel her trembling and her breathing was random. Her eyes were closed tightly and beads of sweat were pouring down across her forehead. He could feel her body burning up.

'Dawn, please, we have to keep moving!' he cried out.

'H-h-he . . . he . . . my eyes, they hurt so much.' Her words trailed out in hysteria. She fell to her knees, crying hard. Mike grabbed her and tried to lift her up. She wasn't heavy, but he wasn't strong either. Feebly, he tried to lift her and carry her. She couldn't bring herself to move. Her breath was rapid. What was wrong with her?

'Dawn, is he close? Is common sense acting up?' he asked her desperately. They were barely moving forward. He peered over his shoulder. He's going to catch them. He's going to kill them. He was sure of it.

'Dawn!' He yelled out in desperation. 'Dawn, move!' Her fingers gripped into his shirt as she forced herself to walk. Mike limped forward as best he could. He could still feel little spots of blood dripping down his leg. He felt her burning with a high temperature.

'Dawn, tell me, is he coming?' Mike continued to ask. She couldn't answer though; the pain was overwhelming.

A fire roared within her soul. But it was no longer within her mind. Her fingertips brushed against her skin. They were hot, extremely hot.

Energy was creeping into her, overwhelming her. She closed her eyes tightly. She felt as though she was going to explode. She screamed loudly, opening her eyes sharply. A bright light shone from her eyes with a fierce nature. Energy rushed out of her in a blinding light. Mike felt a heavy force crash into him as he was hurled away from her. He felt his body smash into a tree. He coughed hard from the impact as he watched in shock. Her eyes, they were shining brightly. Her arms stretched high and wide and shone brightly in a golden glow. Then, she fell to her knees, the light subduing to a dim. Her eyes, that had once been green, were now golden. Her pupils were white. For a moment, she shivered where she knelt. She fell forward; her hands out in front of her, stopping her from collapsing completely. She took in strong breaths, closing her shining eyes and began to laugh while on all fours.

He pulled himself from the tree shakily. Was he safe? He wasn't sure. Hesitantly, he walked over to her. He was terrified he'd be thrown again. Shakily, he placed his hand on her shoulder. She gazed up at him; her golden eyes reflected against his blue ones. Those weren't the eyes he had gazed upon only a few minutes ago.

She laughed weakly as her eyes closed, and her arms gave way; her body fell flat to the ground. Mike stared at her for what seemed like forever. His skin felt tingly from the force that erupted from her. He was terrified of her. Yet she lay unconscious, unmoving. Very slowly, he edged over to her. He placed his hand on her cheek. She felt warm, not hot like she had been before. The girl was definitely not human.

He remembered why they had been running. After the shock of what Dawn had just gone through, he had forgotten.

'Dawn, wake up,' he panicked as he nudged her viciously. 'Dawn, tell me, is your common sense, is it still there? Is he coming?' She didn't move.

CHAPTER 5

Mike opened the back door of a careless neighbour's house. He had dragged his limp friend into a housing estate, every sound making him jump. He pulled Dawn into the kitchen, sweat gathering and sticking to his shirt. He placed her on the kitchen floor and went back to close and lock the back door that the neighbours hadn't locked themselves. His eyes shifted towards the window that looked into the garden. Children's toys and gardening equipment littered the grass. The tools cast shadows—monstrous shadows that made Mike whimper and close the blinds in a panic.

'Dawn, any time you want to wake that'd be swell,' he whined quietly, glancing back at her. Her eyes were closed; her breathing was random and desperate. He knelt next to her; his palm was on her forehead. Her temperature was rising again. Was she sick? Was she dying? Was this his fault?

He flicked on the light and started opening cupboards, searching for a cup. He felt useless as he took it and filled it with water. Water, glorious water that seemed to be everyone's answer when it wasn't clear what the answer was. Wash it out with water. Drink some water. Water it down. He knelt next to Dawn and placed the cup to her lips. Slowly, he tilted it towards her, quietly whispering to her to drink some. The liquid dribbled past her lips and trickled down her cheeks. He parted her lips and tried again. She coughed and squirmed in his arms. Her temperature was rising rapidly. In desperation, he pulled a cloth from the sink, drenched it in the cup water, and placed it on her face, trying to cool her down. He watched as steam began to drift from the cloth. He was only making it worse. He crept away, dropping the cup in the sink. Water wasn't the answer, not this time.

The back gate swung into the side of the house; the smash echoed loudly. Mike took in a sharp breath. The killer had found them. He listened out; his ears strained to hear. Silence. He swallowed hard. The wind picked up, whistling against the windows. Mike opened the draw nearest to him. His eyes struggled to see in the dark. He noticed a glint of metal. He picked up the object—a steak knife. His fingers closed around the handle. He could feel fresh beads of sweat falling. He could feel his heart thudding against his ribcage.

He opened the back door slightly, gripping the weapon as tightly as possible. What was the stalker's plan? Was he going to creep up or charge at Mike? Was his pet going to spring out and ravage him? He gazed out of the small slit, but it was too dark to fully see. The back gate swung in the wind. Very slowly, he opened the door wider. The wind had settled, and there was nothing but silence. He slowly took a step out, staring at the gate. The wind picked up suddenly, slamming the gate against the wall, sending out the loud sound that had emitted before.

He let out a sigh of relief. The wind, that's all it had been, the wind. He walked down the passageway, closing the gate and pulling the bolt across. It may have been the wind that time, but that man must have been coming. Somehow, the man with crimson eyes had found Mike and Dawn as they had fled on the train. If he found them back then, he was going to find them again. Only this time she was unable to move. He thought of checking the garden, but what if they were here? What was he going to do against a dog that slashed through metal and a man who kills without touching?

He closed the back door and locked it, bolted it and barricaded it with a table. He leant against the table, ears perked. His heart was like a rabbit's, beating furiously against his ribcage. He walked back to Dawn, placing his hand on her forehead again. She was in a worse state; her temperature had risen, almost to the state it had been before. She gasped and trembled on the floor.

'Mike', The voice was quiet and soft. Her eyes opened, glowing slightly of gold and white.

'I held back before, but it's burning me. I can't hold it in,' she whispered as a tear fell from her eye.

'Y-y-you can't hold it?' Mike questioned.

'I have to let it all go,' she groaned, holding onto her sides. Her eyes began to shine abruptly. Mike took her hand and held it tightly, realising what was about to happen.

'Get away from me!' she screamed out, slapping his hand out the way. He ran to the door into the hallway, looking over his shoulder at her. Her eyes were brighter than ever before, a brilliant burst of golden rays. He slammed the door between them. His hands pushed against the wood. He felt a strong force catapult into the door, almost sending him flying backwards. His ears rang with the sound of shattered glass as he used all of his strength to keep the door closed between them. Mike could feel the heat lapping at the wooden frame from the light. The hinges groaned against the force. The wooden barrier began to crack and splinter. The door was thrown off its hinges, sending Mike hurtling backwards. He slammed into the wall behind him. The wooden door covered his body from the brilliant light and severe energy as he heard more things break within the house. He trembled violently from under the wrecked door, curling up into a ball. He was going to die. Either she was going to blast him to pieces or that stalker was going to slaughter them.

Mike took in quick breaths as the light slowly began to waver. He watched from the corners of the door as the darkness engulfed where the light had been. The frost of the night crept in; the wind was louder now that the windows were no longer present to stop it. He shuddered, almost weeping in fear. As he felt a hand touch his skin, he whimpered and curled up tighter. The fingertips continued to trail over his arm, checking to see if he was hurt. Slowly, he opened his eyes, glancing up at Dawn.

'It's over, I promise,' Dawn said, her golden eyes staring at Mike's blue ones. He gulped hard, trembling as she checked to see if he was hurt. The door had protected him, besides his previous wounds. He trembled. He had felt the outbursts first-hand, all because her eyes had changed.

'Th-then why are your eyes still yellow?' he questioned, staying huddled under the door. Dawn edged back slightly. Her eyes opened wide; the white pupils focused on him.

'You didn't know they've changed colour?' he asked her. Her eyes were still glowing slightly as she knelt on the floor and picked up a shard of mirror. For the first time, she saw her own eyes. She was silent as she gazed at them. Her pupil had gone white and faintly glimmered. What were once green eyes had now become bright like the sun. Not even amber but a brilliant yellow. Before, she had only felt different on the inside. Now, she stared at the alien in the mirror. What was happening to her?

Mike stayed under the wood as he watched her move around the house in the darkness. They were both in shock. Dawn drifted from place to place, not really focusing. Mike was frozen. He knew he had to snap out of it. He knew the psychopath could come at any moment.

'Dawn, is he coming?' Mike questioned, heaving the wooden barrier and climbing out from underneath it. Dawn was knelt on the floor. The machinery had halted within her mind. She wasn't sure when they had stopped. There was still faint warmth within her chest, and her head felt as though something was pressing against it. Common sense was still present but not as it had been before.

'I'm not sure . . . I don't know,' she answered, concentrating hard. There was nothing stopping her; she was sure of it. She didn't feel powerless. She was in full control of her mind. Yet common sense was there, at a sort of stalemate.

'What do you mean you don't know?' he nervously questioned. Dawn closed her eyes, trying to focus. It was as though the sense had paused.

'I think he's stopped,' she simply said.

'Why on Earth would he stop?' he questioned. She shrugged her shoulders. She didn't know. She had no idea why he had stopped. She didn't truly know why she was being stalked either. All she knew was that he had been chasing her to collect her. He had said so in her dream. He was growing tired of chasing her. That she was acting like 'them'. She finally understood what he had meant by that. She was acting like a human. A creature she knew she wasn't. She didn't know what she was. She was this . . . this thing with glowing eyes, a sixth sense and a *flame* that built up and rushed out of her when it was at its peak. Was there more to come?

'Are you sure he's stopped?' he asked.

'I'm not sure about anything . . .' her voice trailed off. Her attention turned; her eyes focused on Mike. He sat on the floor, rubbing his hands over his jeans. There was a large stain of blood on them. He rolled up the denim himself, licked his fingers, and wiped away the dry blood. A purple bruise had started to form on his arm. She was putting him in danger, in severe danger.

'It's not safe for you to be near me Mike,' she spoke softly. He looked up at her as she spoke. How could she follow Mike for protection anymore when she was putting him in danger? Not just from the Crimson, but from herself as well. There had been a connection, a connection she couldn't pinpoint. But she had to sever it. She would never be able to live with the guilt if he was hurt anymore because of her.

'I don't want you to be hurt because of me. You should head back home. Go to Ricky,' she told Mike as she sat herself on the floor. Mike closed his eyes and pushed grieving tears as far back as he could. There was no Ricky to go back to. She still didn't know. He had made a vow though, and he refused to break it. His fingers curled into his palm, grinding his teeth in frustration.

'I won't Dawn!' he yelled suddenly, slamming his fist into the broken door. She jumped in surprise from his outburst. 'I won't abandon you. You don't deserve it. You don't deserve any of this.'

'But neither do you and this has nothing to do with you,' she pleaded, closing her eyes. How could she put him through anymore of this? He was hurt and had taken so many risks already.

'This has everything to do with me!' he shouted at her. 'Dawn I . . . I . . . care about you.' he glared at her, angry she could consider going on her own. She bit her lower lip. She wanted to protest, but the words were choked by trapped tears. She slumped to the floor and closed her eyes. Awkwardly, he crawled over to her.

'I'm not leaving you, Dawn. I'll figure out something, I will.' He tried to hug her, to reassure her. But she pushed him away, her knees tucked in, and her head buried in them. She closed her eyes tightly. They sat there in silence, in the cold house. Minutes ticked by slowly. Mike didn't know what to do. He slowly got up, wondering how much of the house was damaged. For a moment, he looked back at Dawn. He felt awkward being by her side, unable to comfort her. She had distanced herself.

'If anything changes', he started to speak, 'if it picks up, your senses, tell me immediately.'

He climbed up the stairs and tested the light switch. The corridor flooded with light. The upstairs hadn't been damaged. He looked into each room. He stepped into a bedroom and noticed a TV. He clicked the switch on the side, but it didn't turn on. He thought the upstairs had been untouched, so why wasn't it working? He knelt on the floor and noticed the plugs had been pulled out and the switches off. The family must have been on a holiday. He remembered how his own mum would go around the rooms and pull the plugs out in case a storm came while they were gone. He never understood why the plugs had to be pulled out but they did; something to do with blowing a fuse. But it did mean one thing; Dawn and he were safe to be here, at least from the owners.

He pushed the plug into the socket and clicked the power on the mains, turning on the TV. The screen flashed on. It was set to a sitcom. A group of friends were gathered around a table, drinking hot beverages and talking about how they hated their work. *How selfish*, he thought, *for them to complain about having a home and an income.*

'Janie's like a boomerang. No matter how hard I try to throw her off, that annoying voice always manages to come back,' one of the men tells the others as a chorus of pre-recorded laughter played, to chime in that was a joke. Instead, it made Mike shudder as he turned off the screen in a hurry.

No matter how hard we try to throw him off, he'll keep coming back, his thoughts manipulated the light comedy. If they kept running, he was just going to find them. Dawn had travelled non-stop, and the trains hadn't worked either. That dog had sniffed them out. He had to come up with a much better plan.

'What would Ricky do?' he whispered to himself, looking at the various objects around the room. His friend always seemed to have the answer. His speech was rough, but there was a way about his deceased friend. Ricky had a sense of logic, although blunt and to the point. His friend never overwhelmed himself and took things one stage at a time. He often scolded Mike for thinking too far ahead in the future.

So what was the current priority? Mike's thoughts continued to drag him towards the inevitable. Was it the psychopath and his ghastly dog, Dawn's supernatural power, or the overwhelming ordeal that they could both be dead? He shook his head hard. He couldn't think that way. A little problem, pick a little problem first that could be sorted.

Mike began to open draws and cupboard doors. His eyes scanned the shelves. There had to be something, anything that could help. He charged into the next room, opening each draw and carefully looking through the contents. He checked the third bedroom. A computer was on an untidy desk. It had been a while since he'd sat down at a computer. He remembered how he thought he'd never be able to live without a laptop. Being homeless really changes a person's perceptive on what was really needed. A smile crept on his face as he noticed the object he had been searching for. They were perfect.

'Look what I found!' Mike had run downstairs in excitement, kneeling next to Dawn. Her head tilted upwards. He took her hand, opened it, and placed a pair of sunglasses in them. She glanced at the blue tinted lenses. She held them out in front of her, the dark blue gazing back at her. She understood and placed them over her eyes.

'Yellow and blue make green Dawn. Your eyes are green again!' She looked up at him from behind the glasses. The world had a blue hue to it. He grabbed a mirror shard and held it up. The moons light drifted in, allowing her to see her reflection. She saw that her eyes were a dark green, not the green that they had been, but they were green. Even the pupil had darkened enough that the white was unnoticeable. A smile crept across her face as she began to giggle.

'See, I told you, Dawn. I told you I'd figure something out.' He smiled. She stopped laughing as the words passed his lips.

'He'll still come after me though,' she reminded him. He paused and stroked his chin, deep in thought.

'There's a computer upstairs. We can research,' he led her upstairs, plugging the computer plug into the socket and turning it on. The chimes started to ring from the computer starting up as he sat down and cracked his knuckles. It had been a long time since he'd last been on one.

This guy couldn't have been around and never been noticed. And that dog, something that big doesn't get about without it being posted on the internet. The first thing he searched for was golden eyes. The results were wolf eyes, photo-shops, coloured contact lenses, and a movie. He added white pupils to the end of it. A few articles came up about blindness.

'Can you see okay, Dawn?' he asked her softly. She nodded, sitting on the edge of the bed and watching as he searched. He turned back to the screen; his fingers tapped against the desk in a four-beat rhythm. He would have to try a different approach; nothing was coming up for Dawn. He next typed in red eyes and searched through—Vampires, werewolves, devils, diseases, murders.

'Try crimson eyes,' Dawn advised hesitantly. Mike nodded and changed it to crimson eyes. When the results weren't helpful, he added the white pupil at the end. The results were still worthless yet for a moment he paused. Dawn and that man had the same white pupils. He sat there silently for a moment. Why would they have the same white pupils?

'Is everything okay?' she asked, concerned. He turned and nodded to her before directing his attention to the screen. There was one last thing he could research, one last thing he could try to work out. Slowly his fingers tapped away at the keyboard.

Large black dog with silver eyes.

The results at first seemed as pointless as the ones before. Werewolves and images of the moon were coming up. But then, his eyes drifted to an article. He moved the cursor slowly and clicked the link. The website was plain white with black text except for one image. It was a scanned photo. Underneath it was the date 'March 11th 1950'. The black and white photo sent a chill down his spine. A sharp flash was on the creature lurking in the shadows. Its eyes were bright in the picture. Its fur was dark as one of its paws was raised. Claws like a lions and body of an enormous wolf virtually cloaked in a blackness darker than any other part of the photo.

The Barghest, once mentioned as simply a myth, came to my great grandfather's farm and slaughtered a large bull. By the time he found the camera and started the shot, nothing remained of it but a split skull and dots of blood on the fence, as you can see in the photo. My grandfather found the camera but his own father had vanished.

British folklore describes that the Barghest only appears at night, and the sight of it will bring forth death. They also describe it being ghastly-like, with paws that seem to spread wide like a hand with claws of a cat. Its fur is thick, dense, and is darker than the night sky. Its eyes are described as though they came from the moon itself.

Despite the picture evidence, people still refuse to believe that it exists. But it is out there. It is a spawn of the devil itself, a reincarnation of death. If you even glance at it, you will die a horrible death. The only chance you have is to flee as fast as you can and not look back.

That creature was death. Death had sliced the train in half and had glared directly at him. He felt Dawn's hand on his shoulder. Immediately, he closed the article and turned the monitor off.

'A stupid conspiracy doesn't help us at all,' he whimpered.

'It wasn't a good photo.' She gave his shoulder a light squeeze. Conspiracies are thought up by people that don't truly see something. But that photo, although old and in black and white, looked so much like the creature that had attacked them. Quickly, he got out the seat and kneeled on the bed behind them.

'Right, I think we need a gun, no two. We need two guns. And silver bullets. No, that won't work, silver bullets are for werewolves. That was definitely a Barghest. I'm sure of it. We run from that. But that jerk, maybe we can trick him. Expose him. We get a camera, we take a photo, we ask what he is to a professional. Wait, that dog is Barghest, right? Then that freak is the devil. Must be!' He rambled on.

'Mike, you really need to sleep,' she told him, placing her hand on his chest and pushing him down into a lying position.

'But we have to carry on researching,' Mike replied, yawning half way through his sentence.

'Tomorrow. We both need the rest,' she explained, lying down next to him. He pulled the blanket from off the floor and placed it over her body. She smiled and pulled half of it over Mike. The two lay in the family home, staring at each other. He took in a long breath and exhaled slowly. She was right. He was only getting himself worked up, and he was exhausted.

'Pleasant dreams, Mike,' she whispered as she closed her eyes slowly. Mike watched her. He was extremely tired, but he wanted to make sure she fell asleep first. His eyes began to drift as he was comforted by the thick blankets and her steady breath. He couldn't keep his eyes off her as his felt his heart flutter. He had become so alien to human contact. He didn't know what he was feeling. He lifted the blanket slightly to cover her even more. Her smile grew, and he felt his heart melting. He cared about her, more than he cared about anyone before, not even Ricky.

I will protect you no matter what, he thought to himself as he closed his eyes slowly, *I'll never let anyone hurt you.*

CHAPTER 6

'Mike, are you awake?' Dawn whispered as quietly as she dared. He was sound asleep. They had only been in bed for an hour if that. She leant over, wrapping her arms around him loosely, biting onto her lower lip. She knew what she had to do. A tear ran down her cheek.

'Thank you for keeping me safe, but I can't put you through this anymore.' Dawn whispered, hugging him tightly. The wind outside had calmed. A light snow scattered past the window in the moons light. She remained there for a while as her heart began to ache. She was terrified of going alone, but the way he had panicked earlier, she was now sure that she couldn't put him through this anymore. He had been right. The creature that had attacked them had been the Barghest. The photo, although old, was too much of a resemblance to ignore.

'Please forgive me,' she whispered as she released her grip. His body turned slightly. His hand grabbed the blanket and pulled it closer to himself. He slept soundly as she took in a strangled breath. She edged away slowly. She began to silently cry as she tiptoed out of the bedroom.

The early hours of the morning were an ugly sight outside. The light snow that had settled in the night had turned to grey slush. She felt her boots squelch underneath. She walked alongside the road, her eyes straining to see the road signs. At times, snowflakes landed on her face, but they were few and far between. There was a city several miles away.

She would head in that direction. With her bag on her back, she began to take what she knew would be another long walk.

She questioned herself, whether she had done the right thing. Was it too late to turn back? She shook her head sharply; she couldn't think of that now. She had to get away, had to get far away from danger. Common sense was still a white noise that drifted. In the next city, there would surely be a train station, a way to escape. In doing so, she knew she would never be with Mike again. The thought clung to her as she took in a deep breath. She couldn't think like that. She was keeping him safe, and he always had his friend to go back to.

The night air was cold. She pushed the glasses further up her nose as she continued to walk. When was the sun going to rise? The clouds above were still dark and formidable. She took a quicker pace. She didn't like common sense being so quiet. It unnerved her. There was nobody around. She was completely alone. The thought sent a chill down her neck.

She stopped and listened hard. Something wasn't right. She closed her eyes and concentrated hard. Common sense wasn't there—not a single shred of it. No steam from settled machines or whispers of forgotten people. She turned around, looking behind her in a panic. Nobody was there; it was still just her. She trembled as she took a few steps back. It wasn't possible, not that quickly. He can't have suddenly disappeared.

The clapping sound of her boots against the concrete ground echoed around the empty streets as she quickened her pace. Soon she was running, glancing behind her in panic. It was too quiet, far too quiet. She kept running and running as fast as she could. She had been hobbling for a while now, at times managing to push herself to sprint, but most of the time walking fast, struggling to breathe in the freezing air.

She screamed loudly as she fell to the floor. Common sense was suddenly through as though it had smashed through a brick wall. The machines roared, and the heat was penetrating with such a fierce blow she felt as though she'd be struck with a blade. She wheezed hard, struggling to catch her breath. She had to get up. She had to move. She could feel something engulfing her sixth sense, trying to silence it. She placed her hands on the floor, trying desperately to pull herself up. She feared she'd waited too long as she finally scrambled to her feet. She raced off as fast as she could. Her common sense was there but continued to be smothered by an unknown force. The heat came and went. He was preventing her from knowing. He could have been miles away. He could have been a few steps away.

She needed to get away. She needed to flee. Danger must have been close. She knew it. She felt it. It was instinct that made her drive on. She could hear a heavy clunking sound from far away. Train tracks! Reach the train tracks. Stow away on the carriage somehow. Then she would be safe . . . for a short time.

She kept running. The haunting sounds began to drill into her mind. She felt a heat that was impossible on such a bitter night. The heat lashed at her legs, her arms, and her face. Her fingertips began to trail across her hand and up her arm. There were no marks or burns. Her mind brought the sounds, the burning of fuel, and the clangs of machinery.

Her steps fell into a shaky walk as she stepped near the town's fountain. Tall buildings encircled the ancient stonework, as though they were watching the girl. Her hands pressed against the stones edge, trying to get her bearings. Something seeped into her mind. It was like being poisoned from the inside, making her feel drowsy and unable to move. The feeling was similar to what had happened in the dream she was trapped in. But this was no longer a dream; this was reality. She was completely exhausted; she could not bring herself to move anymore. Her eyes met the moon, tears welling. If she didn't move, he would take her.

Her gaze left the moon and instead caught a glimpse of a shadow in front of her. His figure was hidden in the dense darkness of the night, but his eyes revealed who it was. Crimson. Immediately, fear consumed her, pushing herself away from the fountain into a wavering stance. The adrenaline forced back the venom and spat it out of her head. She heard her voice try to call for help, but it came out as a squeak. He must have been laughing inside. He must have known this was it—that she was doomed. A bead of sweat dripped down her forehead. She blinked once, but when they opened, the villains red eyes had vanished.

Her body jerked into motion, without a thought of where to, she ran for her life. The screams of that girl came back, the echoes louder still; the sound of blood and flesh being torn was more evident. She ran into the darkness, the unwelcoming visions crying within her. She could not see where she was going. She'd run straight into an alleyway, but the darkness confused her. In her panic, she had forgotten about the shades that were covering her eyes. Her heart banged against her ribcage as she whacked her hand into a wall. Her lips met her palm, sucking on the fresh wound as she carried on moving. She tried to feel her way around, arms stretched out, tripping over debris on the ground.

The walls began to turn red before her eyes. She felt as though she was choking on the air around her; the mist seeped into her conscious. It was his doing. The poison was leaking back into her mind. She shook her head hard, stumbling forward in a drunken like state.

'Come to me!' A triumphant yell was heard from above her. Her head tilted up, trying to see in the dark when she felt a tight grip around her small body. She screamed out hysterically for help as the two crimson eyes stared into hers. She struggled furiously as slated structures drooped around her, caging her in, out of sight. She felt his rough finger run across her face up to her eyes. She kicked and fought as much as she could, and the poison in her mind intensified. The glasses were taken off and thrown across the alleyway. A bright glow shone against his face as he did so. Her eyes . . . alien to this world. She stared at her trembling body through the reflection in his eyes. His eyes were an incredible deep red as though the blood of a thousand men had dyed them. Her light bearing eyes shone divinely. The darkness flowed beyond the outside and into her body. It engulfed and drove her to a state of which she could not comprehend until it was too late.

She had blacked out in the devil's hands.

CHAPTER 7

Within the grey clouds, the borderline of life and death, Dawn stood on her own. There were distant sounds, the heavy clunks of metal being tapped, the quiet turning of gears, and the echoes of voices coasting sparingly. She knew she wasn't awake, unable to lift herself from her slumber. There was no comprehending if the sounds from the outside were words or movement. They seemed to never end, forever coming and going. There was simply the great nothing—miles and miles of the grey and desolate sea.

Why did this happen? A distant voice whispered. It wasn't Dawn's thoughts that had murmured those words. Her mind struggled and squirmed, trying to push away the thick mist. The clouds that cloaked her grew darker and darker. A horrible rumble like that of heavy thunder rolled in and out. The grey overwhelmed again and again as she tried to understand.

The Crimson . . . he took me away to the machines. the whispering continued. Dawn ran through the waves towards the voice. In the distance, she was certain she saw a shadow of a person. Desperate to reach her, she accelerated into a sprint.

'What machines? The ones in my nightmares?' Dawn questioned. The world became more sinister. She could barely hear the other girl.

He never cared about the pain he caused the others. They're gone now. His eyes are only for you, the girl spoke out in vain. Dawn felt her heart grow heavy.

'Tell me why!' Dawn cried out. The grey sea had turned a vivid black. Her attempts to push back the developing darkness were hopeless. She could no longer see the silhouette.

'When he took me to the machines, he was merciless. He will give you none of his sympathy,' the voice was barely audible. She was frantic to find out what the demonic stranger had done.

'What happened?' Dawn shouted as loudly as she could. Silence filled the black landscape.

'What did he do to you?' she screamed out. There was no response.

'What will he do to me?' she whimpered. The girl was no longer there.

Immediately, the darkness vanished, and a sharp light forced her into reality. Her eyes opened briefly; her body protested as it was being forced to stand upright. The unnatural light startled her, closing her eyes tightly.

'Wake up!' she was beckoned. She groaned as she felt her body cave, trying to go back to lying. Hands were under her armpits, forcing her to stand.

'Get up, sunshine; I've let you recover long enough!' the familiar voice broke her out of her trance. She opened her eyes and saw, standing in front of her, a heavily built man. He looked human, a handsome man in his late twenties. His body towered over her as though he knew nothing was surely as magnificent as he was. His blonde bangs were covering his eyes partially, but there was no mistaking it. The eyes were crimson. She could feel hot tears behind her eyes trying to escape. He was no human.

'Stand up, sunshine!' He told her again. Her feet struggled to push against the floor. As soon as they did, he let her go and took a step back. Her common sense was partially there, muffled sounds and restricted heat. It was suffocating.

Her eyes narrowed as she glared at her captor. He sneered as he knelt down and squeezed her cheek sharply with his fingers. His fingertips dug into her skin, pressed against her jaw, and pinched slightly. She swallowed hard; her mind began to feel groggy suddenly. He was poisoning her mind like he had done before.

'Remember the dream?' he told her, 'It's your choice, butterflies or chains?'

'Butterflies,' she whispered. He let her go and stood upright again, watching her closely. The venom immediately slipped out of her mind. Common sense was loud, the machines strong and fierce. There was no screaming. There was no heat. It was too late and her common sense knew it. The Crimson had her. Her fate was now in his hands.

He hadn't killed her, which meant he wanted her for something else. There were no windows in this room, and there was no point in insulting his intelligence. If he meant to keep her prisoner, he wouldn't leave a door unlocked or a window open for her to slip through.

His hand outstretched, pointing to the room outside of the one they were in. She made her way towards the room. It was cluttered and stank of mould. The walls were filled from top to bottom with books—old books. Books with worn spines and ripped sleeves. It was an archive of vast information, whether it remained on the shelves, tables, or on the floor itself.

'Let's make sure you know exactly what is going on,' he continued, pushing her into a seat and dropping a bowl of what looked like porridge in front of her. The mush in the bowl was partially grey and unwelcoming. She couldn't possibly bring herself to eat it. Feeling sick at the sight of it, she pushed the food away from her.

'That attitude won't help you in anyway.' He let out a sigh, pulling a book from the many shelves. 'I blame them.' She glanced up from the table. His piercing red eyes stared down at her.

'Blame who?' she asked, the first time she had asked this fiend a question directly.

'The inferior ones', he stated as he dropped the book besides her, picking up the untouched food and walking off. 'Page forty-three', he called out loudly. Dawn stared over at where she presumed the kitchen was. She glared at the book that had been thrown at her. The corners were charred black, and half of the book had been torn out.

Slowly, Dawn opened the book. The encryptions were unlike anything she had seen before. There was no way for her to understand what was written. She slowly turned the pages, counting as she turned them. The handwriting was smooth and delicate; the lettering was written in gold. She turned the pages until she reached the forty-third page and stared at it in bewilderment. Again, there were words that she couldn't understand, but there was something else. There were painted illustrations of two people, a great length of detail in each stroke. They had white pupils and golden eyes, just like hers. Subconsciously, she brought her hand to her left eye before quickly retracting it. The male in the picture stared back at her; his long white hair flowed to his chest.

'Light bearer', the Crimson's voice was suddenly close. She was startled, almost knocking the book as the Crimson stood over her.

'Those that possessed golden eyes were known as the light bearers,' he leant closer. His red eyes stared at the book. He smiled as he flicked two pages forward. Again, there were two humanoids, a man and a woman. Their eyes were red but not as dark as his were. There was something else though, something she hadn't spotted on page forty-three.

They've got wings? She thought to herself, staring at them in shock. Their wings were open wide. They reminded her of a kestrel's wings, powerful, beautiful, and red-brown. But they were not solid, and there were no feathers. It was strange, almost like liquid with a metal sheen, concentrated in areas and solidified in certain positions. She pulled the pages back, looking at the people with the golden eyes, the light bearers. She hadn't noticed before. From their backs came a yellow glow that created the shape of wings. The first time she'd looked at it, she only thought it was a background pattern. The bending light curled and twisted, forming the shape of large wings. She started to flick through the pages with the illustrations. Different coloured eyes. Different wings for each one. He stopped her from flicking so fast, turning each page slowly, finger trailing across each set of eyes.

'The eyes defined your purpose and your strengths,' he stood straight, staring at her, 'and it would appear you're fledging into a light bearer—a bringer of hope and desire.' She was confused and frightened, and he knew it. She glanced back at the book as her fingers were trailing over the person with golden eyes. He spoke of them as though they were the same as her.

'It's not possible.' She denied the evidence, shaking her head quickly and snapping. 'Why are you showing me these creatures?'

'You dare to call your ancestors creatures?' His hands slammed against the table. His face was so close she could smell him and feel his hot breath. She held her own. He closed his eyes, taking in one long and frustrated gulp of air.

'We are the same, don't you see it?' he told her, turning away from her. She stared down at the book turning back through the pages to the two humanoids with ruby eyes. Their faces stared back. Their expressions were hard and stern as though they'd witnessed the worst and were now simply numb to it.

'You are not an inferior, sunshine. You're like them and like me,' he leant forward on the table; his eyes set on hers. She glared back. She wasn't one of these things; she refused to believe it. She wasn't them, and she was nothing like this man.

'I'm nothing like you. I'm human!' she spoke up, getting up quickly from her chair. He turned sharply; his eyes set on her. Her common sense spiked, raging into an intense inferno. His hand grasped her neck. She clawed his fingers frantically with her own as she felt her body being lifted. Her feet were no longer touching the floor. His grip tightened, blocking her airways. She kicked and struggled in the air, desperate to take in a breath. It felt like minutes, but it had only been seconds. He threw her body against the wall; his grip around her neck loosened slightly.

'You are not human. You are not those vile inferior pests. Do you understand?' She felt her body shaking as she took in sharp breaths. 'Do you understand?' He roared at her. She nodded in quick succession, and immediately, she was dropped to the floor. She stumbled to her feet as quickly as she could. He picked the book up from the table and threw it at her. She barely caught it as he walked off. She glanced over at her captor as he stared back at her. It wasn't a coincidence. He knew her actions. She took in a deep breath, unsure if it was safe to talk back again.

She quietly spoke, 'You're wrong. I don't have wings so I can't be—'

'You will do,' he cut her short of her speech. 'For the time being, it's within you, but soon the energy will flow from your shoulders and form into wings. You do remember that sudden outburst you had, don't you?' She looked down, feeling the energy deep within her lapping and whirling. The energy that had built up and exerted when everything became too much had come from this inner energy.

'Why me though? Why not some other alien?' she pleaded. He exhaled deeply in frustration, and for a moment, she thought his hands would be upon her again or worse. He came closer to her, raising his hand. She flinched as it came down, but it only fell to rest on her shoulder.

'First, we are not aliens. We were born on this planet, and we have lived on this planet since the first of us. They had mistaken us for myths, legends, and sometimes even gods. The closet you can call us in human language are angels, or at least an angelic race,' he corrected her. She gazed down at the closed book and back at him. The angels she knew about, which she knew next to nothing of, were messengers of god. Even on the rare visit to the church, she was told they lived in heaven. Not Earth.

'Secondly,' he interrupted her thoughts. 'We are the only ones that remain.' The words didn't sink in for a while as she stared blankly at him.

'We're the only ones?' she repeated his words.

'Yes. I am the last male, and you are the last female. It's a miracle, and one not to be wasted, for we can bring back the race,' he told her triumphantly. His words hung on the air like daggers. She felt her stomach twist sharply and pull tightly at the sound of those words. She felt sick as she began to realise what he was insinuating. He expected her to get pregnant, with him.

She spun round and fled towards the bathroom door, her hand to her mouth. Before she could reach it, the door flung open. She peeked behind her to see the madman. His dark red wings were suddenly visible, with one outstretched in the direction of the door. They were enormous, taking up most of the room, touching both the ceiling and the floor. They were a deep, running red, curved into the template of a bird's wings. She felt herself crumble inside as she ran to the bathroom and vomited violently inside.

'It was never supposed to be this way, sunshine,' he approached her slowly. 'I was to bring you up myself from an infant. No humans could corrupt your mind, but you were cruelly stolen from me and thrown to those creatures. It has taken me over a decade to find you.' His hand rested on her shoulder once more. His intention may have been to comfort, but his fingers felt tense and cold. She slowly turned to look at him, wiping her mouth with the back of her hand. She never really knew where she had come from. She had asked her social workers several times, but they told her it was best not to know. If they knew about him, then they would have fled when she had begged them to. Perhaps, her parents had tried to save her from him by abandoning her. But he had said they were the only two. So many questions swamped her mind as she leant against the toilet, taking in deep breaths.

She spat into the toilet, the taste of bile still strong in her mouth, 'I'd rather die than—'

'I won't allow you to die,' he interrupted her with a grin on his face. 'You will forever be in my constant protection so long as I live. It is my sole duty to keep you in sight and from any form of harm. I will correct the mistake I allowed before. It will not happen again.' She got up slowly, glaring at him. He didn't move.

'I can accept I'm not human,' she spoke slowly, slamming the lid of the toilet down harshly, 'but I will not accept you as being the same as me. I will not . . . repopulate the angels. So you might as well let me go,' she held her head up high as she gave her speech. The man gazed down at her. His dark eyes were still and emotionless. He turned and walked out of the room. She walked out after him after some time. Her sight was on the solid front door.

'So you're going to flee. Is that the plan?' he asked her, bringing the bowl she had abandoned to his lips and gulping it down. His wings were still on full display. She couldn't help but stare at them in fascination. If she touched them as they were, she wondered if her hands fall through them like water or stain her skin like blood. His wings took on a darker colour, the energy solidified. They curved into sharp fingers, grasped the door handle, and opened it. Light shimmered through.

Was he offering her freedom? She took a small step towards it. She begged that she could feel her sixth sense, but he'd drowned it within the toxins.

'If you fully understand yourself and you know how to keep curious eyes of scientists at bay and know how to control your powers both present and future, why, you're more independent than I comprehended. So what are you waiting for?' he asked her. She gazed back at him. He sneered at her, knowing exactly what was on her mind. She took in a deep breath, taking a step towards the door. The sunlight was bright, making her squint. There were no houses. No streets. No roads. It was nothing but a vast forest, stretching from all four corners of the land. This house stood perfectly on its own, unnoticed. She would be lost, and she knew with her eyes the way they were that there was no one she could ask for help. She had no idea how to survive off the land either. Anything would be better than enduring his cruel plan though. She took a single step outside.

'Of course, if you leave, I'll be visiting your little pet Mike,' he slowly spoke. She stopped. Her foot was just outside the door, the winter snap touching her. Mike. He knew about Mike? She turned around, looking back into the house that was lit by electronic lights, turning her back on nature and freedom.

'You're affectionate for that . . . thing,' he remarked, 'There's no use in denying it.' She opened her mouth to protest. He stood up from the table, slowly walking towards her. His demeanour was all that was needed to leave her feeling weak and unable to speak.

'He was in the shambles of that building, quivering and watching from a crack in the door when I killed his buddy,' he continued. Dawn dug her fingernails into the palm of her hand. She'd left Mike alone, thinking he'd go back to his friend when really he'd been murdered.

'I thought that may be enough for him to separate from you, but he's thicker than he looks. I always knew he was accompanying you,' he laughed, grabbing her arm and pulling her close to him, 'I suppose he thought he could protect you, but he made it easier for me.' She could feel sickness rising within her again.

'What will you do to him if I leave?' she whispered. She'd left him to save him, but now she knew as soon as he offered to help, his fate was tied to hers.

'Well then, he wouldn't be of benefit to me.' He licked his lips as he spoke. 'And he knows too much about you and I. The consequences would then outweigh the pros. Do you understand the dilemma put before me? I can be considerate though Dawn. For you I can be and ignore that he exists.' She understood clearly. Be a good little girl, do your tricks, heel by master, and Mike won't be killed.

'I'll do as you ask but don't lay a finger on Mike,' she pleaded. His grin grew. He'd won his trophy, and she wouldn't lash out like some feral thing. He smiled, pulled her back into her prison, and closed the door behind them, the natural light shut out. She shivered as she was enclosed in the house. She edged towards the table; her hands resting against it. She felt suffocated, trembling violently, speculating what she was going to do now.

'You need not worry. You're too young to be burdened with children yet,' he told her calmly, grabbing another book from the bookcase. She felt broken. She couldn't put Mike into danger. Yet she knew what that would entail. That she would have to go through with his plans. Of abandoning everything, she knew about the human world and become this other creature, both in body and mind. She was going to have to play along until she could figure out a plan. She prayed she could come up with something soon.

CHAPTER 8

'The panic sensation you get when something hazardous is approaching is triggered by your eternal eye. A sixth sensory that flows through every vein in your body and reads your surroundings. It sees further than the eyes in your head, hears more than your ears, and feels more than the lightest touch on your skin,' he told her, motioning her to stand on the table. After a week of being locked away, she had become used to being ordered around. She now accepted it and embraced it. She didn't question his commands as she climbed onto the table. The wood groaned underneath her as she stood on it. Because of the food she'd been eating, she had gained weight, enough to cover her bones with meat. She was no longer the skinny thing she had been before. She was kept in prime health, sure. She was challenged mentally through vigorous exercises, sure. But being shut off from the outdoor light, from society, from a true friend and a lack of freedom, was draining her emotionally. She felt like a caged animal in a zoo.

'That sensation is a defence mechanism that is triggered when you go through your most fragile state and will mould into something more refined the more you sculpt it,' he explained to her. She closed her eyes, feeling ill from the thought of what the new exercise would be.

'You can manipulate it with great practice to further benefit you,' he carried on with his lecture. She opened her eyes, watching him carefully. She remembered when she had used it to tell when to strike her attackers.

She had used it to protect Mike and had felt proud that day. She understood manipulation and wondered if she could use it further still.

He walked into the area that was supposedly the kitchen, opening a drawer and taking something from it. She saw a gleam of metal as he closed the draw, hiding the object behind his back.

'Wait, what are you doing?' she questioned. He didn't respond as he stood back in front of her. Her sixth sense intensified drastically. The machines roared and the fire scorched intensely. She knelt down, ready to get off the table.

'Do not leave the table,' he told her. She froze, looking back at him. 'The feeling is drawn from your darkest memory. You must learn to control it and not let it control you.' Dawn shook her head, shivering. How could it be her darkest memory? She never recalled the corridor, the screeching gears, the screaming people, the smells, the heat, and the darkness as her memories. She had never been anywhere like that.

'Please stop. I can't,' she pleaded. He ignored her, bringing out a knife. The sense grew violently. She gulped hard, knowing he would. He'd done it before, and he'd do it again to accelerate her education. He pulled his hand back; his eyes were narrowing at her. He was delaying on purpose, allowing her sense to build and intensify. The pool of energy within her body bubbled and whirled. He pulled his arm back and swung it forward. She yelped, recoiling instinctively.

'Ignore your inferior instincts!' he growled at her, showing the knife was still in his hand. He swung his arm forward a second time. She swallowed hard, flinching but keeping still. The knife was still in his hand. Her eternal eye fed through the same intense fear. Her energy rippled vigorously within her as he pulled back his arm a third time. Then the flames rose in severity, the gears craned louder, and the distant sounds of screaming became closer.

'Stop!' She cried out, seeing the knife leaving his hand. Her common sense triggered violently. She felt it, a quick succession, the moment when she should have evaded. But she couldn't, she was overwhelmed with fear. Instinctively, she brought her hands forward, palms facing outwards. The knife embedded into her left hand. She howled out in pain, trembling against the table. A loud crack echoed across the room. She felt the table cave in, collapsing underneath her. Her chest thumped against the floor. Her head rattled from the drop.

He stood above her as she gazed up at him. His stare was cold and hateful. The knife was still wedged in her hand. She sobbed as her fingers grasped the handle, trying to jiggle it out of place. Each time she attempted to move it though her nerves raged and a charge of pain shot through her hand and up her arm. He slapped her hand away, gripped the handle, and yanked it out in one quick motion. She screamed at the swift movement. The knife was gone, blood seeping through the deep scar. He grabbed her hand as she shook. His eyes lit up. She could feel a soaring hot energy enter her skin and flow through her palm. She whimpered loudly, watching the blood flow stop, the skin patching itself up, and the pain subsiding. He let go of her slowly, taking his hand away. She took in a sharp breath, staring at his left hand. A horrible cut ran deep through his hand, blood dribbling down. He had taken her wound from her and inflicted it upon himself. She ran her fingers across her palm. There were no marks and no pain at all.

He turned his back to her, grabbing a box from a shelf. She knelt on the wooden top, taking in deep breaths as he opened the lid. Full of anger, he snarled, grasping the box in his hand. His fingers tightened around the metal box as it broke inwards. He threw it to the ground, bringing his bleeding hand to his mouth and sucking at the blood. She stared at the broken box—an empty first aid kit.

'Go and study,' he growled at her. She edged back on the table, staring towards the book that was set out for her. It was written in the ancient and forgotten language. She still hadn't learnt the language. She got off the wooden wreck, gazing at him.

'I can't read it though,' she complained. His eyes narrowed, his fingers curling tightly into her palm, his body tensing. She stood up quickly, keeping her head low and walking towards the desk. She picked up the large book that was there, opening it and staring at the scribbles she didn't understand. She heard him storming around the prison. She wished she was somewhere else, anywhere else but here.

He threw a notebook at her, 'Don't expect me to translate it for you for much longer.' She took the notes, English writing on them. Only for part of the book but at least she could now do as she was instructed.

'Thank you,' she whispered quietly, not bringing herself to look up at him. She felt a cold snap behind her. She looked over her shoulder. The front door was open; his figure was standing in the doorway. He had tied a cloth tightly around his hand as he stared back at her.

'Learn every translated page off by heart, sunshine,' he told her, 'If you haven't there will be severe consequences when I get back!' He slammed the door loudly behind him. She sat up, staring over at the door. Had he left her? She slowly got up, edging towards the door. Her eternal eye sparked abruptly. She stopped, realising he was expecting her to try and escape. It was cruel. The exit lay before her, and there were no chains holding her down. Despite that though, she couldn't leave. She sighed, going back to her seat and staring at the English words. One attempt at escape and he'll kill Mike. As she turned the page, she heard footsteps walking away from the door. He had been testing her, to see if she would remain loyal. She closed her eyes and hugged her side, taking in a shallow breath. This was not loyalty; this was repression.

Hours had drifted by as she closed the book and sighed. She was sick to death of her heritage. The book was re-telling the royal family of the light bearers. Pages had been torn out near the end of the chapter, and other areas had been blotched with deep black ink. She enjoyed learning something new, but she also knew he was hiding details from her. The last king of the light-bearers was listed as a man known as Arthur. He had two children, Gyan and Lyra. She could only assume that the angel's son took the throne or maybe had fallen ill and Lyra had taken the throne. The dates were millennia back and Arthur had reigned over two millennia ago. Exactly how old did angels live to be? How old was the Crimson?

'Am I going to be alive long after Mike passes away?' she questioned aloud. The furniture had no answers for her. She leant forwards, closed her eyes, and began to cry. She had never felt so alone and lost before in her life.

She got up abruptly, knocking the chair over. She charged towards the room where she slept, slamming the door. The mirror stood in the corner of the room. She gazed towards it. Tear-stricken golden eyes shone back. She bit her lip, snarling at the mirror. She hated it. She hated what she was. She hated her stupid ancestors. She hated what she was going to be. She charged towards the mirror, grabbing the sides and screamed at it. Her reflection silently screamed back at her, pulled back lips, rage overflowing from every crevice of her face.

She whimpered and slowly descended to the floor, 'I just want to be normal.' She wept in front of the mirror, curling up on the floor. She let the overflow of repressed emotions pour out of her.

'Please, don't cry,' a voice whispered softly. Dawn slowly opened her eyes. She stared at herself. Her blonde hair had grown long, and her skin was roughed up. Slowly Dawn got up and stood in front of the mirror, wiping her eyes. Her reflection stayed where it was. It sat on the floor, looking up at her. The reflection wasn't a perfect copy of her.

Dawn choked back her tears, shocked, 'Hey, you're that girl in the—'

'In the corridor, yes,' the girl in the mirror replied. The teenager's reflection ran her fingers through her blonde hair, slowly getting to her own feet and standing in front of Dawn. The girl's eyes were green with black pupils—eyes that Dawn once had. They now both stood in the room. Dawn stared in amazement.

'Who are you?' Dawn asked quietly, keeping her voice as low as possible. The girl in the mirror remained silent, looking away from Dawn. She would have to try a different approach.

'What happened to you?' Dawn asked her. The girl shrugged, smiling weakly. The reflection placed her hand on the glass. Dawn brought forward her hand, placing it in the same position on the glass. All she felt was the shiny surface. The girl frowned a little, spreading her fingers outwards, then back in.

'He put me through so much pain and torture,' the girl replied, looking away from Dawn and towards the right. 'There were these machines. It was something to do with the machines.' Dawn remembered the loud gears turning in her nightmares, the sound of pistons pumping, the steam whirring, and the metal screeching. Her sixth sense, but of course. It wasn't drawing from Dawn's darkest memory; it was drawing from this girl's darkest memory. The moment before she . . .

'Please tell me what you remember about them,' Dawn begged, not knowing if she would like the answer. The girl in the mirror looked back at Dawn.

'I remember the roaring heat, and I remember him,' she replied. She ran her hand downwards and to the side, still staring at Dawn, 'I remember being enclosed, and I remember the darkness.' Dawn gulped, trailing her own hand downwards, attempting to comfort the girl in the mirror. She wondered quietly how this girl had come to be within her subconscious.

'I wish I could help you,' Dawn told her. The girl gazed up at her.

'Don't worry about me. Worry about yourself,' the girl told her, gazing towards the right and then back at her, 'You need to escape this place.'

'I can't though,' Dawn told her, blinking hard, a leftover tear crept down her cheek.

'You must Dawn!' she told her sternly, both hands pressed against the mirror. 'He can't get away with what he did in the past, what he did to me, and what he's doing to you now. Please, you can't let him get away with it.'

'Well, what am I supposed to do?' Dawn snapped at her. 'Do you have any idea what I've gone through? I've lost the people that were the closest thing to a family. I discovered I'm some alien, duty bound to repopulate. I only have one thing left. I'm not going to be his death.'

'How do you know Mike is still alive now Dawn?' the girl questioned her. Dawn stopped her outburst; her hand trembling. She didn't know if he was still alive. There was no evidence that the Crimson had kept his word.

'He won't keep his word. He tricked people in similar ways. Promising that someone they cared about would be okay. He's a man driven to the edge and will tell you the world is made of gold if he has to.'

'Why was he tricking people?' Dawn asked the girl. The girl's hands rested on her stomach; her eyes were beginning to grow dull. Dawn watched as she saw the girl start to drift away.

'Don't let your guilt hold you back,' she finally answered. Her voice was quiet and weak. 'Don't let him control you. Get away from him, while you have the chance.' Dawn watched as the girl faded completely.

'Wait, don't go, I need your help.' Dawn cried out. 'Don't leave me, please!' She screamed out, grabbing the mirror. Her own reflection stared back, bright golden eyes. The girl had gone again, buried deep within her subconscious.

Dawn let out a scream of frustration, her energy within boiled and lashed out. The mirror shattered, the carpet smoked slightly of dying embers. She had got it all wrong. So long as she was here, Mike could be killed without her knowing.

CHAPTER 9

Mike walked across the street, his sight on the vandalism that occurred days ago. People passed by without giving him a second glance. He made his way towards a narrow alleyway and stared into its darkness. He held a pair of blue shades in his hand. The lenses had been smashed, but he had found them down this alley almost a week ago. His mind was occupied with the thought of his friend. He was worried for her safety but did not know what to do. He placed the shades in his bag as he made his way to what use to be the train station. He was desperate for food and short on money. But he was adamant he wasn't going to leave this location, just in case Dawn came back. If she was still safe, she'd come back to the station to catch a train with him; he was positive about it. Even with the station in ruin, the doors barred off and the windows covered. She would come back here if she could.

The night was growing colder and colder. Mike paced around the station, his body numb and his ears burning. He glanced up, spotting a broken window. It was the one he and Dawn had climbed out of to escape. Awkwardly, he climbed onto the bins and onto the roof. He climbed through the open pane and forced his way into the cafeteria. He scanned around the dark room. He could make out the arrangement of tables and chairs. He turned to the counter to check if there was any food. There was none. He'd already taken the last of it. He was forced to search deeper into the station.

He stepped towards the cafeteria doors and pulled at them. He pressed his foot against the wall and heaved with all of his might, but it would not move an inch. He let go, taking in a deep breath and staring at the frame around it. There were teeth marks across the frame; the metal had bent, getting in the way of the door. He then noticed the glass pane was broken and presented an opening. Mike took in a deep breath and heaved himself upwards, trying to fit in. He wriggled and squirmed before falling onto the other side. Taking in a deep breath, he looked back at the door. An array of claw marks was across the door as well as blood and a single shoe print. Mike had barely made it through himself; there was no way that creep could have got through.

Dust fell from the ceiling and landed on the train tracks as he walked down the corridor. There had once been stairs leading to public toilets, only now part of it was missing. They had been smashed with part of the floor broken apart. The steel and concrete had been twisted together, creating a large pile of debris. What caught Mike's attention was a sign post that was sticking out from the rocks. He walked over to it, running his hands over the destruction. The pole had been perfectly skewered in. Above him, he could hear the ceiling creak and groan against the winter's frost.

Mike's eyes caught a glimpse of something in the rubble. Something was under there, a tiny spark of silver, beckoning him to retrieve it. He grabbed onto the pole and pulled at it as hard as he could before letting go, staggering forward and placing his hand on the clumps of concrete. His fingers felt around them, finding the loose pieces and pulling them away, hoping he wouldn't cause the whole thing to fall. He pulled out a third and a fourth chunk of rock, throwing them to one side. As he reached for the fifth rock, his hand touched something warm and soft. It was too dark to see what it was. He began to pull rocks out quickly. Lumps of concrete and tiles were thrown behind him. More of the dark soft material that had been there before showed.

As he pulled away one rock, he nearly dropped it. Mike froze, realising what the shining object was beneath the rubble. The silver eye stared back unmoving. Shakily, he waved his hand in front of the dog. It didn't move. Mike took in a sharp breath. It must be dead. How could that killer leave it in such a poor state if it was his pet? Had it been down there since that night? Mike noticed that the pole wasn't just skewered into the rubble, but it was skewered into the beast's chest.

His hands clasped around the pole again, and he began to pull at it. He groaned loudly, grunting as he pulled back as hard as he could. Suddenly, he lurched backwards; the pole coming free in a sickening sound. As he did so, the ceiling shuddered violently, and parts of it began to fall. He gasped in horror, realising the building was caving in. He braced himself, arms covering his face.

He felt a tight grip in the side of his t-shirt. As he opened his eyes in those split seconds, he felt his body being lifted with fierce momentum. A flurry of black fur and dust flashed before him as he was thrown backwards. He landed sharply on his side, feet away, his t-shirt torn across the left side. He blinked harshly as the sound of an agonising whine echoed the room. He saw the Barghest being struck by the falling ceiling. The hound howled out in pain as it fell on its side, sliding across the floor. Its bloody body lay next to Mike. Its breathing was deep and raspy. Its black fur was covered in dust, dried on blood and a fresh flow that came from where the pole had been.

In fear, Mike staggered backwards, taking in sharp and quick breaths. The stars were shining through the newly made hole. His attention drew back to the gasping being.

'Did you save me?' he asked it. The Barghest lay where it was, still taking in deep breaths. Mike shook his head. It had been trying to kill him and Dawn only days ago. Slowly he got up, staring at his own chest. His T-Shirt had been shredded, but there wasn't a single scratch on his body. He picked up the ripped half of his t-shirt, staring back at the Barghest. Every instinct was telling him to run, to get out of there. He wanted to run up the stairs and never look back. One thing stopped him. It may know how to find Dawn.

'Don't bite me,' he begged rather than told. He took in a terrified breath as he pressed the cloth against the fresh wound on the beast. He heard the dog groan deeply, making Mike's heart tremble. The two stared at each other, its silver eyes focused.

'Your . . . your eyes . . . the pupil's white,' Mike stated. He remembered the Crimson with his deep red eyes and white pupil. He remembered how Dawn's eyes had changed, from green to golden with a white pupil. Now this creature as well sported the unnatural white pupils.

The monster snarled, and Mike jumped back. It turned onto its front, shaking as it forced itself to stand. The large creature stood there awkwardly, its tongue lapping at the deep wound in its chest, tensing at each swipe. Its head was at the same height as Mike's was, despite being on all fours. Its ears were pointed straight up, curving slightly at the ends towards the centre like a set of horns.

'You're huge!' he whimpered. The Barghest stopped lapping at his wound, staring at Mike. He swallowed back as much of his phobia as he could, taking small steps towards him. The creature lowered its head, its tongue trailing over its sharp big teeth. Mike's hand was outstretched, and his palm was flat. He bit his lip hard and closed his eyes tightly.

The Barghest pressed its forehead into his hand, letting out a soft whine, its ears flat. It sat before Mike, its tail wagging from side to side slowly, its large silver eyes peeking up at him. Very slowly, Mike ran his fingers over the dog's ears and fur, petting him. The fur didn't feel real. It was like running his fingers through warm silk. He stood there stroking the mythical creature for a time before laughing.

'I don't get it. Why were you trying to kill us before?' Mike let out a shaky sigh, running his fingers over its ears and its chest. The Barghest tilted its head, and its ears flopped. Slowly, it lifted up its paw. Mike noted how its claws were long, thick, and sharp. He slowly remembered back. Back to the rundown home he lived in and the boarded up windows. The wooden boards had been broken, and only claw marks remained.

'You were trying to help us get away!' Mike suddenly realised. It raised its head, its tail wagging fast, thudding against the concrete. He gazed towards the tracks where the train had been sliced through. The Crimson was at the station minutes later. The madman had planned on getting onto the train, and the Barghest tried causing a scene so the killer couldn't see them. It even forced the cafeteria door shut to stop the Crimson from getting to them. The two creatures must have fought each other. The Crimson must have thrust the pole into the Barghest and pinned it inside the wreckage.

The creature pressed its nose to the floor, slowly moving across the station platform. Droplets of blood continued to fall as it made its way to the cafeteria doors. It was concentrating on the footprint. The creature turned and jumped down onto the train tracks below, wincing as it landed. Mike took in a deep breath, clambering down. Spots of blood trickled towards the creature's direction. Mike heard more of the ceiling behind him falling sharply. Its nose pressed against the tracks, taking in deep breaths as it padded back and forth.

'Are you trying to get her scent or his?' he asked nervously. The Barghest stopped sniffing the floor and stared at Mike. He took the shades out of the bag and offered them towards the Barghest. It approached him and sniffed around the lenses, then the side of the frame.

'Dawn was wearing these,' Mike told it. 'This was all I could find of hers. They were on the floor in an alleyway not too far from here.' The Barghest grabbed a large metal chain from the wreckage and held it tightly in its fangs. It lay down before Mike, thrusting its head back sharply. The middle of the chain was still in its mouth, the ends now resting on its back. Its tail was wagging slowly from side to side.

Mike approached and grabbed one side of the chain. The dog's paw dragged into the ground as it pushed its side into Mike, tripping the boy over his body. He realised what it wanted. Nervously, he climbed onto the creature's back and grabbed the other end of the chain. Its nose was close to the ground, taking strong strides forward. It then lurched, sprinting down the track at full speed. Mike struggled to hold as the wind rushed into him, coming out of the station and outside.

'I really hope you're taking me to Dawn,' he shouted at the Barghest. He saw its tail wag sharply from left to right. Mike held tightly onto the cable. The beast didn't slow down. At times, Mike could see distant lights beaming from the other side of the tracks. He wondered what the drivers would have thought if they spotted a young boy riding on the back of a beast. Mike knew there were two possible places he was going—to Dawn or to the monster. It didn't matter which. He was positive that the crimson-eyed man had taken her.

Hours had gone by when he noticed the beast was gasping and slowing down. A line of light pierced across the horizon as the sun was rising.

'You've been running all night. You should take a break,' Mike ran his hand through the Barghest's fur. Its fur no longer felt silky but rough and ragged. It slowed down gradually and stopped, letting out a long whine. Mike got off, his legs feeling uneasy underneath him as he stood up. The Barghest was still taking in fragmented breaths as it stepped off the tracks and towards distant lights. Mike followed him closely, not knowing where they were.

He noticed cottages spread sparingly around cobblestone pathways. They were in a village but what village he was in he was unsure. The Barghest lay down on the ground, closing its eyes and taking in strong breaths. Mike knelt next to the canine, running his hands over its body.

'What's wrong?' Mike asked in a panic, wondering if the wounds were too much for it. As he ran his hands over its chest, he couldn't find the deep wound. He continued to search frantically, hoping it wasn't suffering from blood poisoning. As he ran his fingers through its dense fur, he noticed the hairs growing shorter. The sun crept beyond the horizon as the beast shrunk before his eyes. Its paws retracted into soft pads, its fangs retreated within its mouth, and its bulk began to vanish. Mike took a step back as the Barghest slowly pulled itself up from the ground. Its silver eyes shone as it stared up at Mike, wagging its tail once. It was a lanky black mongrel, a fraction of its size.

'Are you okay?' he asked it, slightly confused. It barked three times, high-pitched and normal barks. Mike stood there, remembering back to the article he had read. The Barghest had only been spotted at night. He knelt down next to it, reaching his hand out and stroking the top of its head. Its ears fell flat, whining as it wagged its tail. It appeared the Barghest was cast away when light touched it.

They walked through the village. The dog stayed ahead, checking back on Mike at times before carrying on. They made their way down the side of a series of shops. A few people were out in the frost of the morning, but most were still tucked in their beds. The dog's ears continuously twitched and turned, its head turning sharply at directions before facing forward again. As they passed through a narrow street, the dog suddenly stopped in its tracks. Mike froze as the dogs tail lowered. Something was wrong. Mike watched out from the narrow passage at two people talking.

'The earliest slot they had at the doctors was two weeks from now.' A mother knelt before a young girl. The child looked up and nodded once, smiling sweetly. One of her eyes was covered in a makeshift patch of sorts consisting of a white cloth and medical tape.

'Don't fuss,' the girl told her mother. 'It doesn't hurt me.' Her mother simply shook her head, smiled as she stood up, brushing off her skirt. The dog tilted its head to one side; its ears remain perked. Mike edged forward, trying to get a better look of the two.

'Tell me if it does and we'll go straight to the hospital,' her mother told her as she took her hand. The two walked away and out of view. Now Mike could see behind them. A single shop was in the distance. The dog lowered its head and growled as Mike noticed the door wasn't simply open. It was angled awkwardly from a broken hinge.

The dog paced out of the passage, its head constantly turning sharply, its eyes wide and attentive. As soon as it felt it was safe, its tail jolted upwards as it raced towards the shop. Mike ran out of the passageway, glancing quickly from left to right. Besides the mother and daughter, he couldn't see anyone else. He bolted towards the shop, the '24/7' sign above the door frame. Mike could hear it whining. Arrays of household essentials were stocked on shelves. Toiletries, snacks, cleaners, ready meals, and gloves for the winter snap. There was even a section for first aid.

The dog leapt onto the counter, staring at the woodwork. Mike began to wonder where the shop owner was. Wouldn't the owner have heard them by now walking about their shop? Had they already gone to the police to tell of a break in? He stared at the items for sale. Was anything even stolen?

The dog landed on the floor and grabbed the wooden tablet that lay on top of the counter with its teeth. It pulled backwards, the wood falling to the floor loudly. Immediately, a strong smell invaded the room, a mixture of cheap aftershave and bad hygiene. Mike held his nose as he stepped forward and gazed into the hollow of the counter. A dead man was awkwardly curled in there. His eyes were open in fear, and his neck exposed a clean slash from left to right.

Mike propelled backwards, trembling as images of Ricky returned. The man had been murdered! He had been in here. The scent of aftershave was still strong as he reached over the counter. He touched his fingertip to the man's neck. The blood smudged onto his hand, and the body still felt partially warm. They'd missed the monster by minutes, if not seconds. Mike turned to see the dog staring up at him; its head tilted and its ears flat.

'If he's close by, we don't have any time to waste,' he told the dog, leaving the shop quickly. The sun was rising higher on the empty street. It wouldn't be long before the villagers started to wake, head towards their corner shop and spot the victim's body. The monster must have been close by though and Dawn was likely to be with him. He peered over his shoulder at the dog. It reluctantly left the store, its ears twitching more than ever before. It stepped in front of Mike, its nose high in the air before turning and running down the cobble street. Mike ran after it. Behind the village lay a forest. The dog charged towards its direction. Soon the village was behind them, the forest growing before them. They stepped between the trees, the dog keeping ahead, leading the way.

CHAPTER 10

Mike and the dog walked through the forest. The more they moved forward, the darker it became above from the thick foliage. He wanted to slow down, his legs were beginning to hurt and neither of them had slept. But the Barghest was persistent, striding forward. When Mike dawdled, the dog ran back, tugging at his jean leg until he began to move again.

'I'm not going crazy. You can understand me, right?' Mike asked as the crossed a small stream. The dog looked back at him, still striding forward. Its paws continued to sink into the waterlogged mud. Mike continuously had to grab onto trees and lever his foot out of the thick muck.

'So how far away are we?' Mike asked. It didn't reply, taking faster steps through the forest. Mike was forced to run after it, gasping and wheezing. The cold air made it hard to breathe. They ran deeper into the forest. All Mike could rely on was the dog that ran in front of him.

The forest was closed up entirely at one section. The light couldn't reach past the expanse of leaves. As the dog stepped through in that moment its powerful form came into view. It was almost immediate—its size doubling, its fur bulking, its claws growing. Then it stopped in its tracks, its ears flat. Mike slowly crept towards it, nervous. Mike took in a sharp breath, staring back at the monster. The two stared from the trees at the edge of the forest. Past the scattering of trees was a house. The windows were boarded up. Mike glanced towards the sky. The sun was high, and the shadows were short ahead.

As Mike walked towards the edge, the Barghest followed, reverting back to a flimsy dog. The skinny teen boy wasn't a match for any man, never mind any supernatural fiend. And he doubted the regular dog would stand a chance either.

'What do we do now?' he asked the dog as it lay on its belly. Its paws folded and its eyes set on the house. Its ears curved backwards as it whined, edging backwards and tucking its tail against his body. It was terrified, just like Mike was. He gulped hard, knowing that Dawn was there. The dog had been eager to get here before and now it was petrified.

'You're sort of the same as Dawn and that . . . that guy, right?' he asked the whimpering dog. He knew the creature wouldn't answer. If Dawn could sense when danger was coming, then so could the Crimson. He couldn't wait around, not now. If the Crimson knew he was here, then he'd come after him and silence them. He had to rescue Dawn quickly, before he had a chance to get to them. His fingers dug tightly into his palm, forming fists as he ran out. He heard the dog barking in a high-pitched tone behind him. It was as though it was crying out to him not to do it.

'You know he's coming!' he called out, feeling his heart speed from the adrenaline. 'Either help us or get yourself to safety.' Mike didn't look back as he stood only a few feet away from the solitary cabin. He could hear the dog's shrill yelps getting higher and louder. The door was almost in his reach.

'Be quiet!' he cried back at the mutt, the sound making him sick with nerves. Silence fell. He felt the suns light lick at his face as he peeked upwards. The winter air was still cold, and his hands were numb from the wind. He peered across the woods. He couldn't see the black dog that had helped them before.

He took in a sharp breath with his hand on the handle. As much as he wanted to take his time, he knew he couldn't. Two things could be behind the door, either Dawn or the Crimson. He pushed down hard, expecting it to be locked. The door swung inwards. The natural light crept through, casting ominous shadows from the surrounding furniture and items. He felt his heart knot up tightly. There were books thrown onto the floor haphazardly.

'Are you back?' He heard Dawn's voice for the first time in days. She sounded scared.

'Dawn!' Mike cried out, running into the house. Before he could spot her, her arms were wrapped tightly around him from the side. The two hugged each other, almost crying in sheer joy. Mike pressed his face against hers, taking her scent in, her soft hair, her entire being. He'd found her, and she was alive.

'You shouldn't be here!' Dawn quickly exclaimed, pulling away from the embrace. Anxiety exerted from her eyes.

'Neither should you. We're going now.' Mike told her, grabbing her hand. She pulled it away, shaking her head frantically.

'You don't understand,' she began to speak, 'So long as I don't leave here, he won't kill you.'

'He won't. It's important that you get away from him. You're special. That dog that was trying to kill us? Well it wasn't; it was trying to keep you safe. It was half-dead. I don't know anything that'd go to that length to save someone that's not important. It was trying to keep that freak from getting you. I promise. I know it's hard to believe, but he helped me find you.' Mike rambled quickly. Dawn stood there. Her mind worked overtime, trying to take in the new information. She shook her head, remembering the huge canine ripping the train in half, charging after them, and sending them scurrying in fear.

'The dog has the same eyes as you, but they're silver. You know, they have the white pupil,' Mike told her. Without a word, Dawn turned and picked up a random book from the floor. It was the first book that was presented to her. Her flingers flicked through the charred pages frantically. An illustration of two angels stared back with silver eyes and white pupils.

'He's the same as me then,' Dawn noted, staring at the illustration in the book. From her lessons she recalled that silver eyes were traits of great guardians. She didn't understand though, the Crimson had said they were the only angels left. Had he lied, or wasn't he aware of there being another left on the Earth? That wasn't possible as the two must have met at the train station. That meant that the Barghest was another angel. She smiled, realising someone was out there—not to get her, but to protect her.

They heard a long screech behind them of rusted hinges. Mike turned to face the door, frozen on the spot. The door slammed sharply. The frame splintered from the sheer force. The Crimson glared at him, his blood-red eyes piercing into his soul. Those eyes promised Mike one thing. Death. Mike took in a terrified breath. He felt his lungs tighten in pure fear as he seemed sure he was struggling to inhale. The kidnapper's eyes seemed to grow dark with rage as he took strong steps towards the quaking teen boy.

'Get back!' Mike's voice boomed out from his throat. It had sounded confident and demanding, but Mike's body language told otherwise—his knees trembling, his hands shaking, and droplets of sweat making their way down his forehead. He took a few steps to Dawn's side, and his arms out-stretched.

'I said get back!' His voice broke on the last word, coming out as a high-pitched whimper. The predator smiled. He remembered how Ricky had tried to block his path, and how it had ended. Dawn grabbed the back of Mike's shirt, dragging him further back. No amount of distance would keep her captor away from Mike's life.

'We had a deal,' Dawn pleaded to him. The Crimson stopped in his tracks. The only reason she hadn't tried to escape was the promise that he would not kill her friend. The Crimson surely wasn't going to kill Mike if he still wanted her to be obedient. His eyes met with hers for what seemed to be an eternity before slowly drifting back to Mike. His lips pulled back slightly.

'Vermin will not be tolerated in my home.' His wings curved upwards and into full view. The energy from them moulded at once, becoming as hard as refined steel, each tip pointed and sharp. Mike felt a scream escape, realising that this was how Ricky had been killed.

In desperation, Dawn ran forward. She concentrated hard on the pool of energy that was within her body, trying to claim, mould, and direct it towards the psychopathic angel. She closed her eyes tightly, trying to cling on the little scraps of fire, but there wasn't enough there. The crimson angel struck her with the back of his left wing. She howled out as she was sent hurtling into the far wall. She crashed to the floor; her inner strength had been spilt and thrown out of her.

Mike's frantic eyes scoured his surroundings, but there was nowhere to run to. He fell to his knees, looking up at the formidable foe, taking in ragged breaths. His own life was hanging by a single frail thread.

'I don't want to die.' He wailed out. He gurgled on his own trapped tears as he heard the demon let out a single laugh. The creature's finger nails lashed into the pitiful teen's cheeks, aiming the final blow.

Dawn lifted her head up from her crumpled position. The wind had been knocked out of her from the blow. She lay there, struggling to inhale. She was going to witness her friend being murdered. She was helpless, and it was all her fault. The tyrant's wings drew upwards, each barbed tip targeted at Mike whom was snivelling and crying.

And he stopped, dropping Mike from his clutch and span round to face the closed steel door. As he did so, the door flung open. A black dog came charging through the room. It launched upwards, teeth bared. It threw itself into the Crimson's exposed body, sinking its fangs into his arm. The Crimson was forced to take a step to the side, letting go of Mike, shaking his arm harshly to try and throw the beast off. But it clung on; its paws pressed against his chest, raking its claws against his skin.

Mike scrambled out from the corner in a hurry, racing to Dawn's side. The Crimson glared as he lifted his arm high and swept it downwards in a quick motion. The dog howled out, crashing into the door, slamming it shut. Mike glanced up at the ceiling's lights. No natural light could get into the house. The Crimson turned to face him. Mike grabbed a book from the floor. The Crimson strode towards him quickly, realising what he was about to do. Mike took aim and threw the book as hard as he could towards the light bulbs. The heavy hardback smacked into the lights, shattering them, sending a loud pop across the room. The glass rained down; the lights went out.

The hound tripled in size, howled loudly, launching itself onto the Crimson's back. Its jaws clamped onto his shoulder, retching its head in a backwards motion, pulling the crimson backwards. The Crimson's wings rose as he tried to beat the mythical dog off him. The Barghest snarled loudly, biting down with intense pressure.

There was no time to lose. Mike grabbed Dawn's wrist, dragging her towards the steel door. The two monsters were fighting each other as he swung the door open. The two entered the forest, not stopping. Danger had never been so loud within Dawn's mind. The screaming chorused into a thousand voices. They heard the dog cry out in pain from behind them. They continued running and running. Their legs were cramped, and their chests hurt as frozen air filled their lungs. Mike ploughed onwards, ignoring the pain as best he could. The Crimson had seen him; his face had been distorted with nothing but hate. 'You're dead' had been written all over the monster's face.

Stop at once, sunshine! a voice shot into Dawn's mind with such intensity. She burst out crying. *Do not side with the inferior!* They stumbled over bracken and leaves as they fled for their lives. They followed the stream, having no other path to follow. The ground beneath them squelched, waterlogged. They could hear the dog howling out from behind them. It was trying its hardest to keep the Crimson from them. They both knew that time was precious. The pain shrilled up and down their muscles as they lagged; their stamina dispensed. She stared behind her, knowing he wasn't far away.

Mike spotted a crevice in the ground. He pulled Dawn towards the hole, grabbing a hold of a log that was wedged in there and using it as an aid to climb down. They both touched the bottom, looking up. The ground beneath them was brittle and shaky. The hole was fairly deep. Deep enough that they were out of sight . . . so long as he didn't look down. Dawn closed her eyes, taking in deep breaths. They could no longer run, and she knew this wasn't a good place to hide. They were cornered.

They heard quick footsteps coming from above the ground. They both held their breath, staring upwards. A furry face stared down at them. Silver eyes gazed at the two children briefly. It limped forward, blood dribbled from its jaw. Its left back leg horribly swelled. Dawn gazed back, seeing in detail for the first time the silver eyes and white pupil. It pressed its paw against the log that was in the ditch. Its nose wrinkled as it took in quick snorts through its nose. Its head rose and began to snarl loudly. Dawn's sixth sense spiked through the murk and the poison that was in her mind. The Crimson was here as well.

'Get out of my way, Donahue!' The Crimson snarled out viciously to the dog. Donahue's ears perked upwards; its eyes set on the two teenagers within the small ditch briefly before looking back up. It showed its teeth at the Crimson angel, not backing down.

'You wretched thing, do you not think you've caused enough trouble?' the Crimson scolded the other angel. It growled loudly at the tyrant. Its tail high; its eyes glazed. It hobbled onto the log in the ditch. Dawn felt the ground underneath her sink slightly as it landed on the thick branch.

Mind your step, both she and Mike heard a voice enter their minds. Mike's eyes widened, remembering the voice that had called out to him in the train station. The dog jumped up sharply and bounced into the log, tackling directly into the side of it. The bark splintered; the ground groaned beneath them. They could feel it caving in and then collapsing. The two children screamed as they went hurtling downwards. Dawn stared at the shrinking light above them. She could hear Donahue crying out in pain. She turned in the air, staring downwards. She desperately tried to see around while they descended, accelerating as they went.

A large splash echoed around the place as Dawn and Mike fell into the dark depths below. Dawn's lungs were filled with dirty water, gurgling in a panic. She kicked frantically, swiping her hands forward. She swam upwards with as much force as she could. She emerged, coughing and spluttering frantically. It was far too dark to see anything.

'Mike!' She cried out, swimming around. She could feel the water pushing her with the current. She called out again and again, desperately trying to find him. Dawn closed her eyes and concentrated hard. She tried to pull her energy towards her eyes, to form some light. She felt a heat drawing from them; the light slowly growing. The water pushed her under, interrupting her concentration. As she flailed in the water, she attempted to bring light to her eyes again. The murky water lit in front of her. She stared downwards through the brown water. Mike's body was sinking towards the bottom. She swam down as fast as she could, grabbing Mike's hand. But his body was too heavy to lift up.

She felt a tightening sensation around her lungs, her mind crying out for her to surface. She refused to let go of Mike, turning in the water, her hands still tightly holding onto his hand and arm. Tunnels were coming into view at a quick pace. The current was sweeping them towards an unknown location. They were thrown down the tunnel, water underneath them, their bodies flung to the surface. She gasped sharply, gulping in the air before being thrown down under the water again. She held onto Mike as they were tossed through several tunnels, unable to fight back against the strong current.

Within seconds, the current stopped and the water became shallow. She clambered up, taking in deep breaths of air. Her knees rested on the bottom. She pulled Mike to the side and out of the water. She pressed her hands against his body, trying to feel a pulse. Her arms wrapped around his body in hysteria; her ear pressed against his lips. Not a single sound left his throat.

'You can't die! You can't!' she begged. Her hands pressed against his chest, pressing down sharply a few times. Her lips pressed against his, blowing into his lungs. His chest lifted and lowered. She remembered how the Crimson had simply taken away her wound. She wished she knew how as she pressed her hands against his chest once more. She wept loudly as she brought her lips to his, breathing in as hard as she could.

Mike spluttered loudly, dirty water splashed against her from within his throat. She turned away, trembling as she heard him taking in deep breaths. He was alive. Immediately, she sat him up, hugging him tightly and rubbing his back as he continued to cough out the filthy water. He shivered in her arms for a moment, blinking several times, his eyes trying to adjust to the darkness.

'Where are we?' he asked Dawn. His hand felt the floor, making its way to her leg and then her arm, unable to see through the piercing darkness.

'I think it's the sewers,' she replied, hugging him tighter. She let out a soft sigh. He was alive and talking. He felt for her hand and held it tightly. Both of their bodies were drenched.

'Sewers under the forest?' he questioned, 'I thought the ground was too soggy.' She nodded in acknowledgement, lifting herself from the floor and staring around the place. She motioned Mike upwards, and they began walking close to the water. He couldn't see past his hand but she could. As they walked through the sewers, she reflected back on the lessons the Crimson had put her through. They had been helpful, very helpful. She was getting a grasp of handling the energy within her and using her eternal eye. If she took a step too close to the rushing water, her mind clicked to it more precisely than it had done before.

Mike and Dawn were trembling as they continued to walk through the seemingly never-ending tunnels. Dawn was feeling weak; her light dwindling. She could barely see the ground in front of them, and he couldn't see at all. The stench that had once been overwhelming was now natural to them.

Mike gazed up, spotting a bright light flickering. She noticed his head turn, and she followed his gaze, walking to the walls. She placed her hands forward, finding a steel pole. It was a ladder. She motioned Mike to the rung and slowly he climbed up. Dawn followed behind him as he pressed his hand against the top, pushing hard. They heard the cover move, more light filtering below. Mike crawled up and out of the opened manhole, leaning back and pulling Dawn up. They were covered in sewage waste from head to toe. She trembled as she got to her feet, dragging her fingers through her hair, trying to brush out the clumps of filth. Mike wiped the sludge off his jeans and shirt to the best of his ability. The fresh air was almost like heaven if it weren't so cold to the touch.

They walked closely together. They needed to find shelter. Mike was exhausted, closing his eyes and feeling a little sick. Was this how Dawn had felt when she had run three days solid or had it been worse?

The clouds erupted. A bolt of lightning lashed out, and the rains poured heavily. They took heavy steps as they approached a doorway of a house. They fell to the doorstep, taking in deep breaths. Neither of them could move anymore; their bodies refused to budge. Mike wrapped his arms around Dawn tightly, trying to spread what little body heat they had. She allowed her hair to flow over her eyes, staring out at the rain, hearing the loud claps of thunder. They drifted in and out of sleep; the cold snap continuously waking them up.

CHAPTER 11

Mike slept with his arms tightly around Dawn. She lay there in silence. Her hands were numb, and her eyes were dreary. She had managed to get a few winks of sleep, but each time she had, her nightmare had returned. Each time she'd appeared in the corridor, the girl cried out to her. It didn't help that each time she woke, her thoughts kept returning to what had happened between Crimson and Donahue. He'd sacrificed himself to save Dawn. What was so special about her that she shouldn't be with the Crimson?

The night was growing colder and colder. She closed her eyes and felt within herself. Her pool of energy was resting but not completely dormant. She wondered if there was a way to use it to warm her up, but she was afraid it would backfire and hurt Mike. She pulled Mike's arms away slowly, trying not to wake him.

'I won't be far,' she whispered to him. She edged away; her limbs protested from moving as she stepped out into street and walked further down. The wind whistled, and the cold continued to seep through her. She stepped into the corner shadows, checking back at where Mike was. Taking a deep breath, she closed her eyes and began to concentrate. The energy within her began to rise. She held her hands out in front of her, concentrating harder. She wanted it to warm her. The energy continued to grow and shifted up her arms. She began to think harder within her mind, hoping she could control it. She could feel an intense heat building within her muscles. She concentrated harder, forcing the energy through to her fingers and down to her toes. She began to smile at the thought of controlling her powers.

She heard a bottle smash, throwing her concentration off. Her energy lunged forward and struck the lamppost in front of her. It sparked furiously before the light went out. She quickly retreated deeper into the shadows, checking to see if anyone saw. From the far left, she saw a group of drunken young adults stumbling down the street. They hadn't paid any attention—too busy laughing as one of their friends hurled their body forward and threw up violently.

'Shit, are you coughing up blood?' She heard a voice from down the street. Dawn watched from the corner. A group of men were standing around the hunched figure. A young lady was rubbing her hand up and down his back as he took in deep breaths. She edged forward, keeping herself as much in the darkness as possible.

'It's not coming from my mouth.' The guy snarled at them. The lady walked around him and lifted his face up from his chin. She let out a gasp as the others laughed harder.

'Ew . . . That's gross. It's coming from your left eye,' she whimpered, ignoring the men surrounding them. 'That looks infected.'

'It's not!' He snapped, swiping her hand away and standing back up. 'I've just drank too much, that's all.'

'Alcohol doesn't do that,' the woman objected. The injured man struck her sharply with his hand. The laughter immediately stopped as he seemingly growled at them. He stormed down the street, leaving his mates behind him. Dawn stepped further into the shadows as he passed her. She gasped in horror as a red streak was streaming down from his eye and underneath his chin. He wiped the back of his hand over the blood, smearing it across his cheek and nose. He turned and stared at her. Immediately, she lowered her head, trying to hide her eyes under her hair.

'What the fuck is up with your eyes?' He snarled at her before yelling out. 'You all honestly think my eyes are fucked up guys? Get a load of hers!' Dawn shook her head quickly in fear. The friends yelled at him that they were leaving him and didn't care. She could hear their footsteps growing fainter and fainter. She turned to leave, but he grabbed her by her arm. She closed her eyes tightly, pulling as hard as she could. He leant towards her. His breath smelt of alcohol and of another substance. She opened her eyes as fear overwhelmed her from the smell. It wasn't a scent she knew of at all, but it felt suffocating. His left eye had deep veins of red darting in zigzags across the whites.

'Why are you trying to run? I'm not going to hurt you.' He smirked at her. She closed her eyes and tried to build the energy within her again, but in her panicked state, she kept dropping it. Each time she tried, it slipped and fell further down.

'You're right. You're not going to hurt her.' Mike was behind the man. The drunken laughed, turning to face Mike. Mike remained as he was, fists formed. He noticed new blood forming under the strangers left eye but said nothing.

'Look at her! Her eyes are golden,' he purred out, 'Freak will make me rich.'

'She's wearing contacts you moron, unlike you,' Mike corrected him. 'Been in a scrap?' The drunken man glared at Mike and then back at Dawn.

'Are you asking for a fight you brat?' He shouted, letting go of Dawn and raising his fist. Mike raised his, ready to fight. The man stumbled, about to throw a punch forward when Mike struck him first. The loud impact echoed around the empty street as the man fell to the floor. Dawn stared in shock as Mike grabbed her by the sleeve, and the two briskly walked away.

'Please don't leave my side again,' Mike sternly told Dawn.

'What were you thinking? He could have hurt you!' Dawn scolded him, but he ignored her. Mike had barely slept himself and had known Dawn had left him. He'd watched from the corner, keeping an eye on her.

'I wasn't about to let him hurt you,' Mike told her calmly. 'You're more special than you could possibly imagine.'

'That's not true,' Dawn told him, feeling upset at the thought. Mike kept quiet as he ushered her forward. He had once been a terrified boy, hiding and whimpering from others. His abusive, alcoholic stepfather struck him and cursed him, telling him he was the reason his mother was gone. His stepfather had locked him out of his home, packed his bags, and left. He had been homeless for years. In essence, he had been nothing but a coward, surviving like a rat. Even when Ricky had found him and helped him through the hardships, Ricky himself was a rat, smoking and stealing.

But now, he had found his purpose. There were two supernatural beings infatuated by her, with one wanting her as possession and the other trying to protect her. She was important, and although he didn't know why, he knew he would not let anything happen to her for it.

'There's more to this than meets the eye,' he corrected her. He took his dirty cap from his head and placed it over hers. 'Keep your eyes hidden. We're moving.'

'Moving? But you're shattered,' she told him.

'And so are you, but neither of us are sleeping. We're getting as far away as possible. Think about it, the sewers led us here. He'll check here, so we have to leave.'

Mike strode through the town with Dawn struggling to follow. She didn't complain, knowing that Mike hadn't eaten as much as she had recently. At times, she would ask if he wanted to stop or if they should find food, but he refused. He had a plan in his mind, but he was too scared to mention it.

Soon, dawn was breaking. He gazed from left to right, looking for a signpost signalling a town. Dawn was secretly hoping he would stop, but he didn't slow down. She wondered if they'd put enough distance, but he didn't seem to think so. Her sixth sense wasn't warning her of danger.

Soon, the two of them trudged down a steep hill. At the bottom lay a stream that ran underneath a bridge connecting fields and further on a busy road. Without warning, he slung his bag to the bank and pulled his shirt over his head. Dawn glanced to the side quickly then back, unsure whether she should be looking. He dunked the shirt into the stream, rubbing it between his hands. The grime and sludge from the sewers drifted down the stream and out of his clothing.

'Could you start a fire Dawn?' Mike said without looking at her. She glanced around, looking for something to burn. The grass was covered in frost, but the bank was covered in mud.

'How?' she asked him.

'With your voodoo stuff', he told her, looking back at her. She shook her head, but he continued to stare at her. She had tried to control it before to warm herself up, but it had only ended in her destroying a lamppost.

'I can't control it,' she protested, stepping to the side.

'But you know you can do it. I saw you trying to control it just now,' he corrected her.

'Then you saw I can't,' she whined. Mike felt his heart sink as she told him, but he stuck to his guns.

'And with practice you will,' he told her, 'but you have to keep trying. Bet you'd be stronger than him if you worked at it, a real way to fight back, and you're really the only one that can do it.' She sighed and stared around. He walked towards her, picked up a bin, and threw littered paper that was scattered around the field. She stared at the bin and began to concentrate as hard as she could. She could start a fire. She'd managed to blow that house apart, so a little fire surely wouldn't be a lot of trouble. She extended her hand, hoping it would help in some way. She could feel the energy rising as she focused.

Her thoughts drifted to the Crimson. He had given her a few lessons in how to control her sixth sense, but that monster hadn't taught her how to control this though. Was it so she couldn't fight back? She began to worry. Her anxiety quickly sparked into anger. Her energy suddenly spurted. She quickly tried to recoil it as the energy unleashed, setting the entire bin into an inferno.

She heard Mike shriek from her side. She quickly turned and stared as he knelt into the water, submerging his hand into the stream. Steam rose up in huge waves, and his left hand was horribly burnt. She felt sick, clutching her stomach. She'd hurt him badly. The bin cackled loudly, and she kicked water up at the side of it. The flames surrounding it quickly subsided with the flame within continuing to burn. She fell to her knees and shook her head. Was all she could do was destroy everything around her?

She felt an arm wrap around her as she sobbed. Mike began to hush her, cradling her awkwardly. His left hand was still trembling, and Mike hid his tears from her. He dunked his shirt into the water and placed it over his hand, wincing slightly.

'You mustn't give up,' Mike told her as he placed his wet shirt into the water and onto to his hand again. 'I have to push you. You understand why, right?' He kept his right arm around her as he looked back at his left hand. He wanted to show her that it wasn't that bad, but it was horribly swollen in areas. He didn't care if she burnt all of his skin off, so long as she knew how to defend herself.

He wanted to continue to comfort her, but he didn't want to waste too much time. He washed the rest of his clothes and sat next to the fire to let them dry. He encouraged her to do the same, and eventually, she did. He tried to joke about her fiery personality, but she didn't smile. He tried to explain to her that he'd been through much worse, but she seemed numb.

'I'm going for a moment. If it feels dangerous, run, no matter what,' he told her after an hour had passed. His clothes were still damp, clinging tightly to his body, as he left her under the bridge. He decided she needed time to rest and not to think about him.

He raced across the field and towards the nearby town. He didn't want to leave Dawn for long, but he knew he had to get a few things first. As he entered the town, he quickly located stores and bought as much as he could carry in food and drink with Ricky's money. He shoved them awkwardly into the bag, throwing away his spare clothes to give room.

He approached a corner shop that had a sale on holiday items. The door swung open as a little bell above jingled, letting the owner know a customer was in. In the back, he could hear someone talking on the phone. He walked over to a large container, where sale scrawled over them. He picked up a pair of dark shades, virtually black in tint. He placed the glasses on the counter and looked around the little store.

'Sorry if I made you wait.' A woman came from out back. 'Was checking on a friend in hospital. They're doing checks on a nasty eye infection. How can I help you?' Mike fished through his bag and searched for change.

'Are you going anywhere nice? I'd love to go somewhere warm for Christmas.'

'Just a little trip', he told her as he tucked the shades into his pocket. He held his hand up to say thanks as he turned to leave. In the window, he gazed upon his own reflection. There was still dirt in his hair, and his face showed signs of mud. He unwrapped his shirt from his left hand and observed his burn. Now that the swelling was gone, it didn't seem so bad. Parts of his skin had blistered, but they were small patches, so nothing to worry about. He pressed his index finger to one of the blisters and winced slightly as pain shot through his arm.

'Are you okay?' she called out. He nodded, wrapping his hand back up and opening the door. The little bell above jingled as he stepped out and into the street.

He raced back to Dawn. The fire was still going, but he also realised part of the bridge above the stream was smashed and lay in the stream. She'd been practising and had fallen asleep next to the fire. He whistled loudly, and she jumped, staring round quickly.

'Exhausted yourself?' he asked her as he placed the bag down near the fire. He wanted to stay by the fire forever where it was warm, but he knew what the consequences would be if he did.

'Sorry, I was practising,' she told him, rubbing her eyes. He pulled the glasses out from his pocket and quickly placed them over her eyes. He could faintly make out the outline of her eyes but nothing more.

'That's all right. You can sleep in a moment, but I need you to help me. We're heading to the carriage way,' he explained, pointing to the right. She peered up the bank to where cars were hurtling down the road.

'Why?' she asked him.

'We're hitch-hiking,' he told her as he took a bread roll from out his bag and quickly munched on it. 'Wouldn't normally suggest it,' he spoke with his mouth full, 'but you can tell if someone is dangerous, right?' She nodded, taking a roll from out the bag and taking bites out of it. They travelled up the bank as he held his thumb out. Hours went by as cars stopped. Each time one began to slow down, Dawn shook her head. He paced back and forth along the road, always looking over his shoulder. When the sixth car came, it was past noon. Mike gazed over at Dawn.

'Safe,' she told him quietly. But she wasn't sure and hadn't felt sure for some time. The previous cars could have been safe as well, but ever since the Crimson had invaded her mind, she wasn't sure how much she could trust it.

'Where are you heading at,' a guy asked in his truck. In the back were various odd boxes.

'The way you're going,' Mike said. 'You want a bit for petrol?'

'Nah, mate, just hop in,' he told them. Mike lifted Dawn in first and then himself. He felt nervous sitting in the truck as it set off down the road. He had no idea if they were double backing or heading further away. To him it didn't matter; the more random the trail was the better. Dawn had already fallen asleep and soon Mike drifted off. It was pleasant being in a warm vehicle. Before long, they were woken by the brakes screeching and the engine turning off. They both thanked the driver and left the truck. They were on the outskirts of an industrial estate. The two followed the road and again went to hitchhike.

The two continued to do this for days on end. Dawn told him of everything she had learnt while captive, and Mike told her of Donahue and how he changed his shape. The exchange of information from one was always bewildering to the other, but together they created a more clear understanding of what situation they were in.

Whenever they weren't hitchhiking, he encouraged her to practice her energy. He kept a distance each time she tried and always in an open field. As soon as she lost control and the fires started, Mike would run out and stomp out the patches that were lit. He didn't want to leave any marks. She didn't feel she was getting any better, but Mike had noticed the distance every time was shorter and more targeted.

They had been travelling for two solid weeks since the sewers. Dawn stood on the roadside; her thumb turned out towards the road. Mike was by her feet, curled awkwardly and dozing. She didn't know how much longer they could run for, but Mike had been adamant. There seemed to be no cars on the roads this late at night. She desperately wanted to sit in a vehicle. She craved the blaring heat so the cold snap was not directed at them.

A small car slowed down and pulled up to the side of them. Dawn focused carefully. This person was safe. Her sixth sense wasn't acting out. The window wound down. Dawn doubled back, fear engulfing her as a vision of immense crimson filled her view.

CHAPTER 12

'You poor dears,' a feminine voice filled Dawn's ears. Trembling, Dawn opened her eyes and looked up at the driver. A flow of red locks drifted out from the window, lashing furiously in the winter wind. Her hazel eyes gazed down at Dawn and at Mike. It wasn't the Crimson.

'Oh, get in. Quickly, wake him sweetie. I'd feel terrible leaving you two out here,' she spoke softly. Dawn nodded, nudging Mike. He woke up, yawning loudly, forcing himself to stand. The woman got out, hazard lights blinking from the rear of the car. A rush of warmth filtered out from its heaters as she opened the back door. Dawn could hear clutter being pushed into the boot of the car.

Mike rubbed his eyes, staring at the driver as she leant over the back seats. Her jeans were skinny, showing off her figure perfectly. She was wearing a tight vest top but no coat.

'There's a bit more room in the back now,' she huffed, flicked her hair back, and turned to face Dawn, 'in you hop.' Dawn nodded, scrambling into the back of the car. The car was littered in shopping bags, books, receipts, and stains from spilled coffee.

'Sorry, it's messy.' The woman chuckled. 'Heavens! I never asked where you both wanted a lift to.' She smiled sweetly at Mike. For a moment, his words were stuck in his throat. She was twenty, if that or at least only a few years older than Mike.

'Where you're going,' he finally managed to speak up. She took a step toward him. Before he realised what she was doing, her fingers brushed gently through his hair, down the back of his neck, and rested her hand on his shoulder. That one movement sent a chill down his back and made his hands clutch his cap tighter than before.

'I'm heading back to my place.' She giggled softly, gently pushing Mike towards the passenger side. He climbed in, shaking his head sharply. What had got into him? She closed the door behind him. He felt the heat blurting out from the heaters, making him slightly dozy. He looked over his shoulder at Dawn. She was already fast asleep. Her head rested against what seemed to be a carrier bag of clothes.

'Sorry, if you wanted to sit next to your girlfriend,' the lady closed the driver side door behind her, 'but I really couldn't make any more room.' Mike gazed at her quickly, hugging his bag and keeping it over his lap.

'She's um . . .' he stumbled out, realising he didn't know what their situation was. 'We never asked your name.' She turned the engine back on. The car rattled from the extra weight. She pulled the car back onto the road and started hurtling down it.

'Lucy,' she told him, 'and what's your name?'

'M–My name is Mike,' he told her, 'and she's Dawn.' He wondered if it was smart to give out their real names. He didn't want to leave a trail for the Crimson to follow and previously they had been giving out fake names. There was such a distance now; he was sure they would be safe.

'She's cute,' Lucy remarked as she kept an eye on the mirrors, 'but you both look shattered, even more than I get when I can't put a book down.' Mike nodded, watching as the clouds erupted and rain poured down. He wondered how long they had been running for. He just wanted to make sure Dawn was as lost as possible. He closed his eyes for a moment, thinking carefully on how much food they had left. There were a few tins that would last a day or two, but they had run out of money.

'Look, it's none of my business, but why don't you both sleep round mine?' She offered him. 'I wouldn't mind the company.'

'We wouldn't want to burden you,' Mike argued.

'Oh, heavens! It's no trouble at all,' she replied. 'A little company on Christmas Day would be nice as well.'

'It's Christmas?' Mike questioned.

'Well, it's Christmas Eve technically,' she corrected him, 'but in a few hours it'll officially be Christmas. You both really have been travelling a tonne if you didn't know it was Christmas.'

'You don't know the half of it.' Mike smiled as he leant forward, resting his chin on the bag.

'You're more than welcome to stay at my place then.' Her fingers reached over to the radio, turning the volume down slightly.

'You honestly have no idea what that means to us,' he whispered as he drifted into a deep sleep.

She pulled up to her house, waking them both. Mike and Dawn left her car as Lucy opened the gate that led down a small front garden and towards the bungalow. Mike had offered to carry her shopping in for her, hauling the bags awkwardly on his shoulders. Dawn held a few of her books. She peeked down at one of the covers. She seemed to be a fan of fantasy from the strange creature on the front.

Lucy approached her front door, taking her keys out of her handbag and unlocking it. Dawn awkwardly adjusted her shades, all the time keeping her hair over her eyes. Lucy turned on the light to the hallway. Now they could both see her with more detail. She was remarkably beautiful, even with the rain making her hair heavy and flat. It could have been argued that it looked more stunning that way. Lucy grabbed a towel from the kitchen and rubbed at her hair quickly. She came back out, giving Mike and Dawn towels. They took them and dried themselves as best as they could. Then Lucy wrapped her locks of red hair within her own towel.

'There's a bathroom to the right. You should take a hot bath. You must be freezing!' She stepped behind them and ushered them forward. 'I'll throw your clothes in the wash and dry. I'm sure I have spare robes.' She opened the bathroom door and approached the tub. She turned the taps on and headed out of the room, letting the steamy water run. Dawn wondered why she was being so kind, but she wasn't about to complain. After travelling for so long in the same clothes, she desperately wanted to get clean.

'You don't mind that they're a little bit girly, do you?' Lucy returned, offering two thick and fluffy gowns in their direction. She passed one to Dawn, catching Mike's attention and slowly passing him the other. He smiled as he took it.

'Thank you, ma'am,' Mike replied, rubbing the soft material through his hands.

'Ma'am?' Lucy shook her head. 'Call me Lucy. Madam makes me sound old.' She smiled at him, touched a strand of his hair, and pushed it back behind his ear. 'I'm sure you're a kind gentlemen who will let the sweet dear bathe first.' He nodded and smiled, turning to Dawn. She smiled back, entering the bathroom.

He grabbed her before she closed the door. 'Sixth sense'?

'Nope, not a shred of it,' Dawn replied. Mike grinned, leaving the bathroom and letting Dawn bathe.

'Mike, do you mind helping me bring down the spare bed linen from the attic?' Lucy called out. Dawn listened as Mike ran to her side. She could hear things being moved around. She slowly stripped from her wet and dirty clothes, opened the door slightly, pushed them out, and closed the door quickly afterwards. Dawn slowly got into the hot bath, sighing in relief as the water lapped over her skin, melting away the winter's cold. She took her glasses off and placed them to one side. The world became much brighter. She stared into the water. Her eyes shone back; underneath them were deep bags. She couldn't remember the last time she felt so warm or at home. She lay there for a while, taking up the heat selfishly. She knew Mike would want a bath, but she didn't want to give this up straight away.

It was only when the water started to go cold that she emerged from the water, grabbed the towel, and dried herself off. She grabbed her glasses and put them back on. Her eyes were once again hidden. She stepped out of the bathroom; the robe tied tightly around her. Lucy was across the room, pointing out rooms around the house to Mike. He nodded, staying very close to her. Dawn stood there for a moment, watching as Lucy placed a blanket on the sofa. She gazed up, noticing Dawn was out the bath.

'Go on, honey, you best take your bath while you can.' Lucy ushered Mike. He nodded as he stepped in and pulled the bolt. Dawn looked up at the woman as Lucy smiled sweetly. Her teeth were perfectly white, her skin covered in natural make up, and her hazel eyes seemed to shine in delight.

'Mike told me your home burned down,' she stated, shaking her head and letting out a long sigh. A high-pitched sound escaped as she did so. 'I lost my family to a fire as well when I was very young.'

'I'm sorry,' Dawn answered her. Lucy looked up at her, for once not smiling. There was a sad expression on her face as she recalled memories. Dawn wondered if she should ask what happened but realised she didn't want to talk about what happened to her either.

'It was a long time ago, Dawn,' she replied, forcing a smile. 'I don't want you to feel sorry. I want you to know that . . . time is a great healer.' Lucy grinned, stroking Dawn's hair and walking away. 'It'll be nice to not be alone. That is, if you and Mike would like to stay.'

'It would be nice to be out the cold,' Dawn agreed, 'but only if it's okay with you. We don't have any money to give you.'

'I wouldn't dream of taking any money from you,' Lucy told her as she propped some pillows on the sofa.

'And we won't stay for long,' Dawn mentioned quickly.

'Stay as long as you need to,' Lucy told her as she escorted Dawn towards the sofa. 'It's not my place to ask why you were out there, but it can't be safe being out in the open, while you're in plain sight of awful strangers who could hurt you or worse. I wouldn't want that on my conscious.' Dawn pondered at this. It was true; while they were travelling, they could be spotted by the Crimson. If they stayed indoors though, unless he was knocking on every person's door, they wouldn't be seen by him. Perhaps, it was safer to stay in one spot now that they'd distanced themselves.

'I'll have to talk to Mike tomorrow.' Dawn nestled herself under the blankets and lay her head on the pillow. She yawned as she closed her eyes. Lucy placed her hand on her hair and slowly brushed it to one side. Dawn let out a sigh and swiftly fell asleep.

The next morning, Dawn woke with a smile on her face. For the first time in a very long time, the nightmare hadn't come to haunt her. The light was filtering in through the blinds. She pulled herself out from under the covers and off the sofa. Dawn was the only one awake. She took her shades, tightened the robe around her, and decided to explore the house. She didn't want to disturb Lucy or Mike.

She walked into the kitchen and noticed her clothes hanging over the radiator. She felt them with her hand. They were dry, so she took them and got dressed. She kept the robe on over her clothes though. It was soft to the touch, and she didn't want to give it up. There was an unwashed cup on the side, and beside it a book.

She heard a door open and close. Lucy stepped out of her own bedroom, ran her fingers through her hair and stepped through the living room.

'Good morning,' Dawn spoke quietly. Lucy glanced up and smiled.

'Good morning, Dawn.' She yawned. 'Did you sleep well?'

'Like a baby. Where's Mike?' Dawn asked. Lucy turned on her heels and opened a door. Dawn looked into the bedroom. A king sized bed took up most of the space. Lying on a pillow and curled up in the blankets was Mike, fast asleep.

'Shared the bed with me,' Lucy explained as she closed the door slowly and quietly. 'I really didn't have anywhere else to put him. You should have heard us arguing last night. He wouldn't let me sleep on the floor, so we ended up putting pillows down the centre. Not that you can tell now. Do you know how to make a cup of coffee?'

'Sure,' Dawn answered, a little disturbed by the casualty. Then again, it really was a small house.

'Could you make me one while I take a quick shower?' Lucy asked. Dawn nodded as Lucy smiled and went into the bathroom but not before saying, 'and Merry Christmas.' Dawn filled the kettle with water and turned it on. As soon as she did, she walked over to the bedroom and opened the door. Mike was still sleeping, and Dawn felt bad as she nudged him. He groaned and opened his eyes, looking up at Dawn.

'I was having an amazing dream.' He grinned as she slowly got to his knees. His hair was ruffled, and his robe was swayed a little too far to the right, revealing boxer shorts. Dawn averted her gaze, and Mike quickly realised.

'Sorry.' He chuckled as he tightened the robe. Dawn looked back at him. He seemed half-asleep as he ruffled his hair quickly and started putting the pillows back.

'That's alright,' she quickly mumbled. 'We need to talk though. Should we stay here?' He slowly stood up, picked up the blanket, and tried to make the bed. He turned and glanced at Dawn.

'I was about to suggest it,' he explained, and Dawn smiled. 'We've been travelling but not looking after our health. We should stay for a night or two at the most, and get our strength back up.'

'I wouldn't mind staying here forever.' Dawn frowned.

'It's very tempting,' Mike agreed, 'but until you're strong enough to stop him, we can't afford to stop moving.' She sighed loudly. She really didn't want to give this up. It had been so long since she'd been in a true home, and she hadn't slept comfortably in a long while.

'Isn't it more dangerous if we're always out in the open?' Dawn recalled Lucy's speech last night.

'I think being sitting ducks is more dangerous,' he told her as he stepped out of the bedroom. 'And Lucy would be targeted as well then. I don't want more people killed. Where's Lucy by the way?'

'She's taking a shower,' Dawn told him as she went back into the kitchen, pulling a mug out from the cup stand and looking around for the coffee. Mike reached up to a cupboard, pulled out a jar of coffee, and placed it in front of her. She wondered how much of a tour he had been given of the place. She took a teaspoon and spooned in a heap. She watched Mike as he turned on the TV and sat on the Sofa. A Christmas movie was playing.

'It's two sugars and a little milk. The milks in the fridge,' Mike told her. She nodded, feeling a little left out that he knew more about Lucy than she did. From then on, the day rolled by too quickly. Mike continued to flick through channels and eat chocolate that Lucy gave them both. Dawn found it to be a little too rich, so she kept to fruit and nuts. Lucy continued to apologise for not having a Christmas roast, but she hadn't been expecting any company this Christmas.

'Don't get me wrong. I'm not lonely,' Lucy explained as she ran a hairbrush through Dawn's hair, 'but my friends are home with their families, and I wouldn't like to put them out of their way.' Dawn read two of the books that Lucy had on her shelves. The first novel she really enjoyed. It was filled with adventure and mystery, and all began with a boy simply trying to find his mother. The second one she closed abruptly in disgust. The heroine was a werewolf, vampire, witch, and bounty hunter? Lucy had chuckled when Dawn closed the book prematurely and agreed it wasn't a favourite of hers.

Before they knew it, Christmas was over, and all three of them were tired.

'Would you like to go through town with me tomorrow?' Lucy asked them. 'The sales will be on, and I'm really hoping to get some new books to read.'

'I wouldn't mind window shopping,' Mike agreed as Dawn lay down on the sofa and closed her eyes. She felt happy and sad at the same time. Today had been one of the greatest days of her life. There hadn't been a worry in the world. There had been no fighting, arguing, or catastrophes. She really didn't want to leave this place.

Soon it was Boxing Day. Dawn woke up, went to the kitchen, and started the kettle. She anticipated Lucy waking up soon. She stood in the kitchen for some time. It was ten in the morning, and neither of them had stirred. She shrugged and turned on the TV. The news flashed up.

'A young girl is fighting for her life in hospital,' the news reporter spoke. 'Her brother admits to throwing Sarah out the five story building but says he did so in self-defence. Her brother continues to defend himself, stating that his sister tried to kill him. His defence? His sister was rabid, yet doctors have stated there was no sign of rabies. Officials are questioning why a four-year-old girl would be a threat to a thirteen-year-old boy and highly doubt his claims. The nation is hoping she will make a speedy recovery.'

'There are some cruel people in this world,' Lucy spoke as she took the remote and turned the TV off. Dawn gazed up at her. Lucy's hair was out of place as she walked towards the kitchen. 'Did you boil the kettle for me Dawn'

'I did.' Dawn nodded. 'I thought you might be waking up soon.'

'You're so resourceful,' she praised her as she poured herself a coffee and sat down at the counter. She pulled out a book, which she was nearly finished with, and began to read. 'You should leave Mike for a bit. He didn't get a lot of sleep.'

'How come?' Dawn asked. Lucy didn't reply as she took a sip of her coffee and carried on reading.

'Help yourself to breakfast,' she told her. Dawn nodded and poured herself a bowl of cereals. An hour later and Mike crept out of the bedroom and quickly went to the bathroom to take a shower. An hour after that and the three of them left for town.

It was another day that went by quickly. Lucy had bought several books and clothes for herself. She'd bought Dawn a silver necklace and insisted it was a Christmas present. She bought Mike a new cap, and he quickly threw away his old one. They ate in a café and talked about fantasies and dreams.

'I always wanted to be a police man,' Mike confessed as Dawn took a bite out of a scone. 'I've always liked the idea of protecting civilians.'

'Why don't you try?' Lucy questioned him. 'They do all kinds of catch up courses at college, and the government pays out for those down on their luck.'

'It's a silly dream I had when I was much younger.' He chuckled, dismissing the idea entirely. 'Besides, Dawn is enough to protect.' Dawn gave a weak smile as Mike laughed to himself. Mike's spirits had lightened a lot since they had arrived. He'd opened up a lot to both Lucy and Dawn. But as the two talked about their future ambitions, Dawn felt a bitter taste in her mouth. She had no idea what she would do with her own life. She remembered being in school, a little better than average grades. Never had she thought of what her future would be, and now it seemed unlikely it could ever be normal at all.

'Lucy, tomorrow me and Mike are going to leave,' Dawn told Lucy as they sat in the living room that evening.

'Do you have to leave, you two?' Lucy frowned. Dawn and Mike nodded. They didn't want to leave, but they had already decided they weren't going to stay another night. Mike looked down at his feet, knowing it was his suggestion that they left after tonight.

'We really appreciate you putting us up,' Mike insisted.

'I'll be sick with worry,' Lucy complained as she sighed. 'I don't like the thought of you two wondering the streets.'

'We know how to look after ourselves,' Mike tried to comfort her, 'but we can't stay any longer.'

'I won't pry,' Lucy murmured. 'It's not my place to. I just feel so sad for you two.' She shook her head and went to bed earlier than she had done the previous nights. Dawn felt guilty. Lucy had been so caring, and it had become apparent she was very lonely. She had no family, and they had found out her friends travelled a lot, rarely meeting with her.

'I think I'll get an early night,' Dawn told Mike. He nodded as she crept onto the sofa and closed her eyes. She felt sad. Why couldn't they live normally? She would love to stay here. It had felt more like a family than she had ever known before. Mike sat awkwardly on the floor, staring at the TV but not watching the show.

He heard a soft whimpering sound coming from the bedroom. He got up and opened the bedroom door.

'Lucy . . . are you crying?' he whispered. She peered over at Mike. Her eyes shined as a tear crept down her cheek.

She sniffed, holding a tissue to her eyes and dabbing them dry. 'I'm just a little emotional.' Mike sat on the edge of the bed, placing his hand on her back attempting to comfort her.

'I'm going to miss you,' she whispered to him.

'I will as well,' he declared, 'but we can't stay.'

'Why can't you?' she asked him, turning to face him. 'I know I said I wouldn't pry, but I'm really worried for you both. What's so important that you have to live roughly and on your own and to have to go through so much?' Mike gulped, feeling sorry that he couldn't tell her. She wouldn't believe him anyway. Surely, he owed some explanation. But what was he to say?

'It's okay, darling.' She hiccupped as she lay down and closed her eyes. 'You don't have to tell me.' Mike lay down next to her. She sighed as she opened her eyes, lying on her side and gazing at him. She seemed so lost, and alone it was hurting Mike to see her this way.

'We'll be okay,' Mike tried to reassure her. She let out a long sigh as she closed her eyes.

'I hope you're right,' she whispered.

CHAPTER 13

They would have to leave. It was going to be difficult, but they had to. Dawn was swamped under the silken blankets and plush pillows. The sweet scent of flowers drifted into the living room. The birds sang outside as the sun shone into the place.

She sat herself down at the kitchen counter. She'd helped herself to a large meal, spoilt herself with a generous helping of strawberries. One last full meal before they set off. A soft sigh escaped as she swallowed a spoonful. It was amazing here. She never wanted to leave.

'Good morning,' Mike sung the words as he walked into the large living room. His hair was scruffier than it had ever been. As he gazed over at Dawn briefly in a dreamy state, it seemed his eyes were shining, and his smile had crept into place. His clothes had been haphazardly put on. She couldn't help but notice his entire body seemed to glow. He gazed back at the bedroom, not paying much attention to her. He wasn't fully there, staring at the door for a moment before he walked away, heading towards the bathroom.

Dawn shot up from the table and went to the bedroom door. It was partially open. From the gap she could see Lucy. Her long red hair was messed up and drifting awkwardly down her shoulders. She looked more stunning and wild like that than before. She was smiling to herself as she bent over, picking up a hairbrush. Alarmed at Mike's casual approach to her, Dawn marched towards the bathroom. He was humming a tune from the room as Dawn opened it.

'What did you two do last night?' Dawn noted rather than questioned. His eyes met Dawn's in a trance, letting out a soft laugh as he did so, shaking his head a little.

'Oh, come on, Dawn. Stop being paranoid.' He ran his finger across his lip and chuckled to himself again.

'Mike, the Crimson might come at any day,' she whispered to him, looking over her shoulder to make sure Lucy wasn't within earshot. Mike snapped out of his trance for a moment, staring at Dawn as though she had slapped him.

'Dawn . . . come on. We have everything here. Food and shelter and . . .' His words trailed off again as he closed his eyes and giggled. 'Why should we leave? We're perfectly safe here.' Dawn felt sick, but she couldn't work out why. He seemed completely different; his concerns only the day before thrown out the window. They were putting Lucy in danger as well. He was putting her in danger. He himself had said they needed to leave, and now he changed his mind?

'Mike?' Lucy called out from the bedroom. Mike's eyes shone with excitement. If he were a puppy, his tail would be wagging a mile a second. His grin spread across his face even more as he barged past Dawn and headed back to her. Mike was completely out of character. This wasn't like him at all. Dawn huffed angrily, snatched her shades up, and put them on.

'I'm going out!' Dawn yelled out loudly, grabbing her jacket and the bag, slinging it over her shoulder. As she pulled the handle of the front door, she glanced back. She could hear Lucy mumbling something about trust and kindness.

She slammed the door behind her, biting her lip hard. Couldn't Mike see they'd be putting more people into danger? In frustration, she kicked out. Her boot met with a garden ornament. It struck the window and shattered. The wings of the angel fell in clumps, the main body indistinguishable. Dawn took in a sharp breath. Why was she so angry?

'Dawn would you like to talk?' Lucy's head appeared from the window as it swung open. Dawn gazed across to Lucy.

'I'm sorry,' she apologized immediately, walking briskly over towards the shattered remnants.

'Oh, don't worry about that.' Lucy smiled sweetly. 'I never really liked it.' She closed her eyes for a moment before pushing the window open all the way. She lifted herself from the windowsill and to the ground. A wing crunched under her bare foot as she walked towards Dawn, her arms open wide. The welcoming gesture of a hug well needed.

'I'm sorry. I–I need to go for a walk.' Dawn smiled weakly back.

'I understand.' Lucy gazed down at the grass with her hands to her side.

'I'll clean this up before—'

'Oh, no, go for your walk,' Lucy interrupted her. 'You seem so riled. I think a walk will do you good. Just promise me we'll talk when you come back?'

'I promise, Lucy.' Dawn smiled. She opened the garden gate and closed it after her. She peeked back at the small house. Lucy remained in the garden, waving her off. Dawn felt better about herself as she started heading towards the town. She looked over her shoulder a few times. Lucy remained there until she was several yards away before climbing back through the window.

Dawn started to hum as she walked towards the shops. While there was no sixth sense telling her of danger, why shouldn't she enjoy herself? Her eyes glanced across the several shops. Big sales had started, the Boxing Day shoppers seemed to reappear and were more frantic than the eve shoppers had been. Perhaps, Dawn could replace the ornament for Lucy. She had a little money with her since the outing yesterday and knew she may need it in the future. Lucy had looked after the two of them though. She owed her for all the food and shelter the two had been given. She reached for her neck, touching the small silver necklace that hung around her neck.

After some time had passed, she sat down on a bench, taking in a deep sigh. Dawn had checked from shop window to shop window. There seemed to be no suitable replacement. She glanced upwards at the large clock that stood high in the centre of the street. It was close to noon already. She took out a sandwich she had bought earlier and began to eat it, staring at the clock.

Maybe they didn't have to leave. They had been travelling for so long that how could he possibly find them now? Lucy seemed so lost without them as well. It would be really painful to leave her. Then again, the longer they left it, the harder it would be. Mike may have been right. Why leave when she can simply wait for her sense to kick in and warn them of him approaching?

From the corner of her eye, she noticed someone sitting on the other side of the bench. She scrunched up the wrapper for the sandwich and slowly stood up. A hand grabbed her wrist and pulled her back down to a sitting position.

'Dawn, I need you to come with me,' a warm breath exhaled on her right ear as the strangers voice whispered. Her eyes jerked open as she stared at the person. He was wearing a dark set of shades, stylish and designer. Immediately, she pushed him back sharply and ran away from the bench. She charged through the streets and looked back at the bench. He was gone. She went round the back of the clock tower and was forced to an abrupt stop. He'd managed to cut her off, standing in front of her with his hands held out signalling her to stop. She extended her own arms. Her hands held out flat. Her energy exerted and slammed into him. He was thrown backwards and onto his back.

She stared at her hands for a brief moment, astonished she had been able to take control. The backdoors of shops faced her, large waste bins on the opposite side holding recycling and trash. She went to run past him, but he was too agile. He stood and grabbed her. He pulled her close to him. His hand covered her mouth. She could smell burning coming from his arm as he struggled to keep a hold of her.

'Dawn, wait!' the man whispered to her. She didn't recognise the guy's voice. Before she could react, he lifted her up over and into one of the bins. Everything went dark as the lid was closed. A loud clash echoed from above her and sound rung in her ears. It caved inwards. Something kicked at the side of the bin. She was about to scream for help that a mad man had abducted her and thrown her in the trash when she heard an unmistakeable voice.

'Where is she?' the Crimson's voice spoke coldly. Dawn placed her hand over her mouth, stifling her own breathing.

'I-I spooked her,' the stranger replied to him quickly. 'I thought she went this way, but I can't see her.' The bin screeched as it was pushed backwards. Dawn swallowed loudly, containing the shriek that wanted to come out.

'Stop! You'll break it! It's still not fully healed,' the stranger whimpered. It was clear that the Crimson had a hold of him, pushing his weight against the lid. Dawn wasn't as worried about the lid smashing into her body as she was the Crimson realising that she was right underneath his nose.

'I'll be glad to break it off for you then!' the Crimson yelled at the man.

'She's not here!' He gasped out. 'Y-you know I'm not lying. You can see that.' Dawn's ears strained for the answer. The lid stopped groaning in protest.

'Y-you've had to close your eye, haven't you?' he spoke in a softer tone. 'She's gotten use to you.' What did the stranger mean by that? The man that had thrown her in the trash knew far more about the Crimson than she did. Who was he?

'Where do you think she went, dog?' Crimson asked coldly.

'I can tell you she ran down this way. Don't think she trusts anyone. She's probably jumping a train or hitch hiking again.' Dawn heard the Crimson let the man go. His footsteps were heard walking past the bin. She kept her hand to her mouth as the footsteps grew fainter and fainter.

The lid opened, and light flooded the filthy containment. She slowly stood up, and her were legs trembling. Had he gone? She took a hesitant step out and looked left and right. He wasn't in sight. The stranger rubbed his hand up and down his arm. He limped forward; his left leg was lame. He gave a sly smile as he slowly took his shades off. A set of silver eyes gazed at her.

'Donahue?' she questioned as she stared at the angelic eyes. He nodded, wiping his shades on his jeans and pressing them back up the bridge of his nose. She couldn't believe it. This man was the dog that had rescued them?

'You don't know how thankful I am you didn't hit me in my leg.' He chuckled as he continued to hobble towards her. She took a step back, holding up her hand. He held his hands in front of him, leaning against the wall and letting out a sigh.

'I'll keep my distance, but there really isn't a lot of time,' he told her, taking in a deep breath.

'How did you find me?' she interrupted him, 'And why the hell did you let us fall into the sewers? Mike almost drowned.' She kept her distance from him.

'I'm sorry. I didn't think straight. I didn't mean to hurt either of you. But I knew he would hesitate to follow, and you'd have a chance to get away. More than anything, I hoped he wouldn't keep hunting you, but he won't let you go. You've been leaving a trail, and I've been following it.' He grinned, rubbing his arm, leaning against the wall. Had her practising her powers caused a trail to be left?

'I bumped into Mike just a moment ago. He looked worried then, well more than he is now.' Dawn's eyes widened. Mike had come out looking for her?

'He's been following the trail too. Minutes away,' he told her quickly. 'I told Mike to meet me at my truck after he collected your things. I can get you both to a safe place where he can't get to you.'

'Why isn't my sixth sense—'

'I keep forgetting you have no idea,' he mumbled, 'Experienced angel's, like him, can make other angel's eternal eyes close, so long as he knows who his target is but in return he must close his own.' Dawn closed her eyes and remembered back. She remembered how her sixth sense had been deathly quiet. She closed her eyes tightly and concentrated hard. She could feel a thick layer of toxins that had blocked her sight before and realised it wasn't poison at all. It was blindness. The Crimson had prevented her from seeing.

'Where are you taking us then? Are you sure we'll be safe?' Dawn questioned him.

'I give you my word Dawn that I will do everything in my power to stop him from using you,' he reassured her. She nodded and walked slowly towards Donahue. He smiled and started to walk through the alleyway. She noticed he was limping badly on his left leg. It seemed the Crimson hadn't broken it, but it was in a bad state.

'If he realises I lied. . . Just find Mike. I'll do what I can to keep him off, but I'd rather not fight.'

'Does it hurt?'

'I've been through worse.' He trailed off. Suddenly, he applied pressure on his bad leg and ran forward. Dawn followed in a panic, looking behind her. The Crimson wasn't in sight. His leg gave way as he fell down sharply. He cursed under his breath as he tried to pull himself up.

'What's the matter?' she asked, alarmed by his sudden change.

'Mike's in danger,' he spoke frantically, pulling himself up and gasping loudly. He forced himself to his feet and tried to run again. Dawn sprinted after him, terrified for Mike. What was going to happen? Dawn span round the corner and noticed Donahue had fallen, writhing in pain from his injured leg. She darted towards the left. Her sixth sense was calm, but Donahue was adamant something was going to happen. Danger was not aimed at her, but for that moment, she wished it was, at least then she would know.

Time slowed down. Dawn pushed harder; her steps seemed to slow with the world. She turned the corner. Across the busy road was a mongrel of a boy. His hair was shaggy, and his expression was worn. Their eyes met within that moment. He was charging towards her. His lips parted, about to call out to her. There was sweat covering him. In the corner of his right eye she could make out a deep red. There was a horrible gash to his forehead that hadn't been there this morning. The world was silent for that one moment as Mike's voice echoed loudly to her.

'Run!' he bellowed. Dawn's eyes widened as she desperately tried to get to him; the seconds ticked by at a sluggish pace. As Mike stepped onto the road, the sound of a blaring horn rang out. A lorry was going at an incredible speed, but its wheels did not touch the road. Like a toy that had been thrown, it soared through the air sideways. Its wheels spun in the air. The horn continued to blare loudly. The heavy vehicle was descending at a fast rate, headlights pointed directly at Mike. With a thunderous crack against the tarmac, it crashed into his side. Mike's body disappeared underneath it. A hysterical scream roared across the scene. Dawn realised it was her voice as she made her way towards the accident.

She felt herself being pulled back. In a fit of rage and grief she turned on her suppressor and lashed out. Donahue put up with the kicks and blows she was raining down on him. The smoke and rubble began to clear. She couldn't see Mike at all but only the crimson blood that was scraped across the road and the lorry lying on its side with no driver in sight.

'Dawn, he's coming!' Donahue pleaded. She was still screaming, frozen to the spot, and in shock. She was jolted backwards, Donahue cursing and struggling on his leg. He couldn't run, but he marched in an odd fashion. She cried loudly as her sixth sense picked up dramatically. The Crimson was coming for her and was extremely close.

She felt herself being thrown into a truck and the door slammed behind her. She turned and stared out the back window. She was hyperventilating. Danger was only a few feet away; she could feel it. A tall figure stood near the lorry. His blonde hair was swaying in the sharp winter air, and his red eyes were partially hidden behind them. He was focused on the blood that was underneath the vehicle. The car revved loudly as the silver-eyed being forced it forward. The Crimson's attention turned and their eyes met briefly.

He'd killed Mike. Her tears turned hot as her energy boiled within her. She was going to destroy that fiend if it was the last thing she ever did.

CHAPTER 14

The truck rolled to a stop. They appeared to be in a rundown service station. Most of the stores were barricaded or closed down. Only one building remained used as its lights blared out in the velvet black of the night. Dawn had wept until there were no more tears and now simply stared at the man with silver eyes. Not a man but an angel. He hadn't spoken to her the entire time they had driven. He had taken sharp turns and bolted down country roads. It had been hours since she had felt the presence of the Crimson and figured they had lost him. Donahue faced out of the front window; his black hair only partially covering his eyes. His shades had slipped somewhat, but she could still see part of his eye, bright and silver.

'Go on', Donahue slowly spoke, not looking back at her. 'Scream it out. I should have saved him. I failed you both.' Dawn pulled the bag close to her, hugging it tightly. She could still smell the sewers, the last remaining packet of food and most importantly, Mike. She stared into the bag, as though holding it would somehow reassure her that Mike wasn't gone.

'What's the point?' she questioned dully, leaning back into the car seat and sighing. 'He's gone. I could complain till my lungs go blue, but it won't bring him back, will it?'

'No,' he replied, resting his arms over the steering wheel. 'It won't bring him back, but it might make you feel better.' The scene ran through her head over and over. Mike running towards the road, his head wounded, yelling out for Dawn to run. She couldn't stop the vision of the Crimson standing over what remained of his body. She began to shudder violently as the memory continued to replay over and over.

'If we travel through the night and the day, we'll reach a safe house,' he told her. 'Built it myself. Lived there for a good decade, and he hasn't found it. Even if he did, I've secured it, so he couldn't get in.' She was putting her trust into a man she barely knew. She didn't reply, and after a long silence, he eventually left the truck and walked towards the one lit building. She felt as though she should sleep, but how could she? She wanted Mike back, more than ever before.

She opened the passenger door and stepped outside. The wind had picked up and gusted loudly against her. From Mike's bag, she took out the last chocolate biscuit and slowly ate it. It felt dry in her mouth, and the chocolate had a strange tang to it. The biscuit was fine, but her ability to enjoy its taste had left her.

'Hope you don't mind I took the last one, Mike,' she spoke to the air as she continued to consume it. She wasn't hungry, not really. She wondered if she was doing the right thing, allowing Donahue to take her away. She still had the option of going it alone. That was a daunting prospect, to be alone. Who could she turn to? If she went to people, with the way her body was changing into something very not human, would they even consider helping at all? The thought of going back to Lucy when the Crimson had been in the same city worried her. She didn't want any more people to die because of her. The best chance she had was an angel, and she only knew of two. The one with silver eyes at least seemed to be trying to help, not capture and force to conceive children.

'Miss?' a young voice called out. Dawn peered in the distance. On the opposite side of the road was a young girl no older than five or six. In the silent night, she could hear the wind picking up behind her, whistling and moaning. The sound of snivelling echoed across the breeze. Dawn took a step towards the road, wondering if the young girl belonged to one of the people in the shop. The child continued to sob softly as Dawn made her way across the road. The young girl's right hand was over her eye, rubbing it awkwardly. As Dawn reached her on the other side, the kid ran to her and hugged her leg tightly. The young girl's hair was tangled, and her clothes seemed to have stains on them, although it was too dark to see what the stains were. Dawn hushed her softly, and as the little girl clung to her tighter, Dawn recognised her.

'I know you,' Dawn exclaimed in surprise. 'You're Sarah! I saw your photo on the news a few days ago. But from the way the reporter spoke, I thought—' She trailed off. She thought her brother had pushed her out the window and put her in a critical position.

'You are Sarah, aren't you?' The young girl nodded and grinned. Her right hand furiously wiped at her eye as she hugged onto Dawn's leg. Her nails were digging into the fabric of her jeans. Something was off about the child. Dawn could no longer tell if she was crying or laughing.

'You are very special.' The young girl smiled with her teeth on full display, and the edges of her lips were curved upwards. She pulled her right hand away from her eye. A sticky red liquid slipped from her hand and drooled down her cheek. Her right eye was almost completely red, and her left eye now started to show spots of crimson forming. Taken aback, Dawn tried to step away, but Sarah held on.

'Don't . . . go,' Sarah stuttered, more red liquid dribbling from both of her eyes and dotting the ground. 'You're needed!' Dawn pulled the child off her. Sarah let out a feral screech; her left eye burst into a deep red as bloody tears fell from it. Common sense flared up quickly, recognising the danger too late. Dawn turned to run back to the truck. A sharp pain dug into her ankle. She tried to pull herself free, realising Sarah was clung to her leg, and her nails were dug deeply into her skin. Dawn let out a scream, lifting her leg up sharply. Sarah clung to it, her nails ripping through her skin and exposing fresh blood. Dawn closed her eyes, and her breathing was quick and frantic as she transformed the energy inside of her. She dispersed it sharply in defence. The dirt flew into the air as Sarah's nails slid out of her skin. Her hair smelt of burning and began to smoke. The tiny girl laughed hysterically; her left eye enveloped completely in crimson. The child wasn't fazed from being burnt.

The sound of sprinting paws echoed as a dog barked loudly behind her. Sarah lunged towards Dawn when suddenly a figure sped past and grabbed onto the child's arm with his jaw. A black paw thrust down onto Sarah's body, pinning her to the ground. The Barghest growled at her, tail high, licking its lips, and bloodied teeth.

'Master needs the girl,' a demonic voice creaked from the girl's throat. Blood continued to weep from her eyes, dribbling down her cheeks. At that moment, the two heard a loud racket coming from down the road. The beast grabbed the girl by her torso and charged down the road towards the others.

Get to the truck now! he ordered into her mind instead of verbally. Dawn peered into the distance, her golden eyes shining to see better in the dark. There were two people sprinting down the road. Although difficult to see their features, there was one thing that was apparent. Their eyes were also completely crimson, blood drooling down their faces and onto their clothes.

The door swung open as she hurtled into the passenger side, slamming it shut. Her fingers felt for the locks and pushed them down, a clicking sound signalling that the outside couldn't get in. She hoped.

She took in a deep breath, clutching onto Mike's bag once more. In the distance, she could hear inhuman screams. Her common sense was still loudly calling out within her mind, demanding that she pay attention to it. What were those people?

The car shifted forwards abruptly. The brakes creaked as they were forced out of place. Dawn's hand struck the dashboard, stopping the rest of her lunging forward as she gazed behind her. A woman clawed against the back window. Her eyes were completely red and her fingernails showed cracked nail polish and blood. The tips dragged down the glass and leaving long red marks.

'My master requires you!' The bloody woman screeched out coldheartedly. Within the night's darkness, a pair of hands grabbed her by her shoulders and threw her to one side. Donahue came into view; his mouth seemed to be splattered with dots of blood as he grabbed the handle of the driver's side. Dawn pulled the lock upwards, allowing him in.

'What's happening?' she asked as he fumbled the keys into the ignition.

'There's more coming,' he spoke, forcing the gear into position and slamming his foot onto the pedal. The truck coughed and spluttered as it was forced to go speeds it wasn't use to. It raced away from the service station; his fingers scrabbled for the radio and switched it on. He started flicking through stations, trying to find some form of news, but nothing seemed to be coming up.

'I think they're after me,' she said, staring back behind her. It was too dark. She couldn't see a thing out there.

'I think you're right.' He gulped, grabbing a tissue from the glove box and wiping his mouth. He spat on the tissue, blood on the paper as he rolled it up and shoved it into a carrier bag. His front teeth were stained with blood.

'Oh, god, do you think he's done this?' She began to tremble.

'Even for him, this seems—' he began to speak when a large thud thundered through the truck. Something was on top of the truck, screeching incoherently. Donahue spun the stirring wheel sharply, throwing the person off the vehicle. The truck started to jitter as it was forced to speed off the road. The panicked acceleration was taking a toll on the truck. The dial began to signal that the engine was overheating.

Dawn peered through the darkness. Her eyes glowed intensely, so she could see into the night. Towards the right, she could see a tall building coming into view.

'Donahue, if we can get to the building, we can barricade ourselves in.' Dawn pointed out to him. 'Can you see it? It's just to the right.' Donahue shook his head, unable to see as far as she could, but he pushed the truck onwards. The noises began to subside behind them. They were losing the creatures. Smoke started to filter from beneath the bonnet. The vehicle was about to give in.

'How far away is the building?' he asked her. She didn't need to reply because the walls encroached in view of the headlights. The truck rolled slowly to a halt as he stared up at the building. It was in the middle of nowhere—a single structure that was three storeys tall. It was formidable. His fingers drummed loudly and quickly against the steering wheel. Dawn's stomach turned, an uneasy feeling flooded into her from the building. She shuffled in her seat and clicked the seatbelt buckle off.

'This isn't good,' he spoke. 'It's his . . . Was a place he . . .' The two could hear screeching from far behind them. They'd created a gap between them, but the truck would struggle to carry on.

'Whose building?' she asked, peering behind her into the night. He stepped out the truck and ran to the large doors. She followed as he grabbed the door handle of the structure and pulled it open. Black dust fell from the doorframe and landed onto the ground as he edged in. They could both hear the cries of the people behind them. She stepped into the building. Her boots crunched against something on the cold floor. She glanced down at the broken shards of glass that were littered sporadically. She looked back up. Ahead of her were large cylinders that rose from the floor and touched the ceiling. Black marks covered the remaining glass on each cylinder. Each one was broken and cracked in places; glass scattered beneath them. She stepped towards one of the large tubes.

She could hear Donahue behind her, pushing the door closed. He grabbed something from the side and thrust it between the handles. On some of the remaining glass, she could see a faint computerised light. There was a name, Tony White.

'Donahue, what is this place?' she spoke out, her voice echoing off the walls. His index finger quickly pressed against her lips.

'Shh, please,' he told her sharply. The room was pitch black dark. Even with Dawn's eyes, she could just about make out her own hand. The room remained silent.

'This is private property, and I really don't want the owner to know there are trespassers here.'

'You're saying we're trapped?' she whispered. They could hear the bloody eyed beings getting closer to the building.

'Truck just needs some time to cool down. I'll figure something out. I will. We can carry on then. Unless they suddenly sprout wings, they can't get in.' The two fell silent.

'Master requires you,' one of the people yelled through the door. 'Come out girl!' Nails clicked against the metal structure, voices and hissing grew louder. They had caught up.

CHAPTER 15

'See? They can't get in,' Donahue reassured her after some time had passed. The building was incredibly cold to stand in and Dawn had decided to sit close to the door. She could feel the soot under her fingers; the ashes sometimes lifting and forcing her into coughing fits. Donahue was stood close by.

'What happened to this place?' Dawn asked him.

'There was a fire,' he told her rather quickly. His silver eyes were just about visible in the darkness. He wasn't coping well in the blackness. He was taking in deep breaths. The Barghest was a beast of the night but Donahue kept his monstrous form at bay.

'I gathered there was a fire. There's soot everywhere!' she said irritably.

'You're best not knowing,' he interrupted her line of thought. 'Look, it's starting to get light. You can see the sun trying to get through.'

'Donahue,' she tried to cut in.

'We only have to wait a little longer, and then I'll push them back. You get to the truck. I'll follow, and we'll be at the safe house in no time,' he continued his speech.

'Donahue, please,' she tried again.

'Once we're at the safe house, it's a lovely place. I'll teach you things if you like. I can provide you with a normal human life, or I can teach you how to use your talents as an angel. I'll do anything I can to make things up to you Dawn.'

'Donahue!' she shouted out.

'I don't want to tell you about this place,' he snapped at her. He didn't want to tell her about the building; he had made that very clear. Something else was on Dawn's mind.

'I'm trying to listen. Something doesn't seem right,' she told him as she pressed her ear against the cold metal door.

'What can you hear?' he asked her. The problem was Dawn couldn't hear a thing. It was perfectly silent. For ages, she could hear them clawing at the door and talking in broken sentences. She had heard them pacing and breathing deeply. She couldn't hear a thing now. Her eyes focused on the wreckage in between the handles and pulled it out of the way. The door opened slightly as she peered out. The sun was starting to rise, light pouring onto the surroundings. On the doorstep lay four bodies. One body lay on its back, its eyes wide open, and blood dribbled from its eyes and down the cheek. The man's neck had one deep cut across his neck.

'He's here!' Dawn panicked as she looked back into the building.

'Is he now?' a cruel voice replied. The slither of light entered the building from the outside, hitting the left hand side of the Crimson. His hand was clutching Donahue from the back of the neck. He was limp, breathing but limp. The hand let go, dropping her guardian angel with a thud.

'Not the smartest idea you had, sunshine,' he spoke, his crimson eyes narrowing and staring at her.

'What have you done to Donahue?' she asked, trembling as she spoke. He didn't reply. How had he managed to sneak up on her and Donahue? She tried to feel her sixth sense. Instead, she felt a thick poison overlapping it and making it dull. It hadn't been nerves before that made her feel queasy. It had been him. She could hear the glass crunching underneath his heavy shoes as he approached her. She wasn't going to let him take her again. She wasn't going to let him get away with what he had done to Mike. But the courage she had before and the desire to take revenge rushed out of her soul, was replaced by fear. She took quick steps backwards, her hand flailing behind her to find the door.

The door slammed with a mighty bang, and the light was replaced by darkness. Dawn looked up; her eyes shining to view the Crimson towered over her, his hands pressed against the door.

'If I have to chain you to keep you from running, then, so be it,' he snarled at her, dragging her quickly by the arm and deep into the building. She dug her heels into the floor as much as she could, but her heels tapped against the smooth surface in vain, sending glass fragments across the floor. Doors were being swung open by invisible arms, smashing against the walls and echoing loudly.

'Perhaps, the chains won't be necessary if you decide to cooperate,' he warned her, dragging her down flight after flight of stairs. The sheer size of the place was now sinking in. She desperately tried to keep a track of where she was going, where she was being taken. At times, she saw glimpses of cages, long steel bars, littered glass, and stains of red and black spread from the floors and walls. She kicked out at him, dug her nails into his hand, and punched him as hard as she could. He didn't flinch or strike back at her. She heard a set of large doors fly open somewhere in the distance. The path ahead was blanketed in darkness; the lights were broken. She squinted, spotting giant doors ahead of her. She concentrated hard on them as they quickly approached them.

'This is your last chance, sunshine. Understand and take on your destiny,' he spoke loudly to her. He took another step forward, entering the doorway. She remembered what Donahue had said about blinding the sixth sense. If he was covering her eternal eye, then his was also blinded.

'No!' she screamed out, unleashing the energy within her sharply at the doors. They swung outwards and then inwards. The left door slammed directly into his body. The steel crumbled against him. She felt his hand spasm in shock from the impact. She jerked backwards, pulled herself away from him quickly, and ran down the corridor. The adrenaline within her peaked. The poison rushed out her, and her sixth sense heightened dramatically. Her eye was open, as was his.

She turned on her heels abruptly. His red eyes shone brightly, directly in front of her face. He was much closer than she expected him to be. Her attempt to throw him back was halted as his hands clutched onto her wrists, throwing her to the ground. The floor creaked in protest beneath them as she felt in cave in slightly. Her stomach pressed tightly against the floor, and her head shook from the impact. She could hear him taking in deep breaths of frustration. Her head throbbed from the collision as she felt a warm liquid trickle from her forehead. She peered back at him over her shoulder. His expression changed from anger to concern as he let go of her left wrist and placed his hand on her forehead.

To the ends of the Earth, he would chase her for she was the last female angel. Dawn was his last hope to bring back the angels, and if she was right, he would do anything to prevent her from being lost, even by death. Her hand swiftly pressed against the floor. He noticed too late as he tried to pull her body up. The energy flowed from within her to her hand and blasted through the floor. It gave way. The two fell downwards into the darkness. Within the air, he grabbed her body, and his wings came forth in a bright fiery red. They turned in the air as the wings enveloped her.

His body struck the ground sharply. Her body pressed against his. The wings softened the blow to her. His wings parted and lay flat on either side of his body. Shaken, Dawn rolled her body, landing on his right wing.

The Crimson lay on the ground. His body was trembling; his eyes closed tightly. The impact would have killed a normal person. She would be so lucky he would be as weak as them. If there was a time, she could have destroyed him it was now. Visions of Mike flashed in front of her. Anger filled her, taking in deep breaths. Her hand reached over his chest, feeling it rise and fall as he breathed. If she could muster the strength, she could burn his heart out. Her chest felt tight as she inhaled soot and coughed loudly. The pain she felt was awful and sickening. There was no way she could exert her energy.

She felt fragile from the abrupt outburst as she pulled herself to her feet. The sensation to lie down was overpowering, but she pressed on. She couldn't kill him, so she would have to leave before he came round. The corridor was long and narrow. Most of the lights were gone with only a few remaining dim. The walls were a dark red, covered in a mesh of steel wiring. Her hand pressed against it as she took in a deep breath. Something stuck to her hand. Disgusted, she pulled her hand back quickly and inspected it. Dirty red lines crossed over her palm. She ran her index finger over the markings, and the lines vanished into soot and red dust.

This was the corridor. This was the corridor that appeared in her nightmares. Had she fallen unconscious, or if this was reality, she couldn't tell. Her mind was expecting to hear gears turning and people screaming for help. The room was perfectly silent. She closed her eyes and took in a deep breath from her nose. A lingering scent of burning filled her nostrils. In her nightmares, the smell choked her, no matter how hard she had refused to take it in, but the scent was almost gone now.

Her legs were trembling horribly as she went around the corner. There were flickering lights in the distance—an assortment of colour. There had been a fire, a horrible one at that. That must have been the flames she felt when her eternal eye spiked during danger. As she got closer, she noticed the lights beneath cylinders, similar to the ones she had seen upstairs. Words were flashing slowly. Josh Faust followed by the strange language that she had been presented with before. She could only assume it meant gone or offline as when she pressed her head close to the glass and took in a strangled breath. The gaze of a skeleton met her own. It was a quarter of the size of her. A child, maybe even a baby. She fell to her knees, the impact from the ceiling taking its toll. She crawled along the sooty floor. Cylinders stood tall around her, judging her. The names underneath each were red. Melody Hughes, Ronald Smith, Alicia Jones, and Scott McLeod were all repeating the same word. Each cylinder contained charred bones, some cylinders with scratch marks forever etched into the cold glass.

She slowly approached the last cylinder in the room. The same words glowed dark red like the others had. Sky Moore. As she read the name, she felt a delicate presence within her mind stir. She placed her hand against the glass, trying to peer in. At the back of the cylinder, the glass was shattered and broken. There was no body within. The lights flickered frantically, changing colours in rapid succession. The word had changed green, no more than that. The word itself had changed and from what little of the language she had learnt she knew its meaning. The word translated to present. The other cylinders hadn't reacted in that way. Why was Sky Moore's cylinder different? Why was it reacting to her? Her eyes widened as she began to understand. She curled on the floor, staring behind her. The vision of a lady came into view—her long white and wild hair partially hid odd eyes. One was green, the other purple with a discoloured pupil. The building seemed to shriek out from beyond, shattering the silence. A hand stretched out, ready to take Dawn's.

'Why?' Dawn whimpered. Her mind and body gave in, and she fell unconscious.

CHAPTER 16

When she opened her eyes, the world seemed different, as though looking through a window. The light was bright, spreading down the corridor she was sure she had already passed. The black ashes were no longer present, and the place was clean except for a few footprints on the floor. There was lighting above her head, and the walls seemed smooth and well kept. It hadn't been this way a moment ago.

The sound of crying emitted from the corridors. Dawn turned on her heels and headed towards the noise. The prison cells she had passed before were all empty; the doors wide open. There was a single cage that remained locked. Within it was a teenage girl, curled up on the floor. Her tangled hair had fallen over her face. The sound of footsteps grew louder and louder. The prisoner must have heard as she rose slightly from the floor. Her face appeared from beneath her locks. It was the girl who had been within her memories, the one that came before her and spoke to her directly. Dawn went to grab the bars, but her fingers slipped through the metal. The person walking down the corridor was almost within reach. Dawn glared at the man as he approached. His red eyes stared at the prison door.

'Leave her alone.' Dawn turned around; her hands held out. The Crimson stepped through her, sending a ghostly shudder down her spine. It was like she wasn't there at all.

Because I'm not, she thought to herself. This was a memory, but was it hers? Dawn watched as the Crimson produced a key, realising that she wasn't present in this time. The girl's eyes were filled with tears as the door swung open. It was the girl from the corridor, virtually identical to Dawn besides her dirtied long hair and green eyes.

'Stand up, Sky,' he spoke coldly as he entered the room, giving Dawn a name to finally place to her alter ego. Sky wept loudly as she shuffled backwards; her body pressed against the wall in hopes it would open up. The Crimson took no notice as he grabbed her arm tightly. She tried to fight him off as he began to drag her. Her fingers reached for the bars, but her grip was too weak. Dawn watched in horror as Sky began to scream, kicking and fighting back as hard as she could, but he didn't acknowledge her struggles.

'I don't want to die, not like them!' Sky pleaded. Dawn watched in horror as they entered the red room. The cylinders contained naked children attached to tubes and surrounded by liquid. She placed her hand on one of them, reading the name underneath and watching the lights flash. The name she read was Ronald Smith, one of the names she'd read before passing out. Directly behind it was an empty cylinder. It was labelled Sky Moore.

A heat lapped at her side. The machine stood tall and menacing, fully functional. He took Sky to a table nestled within the machine, clamping the girl's wrists into shackles as he leaned to one side and flicked a switch. Her body lay flat and stretched; her head fixed into place as the gears began to turn and hiss.

'Don't make me one of them,' she begged one last time. He ignored her as he took a needle attached to a thick tube and struck it into her chest. A dribble of blood slithered from the wound and onto her shirt. The gears sped. The machine roared. The electricity sparked. Sky began to scream as jolts of energy ran through her. The tube started to fill with her blood and entered the confinements of the machine. Tears crept down her face; her skin turned white.

Sky's pain was Dawn's darkest memory.

Dawn turned her head away, no longer able to look. It was then she noticed the cylinder, and as Sky struggled against her shackles, blood began to pour into the cylinder in front of the machine. It mixed with other substances and bubbled furiously. The two were connected. Dawn read the sign underneath it. The words had changed to the same words she had seen before when her hand had pressed against it. A tiny embryo formed within the container. It started to grow, gaining limbs, eyes, fingers, and toes. Within minutes, it turned into what appeared to be a baby. Tubes came down and inserted themselves into the baby in a similar fashion to the other naked children.

Sky's screaming became louder than it had been before. Dawn covered her ears, unable to look away from the baby created with the dying girl's blood. She looked up at the ceiling, trying to avoid the scene. In the rafters above, she noticed a man with black hair and silver eyes.

'Donahue?' Dawn questioned aloud. As she spoke, the Crimson also noticed the guardian.

'St-stop this now . . . or I'll . . .' Donahue's voice called from the ceiling, his hands holding onto the mesh that supported the building. She could see the terror in his face and sweat on his forehead.

'Her life will have greater meaning in death,' Crimson spoke coldly. 'She has one of the strongest strains of our bloodline.'

'Stop this madness,' Donahue called out. 'All of the angels are dead. You can't bring them back!'

'I can and will,' Crimson snarled at him, his red wings coming into view. 'Sure there have been set backs, but I will bring back our legacy. They are surviving, and when the strongest emerge into adults, we can start again. This world is overflowing with humans. A few hundred deaths won't leave a dent.'

'It's not right. If you don't stop this I'll—'

'You'll do nothing,' he interrupted the angel in the supports. The Crimson turned his back to Donahue; his attention back to attending the machine that Sky was still being tortured by.

Donahue leapt down from the rafters and collided into the monster. They both crashed into the machine. The mechanic beast cried out as vents of steam rose from its frame. The bolts of electricity that had been coursing through Sky seemed to halt, but the blood was still making its way towards the tank.

'Please . . . help,' Sky whispered. She was no longer screaming. Her chest was lifting up and down rapidly for breath. Donahue pulled himself up awkwardly, blood etching down his lip. He rushed to the shackles clamped around Sky. His fingers dug into the braces around Sky's ankle. The smell of burning plastic and copper began to drift. Flames lapped at the circuits within. The Crimson had lost himself in a fit of rage, launching himself towards the guardian angel. His fingers wrapped around Donahue's throat, squeezing the air from his neck. Donahue tried to fight back, kicking and struggling against him.

The fire erupted from the machine, growing beyond the metal cage and making its way across the floor. It edged its way towards a large tank that smelt of fuel. The gears spun faster; the smoke began to rise. A roar of energy filled the room with a fierce fire that consumed everything in its path.

This is what he did to us. Sky's voice spoke numbly to Dawn. The lab was burning, flames engulfing the tanks and machinery. Donahue lay on the floor, motionless, curled awkwardly against Sky's tank. Glass shattered from the extreme heat. Liquid poured out from their crevices and forced the flames to spread further. The sleeping children were being destroyed. Some were conscious. Some were crying out and struggling. They couldn't escape. They were doomed to die. Dawn stared at the cylinder where she was conceived. The flames did not touch her. They died out as they touched Donahue's body.

You were the only survivor. He had no way of restoring that machine. Don't let him be your doom like he was ours.

Dawn screamed in horror, waking herself in the process. She had witnessed her birth and hated it. With another person's life, she had been created by the Crimson. He was now obsessed with her—the only surviving child from his mad experiments. Somehow, she had escaped, but why her and only her?

'Are you awake, Lady?' a woman spoke out. Dawn peered from where she sat. She wasn't in the building. She was back in the truck. She edged forward in the seat. The seatbelt pressed against her chest as she peeked over the headrest in front of her. Donahue's body was collapsed in the chair, taking in shallow breaths. The person driving the car was an elderly woman with long and matted white hair. The lady she'd seen before she had passed out. The truck was rolling forward at a casual pace, and her green eye was staring at the road.

'I'm awake,' Dawn responded, sitting back into the seat. 'Did you get us out of the building?'

'Yes Lady,' she replied, a grin appearing on her face. 'Angelica, worried she did. Came out to look and noticed skid marks.' She turned her head to look directly at Dawn. 'Are you a friend of Donny's, Lady?' Dawn was left speechless. The woman had different coloured eyes, one green with a black pupil. The other one was a strange shade of blue, almost purple, and that pupil was clouded, a mixture of grey and white. She was wearing a long and white summer dress, despite how cold the winter was, and yet there were dots of red in random areas of the cloth.

'This is my mother's eye.' She pointed to the clouded eye with her finger. 'Her father was an angel and her mother was human. Father was . . .' she paused midsentence. For a moment, the two stared at each other. The woman didn't finish her sentence as she turned her attention back to the road. The conversation had ended, not paused but was ended at that moment.

'Right . . . Erm, Donahue's helping me,' Dawn told her.

'What is he helping you with? He should have known not to go to that building. It smells wrong. Don't you agree, Lady?'

'It did smell bad,' Dawn hesitated in her response. 'My name's Dawn. You don't need to keep calling me Lady.'

'Dawn is not a good name to have, not these days. A very bad name.' Angelica sighed. 'They're after you.'

Before Dawn could respond, a groan came from the passenger side. Donahue opened his eyes slowly. When he noticed he was in the truck, he bolted upright, staring left and right. When he spotted Dawn, he let out a sigh of relief, then his lips pursed as he spotted the elderly woman.

'Angelica?' he asked in surprise. 'Did you get us out of the building?'

'Yes, Donny. Angelica knew to meet you here. Angelica saw it ahead of time.' She patted her purple eye as she spoke. Dawn thought back to what she knew about the angels. In the book she'd been given it had shown angels with purple eyes could foresee parts of the future. Was it possible for a half-blood to possess the same power?

'I haven't seen you in years,' he murmured. 'Why are you driving the truck?' he asked her.

'Must go to the city. They are gathering there,' she told him.

'Who's gathering there?' Dawn asked in confusion. At that, Angelica turned the radio on.

'Numbers of the outbreaks being reported keep rising in level, and it is suspected it has reached hundreds of people. The government has issued an evacuation on the city until further notice. Experts have stated the majority of reports are coming from the city and that other infected people seem to be gathering there. If you spot any individual which appears to have blood tears, do not approach them and call the local authorities.' The radio gave its speech. The world now knew of them. These were real people and families that were being sucked into this—all to obtain Dawn for their master. The two in the front were talking to each other, but Dawn had blanked them out. She tried to recall how long it had been since she had left the children's home and left for herself. The children had died. Ricky had been murdered. Mike had been killed. Hundreds more were now being turned. All because she was a science experiment; the end results of the death of so many people. Dawn felt the truck slowing. She flung the door open; her seatbelt unbuckled as she threw herself off the seat and onto her feet outside.

'Dawn, get back in the truck!' Donahue called out as the truck screeched to a halt. Dawn walked away and stared out across the empty fields. Her knees buckled. She knelt on the floor and vomited loudly. It was too much to take on. Why was she still trying to escape? Why was she still fleeing? There was no end in sight.

'Dawn, please get back in the truck. It's dangerous out here,' Donahue approached her.

'I'm a monster.' She spat on the ground.

'You're not.'

'He killed them. He killed Sky Moore. He killed Mike, and he's turning people into . . . into bloody messes to get me. He won't stop. He'll never stop.'

'I'll protect you. The safe house isn't much further. Another day of driving at the most. Nothing will get to you there. You deserve better than this.'

'No.' she gritted her teeth. 'Sky Moore was tortured to death. That's how I was born. I shouldn't be alive.'

'Neither should I,' he sat next to her. 'The reason there aren't any angels anymore besides the three of us if because of a war years ago, and all of the angel's should have died back then. There was a fight for power and for strict traditions. I was about your age when they had nearly wiped each other out,' he began to speak.

'What happened to them all?'

Angelica piped in, 'Fires as strong as the sun engulfed them all, so strong there was no trace left, but a demon and a coward.' The two looked behind them, staring at Angelica. Her hair whipped wildly in the wind.

'Don't call me that!' he yelled at her, 'You think it doesn't get under my skin?' Angelica went quiet. He picked himself up, heading to the driver's side of the vehicle.

'Why didn't you protect them Donahue?' Dawn asked. Donahue's hand rested on the door handle. He didn't move. He began to snivel, trying to hold back tears as he wiped his eyes with the back of his hand. He took in a strangled breath.

'I'm sorry Dawn. I'm so sorry,' he wrapped his arms around her without warning. She didn't push him away as he leant into her, holding her tightly. 'I'm so sorry. I couldn't save the angels, but I could have saved those people. I knew what he was doing. Kidnapping innocent children because they were hybrids, humans with angel blood mixed in like Angelica. I was too scared to intervene. He promised he wouldn't hurt my friend if I kept my distance. But every night I heard them scream for help. He only cared about bringing back the angels.' She could feel him shivering.

'You don't have to carry on,' Dawn whimpered as he held onto her tighter still. The memories were flooding him though as he shook his head, tears running down his silver eyes.

'When I finally did decide to stop what he was doing, I charged in recklessly. I caused the machine to malfunction. It set the lab on fire. I'm the reason they're all dead. He left me to perish, and I was going to let myself die there. But you were still alive. I knew I had to save you. I broke you out and ran as far as I could. I ran to the closest and safest house I could find and frantically knocked the door. When they saw me in that broken state, they went white in the face. I was a bloody mess. I literally thrust you into their arms and fled.'

'I didn't know what happened to me,' Dawn choked on her words, almost crying herself. Donahue had broken down completely, sobbing uncontrollably. 'The home always told me it was best I didn't know.' He nodded in agreement.

'The owners took you to an orphanage,' he carried on rambling. 'When he realised one of the angels had survived, he tracked me down, and I was forced to tell him where I had left you. But you had been given away, and he had killed the couple before he had thought that was a possibility. Neither of us had any idea where you were. All I could do was follow in his shadows in hopes I could keep you safe if he found you.' He let Dawn go, hugging his sides.

'Perhaps, your friend could help if we asked?' Angelica questioned. Donahue glanced at her, smiling shyly and let out an exhausted laugh.

'Oh, my friend has been . . . gone for some time.' He smiled. 'We'll all go to the safe house. We've got to keep moving, right?' He wiped the tears aware as he pulled himself into the driver's side and shut the door.

'Angelica's sorry Donny, but she didn't see the house,' Angelica spoke out.

'I'm really glad you saw the future with us in trouble. I have no idea how we'd have escaped otherwise,' Donahue commented, 'but there is no way I'm putting Dawn in anymore danger.' He averted his gaze as he pushed the passenger door open, coaxing the two women to get back in the truck.

'Did you know his friend?' Dawn asked Angelica as the elderly lady approached the passenger door.

'I'm afraid I've forgotten lady. A very important person to Donny for sure, but I can't remember. My mind seems to miss points, and it hurts so much,' Angelica's hand instinctively grasped over a silver necklace around her neck. 'We shouldn't worry about the past lady. We should continue through the present. But I fear going to this house will not happen.'

CHAPTER 17

'Donny, you're driving the wrong way,' Angelica spoke out. Dawn stared out the window as the truck continued forward. The forest was hanging on either side of the road, casting shadows over the truck.

'We are going the right way Angelica,' he told her sternly, 'we're going to the safe house. Do you know why? Because it is safe. It's away from him and this army of . . . of—'

'They are after the lady. They will not stop until they have the lady. You know this. These are demons like in the war.'

'They are not demons!' Donahue spoke out, 'Only the mad king knew how to create demons, and they did not bleed from their eyes or were screaming like strangled cats.' He gritted his teeth, rubbing his eye with his hand. Dawn edged forward in her seat, trying to put pieces of the puzzle together. A war, a mad king, and a fire led to the end of the angels it seemed.

'They're very similar though,' Angelica continued, 'Angelica has a cure like the last time. It works a little it does. Angelica knows it does. Angelica has tested it, but so far, it only delays. There is a way to get it to cure.' Dawn wondered if both had been in the war that had wiped out the angel's. They seemed to both be very familiar with the war.

'You have a way to turn them back?' Donahue asked.

'There is a man in Angelica's vision who can complete it. The city, Donny, is the way, and that is the way we must go.'

'Do you honestly think going head first into the nest of these things, especially if you say they're like the demon controlled shells from the war, things we know are after her. You think going with Dawn is clever?' Donahue scolded her, 'We'll go afterwards, not before.' The two in the front fell silent.

'We should go then,' Dawn spoke out. She agreed with Angelica, whether visions were right or not. These were people that were being turned into monsters against their will, people who were specifically after her. Whether they managed to cure them or they got a hold of her, either way it would end the carnage. It wasn't that Dawn wanted to be taken, but she did not want to be the reason for people being hurt, not anymore.

'We don't,' he angrily told her. The truck continued to roll forward, tyres squelching against the muddy and damp road.

'I don't know much about the past, but from what I can tell, the demons were a big part of the end of the race. Am I wrong?' Dawn asked.

'You're not wrong, but that is exactly why this truck is not turning into that city.' Donahue explained.

'Well, then I am,' she responded, 'People are being overtaken and—' Before she could finish the tyre's screeched as it was forced to stop. Dawn felt her seatbelt tighten against her chest from the sudden brake. Angelica's hair was thrown over her face as she let out a shaky wheeze. Donahue turned to face Dawn.

'Did I say I was ignoring it?' Donahue's heightened voice came out.

'No, you didn't but—'

'I'll take Angelica and her part cure after I know you're safe,' he told her sternly.

'I don't want to be locked away for my safety,' Dawn argued. 'They're out there because of me.'

'So putting yourself out there will solve everything?' he snapped at her. Dawn withdrew in her chair.

'I didn't say that.' Dawn gritted her teeth.

'No, you just think that throwing yourself to the dogs will help.'

'Donny, please, I know you are scared . . .' Angelica softly spoke, her hand rising to touch his face. He pushed her approach away with his arm, raising it and pressing his hand to his forehead.

'You both need to shut up. You are making my head ache.' He yelled out. The trio fell silent for a time.

'Donahue, has the outside invaded?' Angelica piped up. Dawn remained silent. The half-angel opened her bag and pulled out a small bottle. The bottle was a see through plastic, and in it rattled three individual capsules.

'Donny, I have some medicine,' Angelica continued, 'I have three left, three pills. If the outside has got in, it will slow it down.' Donahue didn't respond. Dawn pulled herself closer and stared at the pill. Angelica popped the lid open and poured one of the capsules into her palm. Her hand lifted to her mouth and tilted backwards, allowing the strange medication to go down her throat with a gulp.

'Angelica shows it is safe. There are two left. You can have one, if the outside has . . .'

'You don't even know the rubbish that comes out of your mouth,' he snapped at her, 'You're still the same as you were the last time we met. Bat shit crazy!'

'Don't talk to her that way!' Dawn shouted. Donahue glared at Dawn coldly. She pushed back into her chair, unsure what to make of him anymore.

'Angelica is sorry if she has upset Donny,' Angelica withdrew, pushing the bottle back into her bag, 'The mind has wondered with a lot of memories. Has something important been forgotten?' Donahue let out a deep groan, one hand tightening around the steering wheel. His other hand was firmly against his forehead, his fingers pushing against the skin to try and nurse his headache.

Dawn stared out of the back window of the car, finger prints were still smudged on the glass from the encounter with the possessed woman. Something clicked within her mind, as though a shutter of a camera had gone off for a second. The outside was silent, no sound of animals or creatures. The truck had been stopped several times on the journey, whether for the engine or to rest. She looked back at the two arguing, who were completely lost in their own worlds.

'You need to drive,' Dawn spoke up quickly. Neither heard her. A streak of red entered her vision to her left.

I know you are out there! She screamed within her head, *Why won't you give up?*

'I do not care about your vision,' Donahue growled at Angelica.

'Angelica's vision is correct.' Angelica yelled back. 'Angelica saw the building, the lady, and you.' Dawn watched in horror as a tall man stepped onto the muddy road in front of the truck. His dark red eyes stared directly at Dawn through the windscreen, his wings stretched out. His right wing showed dark cracks, revealing his injury from the fall.

Step out the vehicle and the others do not need to be involved. The Crimson's voice slipped into her head. Dawn shook her head, leaning forward and grabbing Donahue by the shoulder.

'Move the truck!' Dawn yelled at the top of her lungs. Before either Donahue or Angelica could react, a blaze of red smashed through the windshield. Dawn felt two hands grab her body. The red wings wrapped around her. The back of the truck pierced outwards as a shower of glass hit the road, and the two fell through onto the mud-stained tarmac. Her body was lifted as she heard the truck lift from the road and collide into the trees to the side. He pressed her against a tree, one wing behind her back. The Crimson kept his hand firmly against her chest. She felt her energy boil inside of her, stretching out her hand awkwardly in his direction.

'Do it, and the truck will explode with them inside,' he warned her. His free wing drooped awkwardly, a discoloured red. The truck lay on its side, the doors smashed inwards. Donahue was visible in the driver's seat, his hands covering his face. Angelica was lying beside the truck. Her hands were scratched from the gravel as she began to lift herself from the road.

'If you drag me back to that prison or that cabin in the woods what are you going to do?' she snapped at her creator.

'I will bring back our people,' he told her, gripping her more tightly. 'You are the only one that can do so. I will do all in my power to make sure of it.'

'And each time you take me I'll grow stronger, I'll fight back. I'll run from you forever. I gain nothing from your plan and you have nothing to barter with me anymore.' She took in a deep breath and exclaimed, 'You killed Mike!' His grip remained firm on her as he leant back slightly.

'Sunshine, I did not kill the boy,' the Crimson spoke. Hot tears surfaced behind her eyes as she took in a deep breath.

'Liar!' she cried out, 'I won't help you. You are all monsters and I don't want to become you or him!' Behind them, they both heard steel crunching. Dawn looked across to see Donahue emerge from the truck, awkwardly opening the car door and dragging his own body out. He took in deep breaths; the impact of the collision had shaken him.

'You cannot keep her from me Donahue,' the Crimson let out a deep sigh as he turned to peer over his shoulder. Donahue dragged his body forward with his right hand, his knees scuffed from the gravel. His left hand was placed over his face, blood secreting between his fingers.

'Why? Why are you doing this?' Donahue growled in a beastly manner. The Crimson's eyes narrowed as Donahue's right hand fell to the floor. His face was bloody and as Donahue looked directly at the Crimson it was apparent that the truck colliding was not the reason for the blood.

His left eye was cracked horribly with a deep red that covered his pupil. Blood etched and dribbled from the socket. Only his right eye remained silver. Before Dawn could react the Crimson did first. He hoisted her from the tree trunk and pushed her to the side and behind him. He turned to face Donahue, wings outstretched and blocking her vision of the wreck.

'Leave... her...' Donahue's voice began to break. The Crimson ignored the warning, taking strong strides towards the man. His wings deepened in colour, forming into physical sharp tools that encroached towards the man. It was now that Dawn had a chance to flee. She chose to sprint onto the road, keeping a wide birth of the two angels. She stared at the man whose jaw began to fill with the canines of the Barghest. A slither of blood crept from his left eye. Dawn knelt next to Angelica who was trembling on her knees.

'Angelica thought it had invaded. How? How did it invade?' Angelica had started to tremble. 'If Donny is invaded… if… if he… Angelica wishes she saw this.' Dawn placed her arms under the trembling elder.

'What do you mean invaded?' Dawn asked her. She could feel the Crimson's eyes on her back as she helped to aid Angelica to the side.

'Do not set your eyes on her. She is not yours to take,' Donahue's voice was breaking into an animalistic tone. Dawn gazed back as the Crimson picked up the bleeding man by his neck.

'Do you wish for me to cripple you?' the Crimson spoke coldly to him, 'Your constant interference is—'

'I am not speaking to you,' Donahue let out a long whine of a dogs as he spoke, ignoring the pressure that was being applied to his throat. In that moment, Dawn felt the ageing quarter-blood push a small object into her palm and close her fingers around it.

'This is your final warning to stay out of my way,' the Crimson let go of Donahue and turned on his heels. He approached Dawn, his deep crimson eyes set on her. Dawn's hand left Angelica's as she stepped away from him. The angel was still too close to the truck for her to release her energy, and she didn't want to risk hurting Angelica or Donahue.

What happened next was almost a blur. Donahue roared loudly, partially transformed. His arms and face were covered in dense black fur, and his clothes were torn. He sprinted forward on his hands and feet, one bloody eye, and one silver eye fixed on the Crimson. Before her creator could even turn, the beast collided into the Crimson. His hand's clutched onto the Crimson's leg, throwing him off balance and was hurled to the floor. He snarled loudly as he gripped onto the angel's torso with fangs and ran with him deep into the woodland.

The red angel was thrown deep within the forest, trees breaking under the force and crashing to the leafy floor. Birds and insects scarped from the remains of their homes as the two angels collided. Dawn watched as the Crimson's eyes glowed a fierce red. His wings darkened and drew downwards like a thousand swords into Donahue's body. The beast howled out as blood poured, letting his grip go. Blood zigzagged down the Crimson's chest.

Donahue kicked out sharply at the Crimson's leg. The Crimson's wings trembled as they folded slightly. Donahue transformed fully into the Barghest under the foliage of the thick woods. His jaws opened widely and snapped shut onto the Crimson's damaged wing. The red blades pierced through the dogs muzzle as it growled loudly. For the first time Dawn heard the Crimson angel scream out in pain, withdrawing his other wing from the beasts body. The beasts back paws fell to the ground as it pulled backwards, turning its head sharply. The sound of tearing rang out through the forest as the Crimson cried out both in pain and fear. The angel's wing was being torn; she could hear it being pulled from his back. The beast lunged forward, a snapping sound echoed through the forest as the beast pressed its head into the Crimson's torso and let go, sending the bleeding angel deep into the woods. Trees toppled within the far distance.

The Barghest turned to face Dawn, its left eye completely red and its right starting to crack. Its lips pulled back, revealing bloodied teeth as it strode towards her. As the light touched his skin, he became a mixture of beast and man. In a panic Dawn fled to the turned over truck, the only shield she could think of. The Barghest cut her off, standing tall at her side, snarling loudly at her, blood drooling from its mouth.

'Don't do this,' Dawn begged. Donahue took in heavy dog like breaths. His narrow eyes widened, patches of silver still remaining. His paws squelched against the muddy floor as he sat on the road. Donahue howled out from his beastly muzzle, turning his head away from her.

'Stay back... I... I won't be taken! You won't take me!' His voice was contorted, a strangulation of human and wolf. Angelica was snivelling as

Dawn looked at her hand. Angelica had pushed one of the pills into her palm.

'Donahue, take the pill,' Dawn thrust the capsule into his vision. He looked up at her, his right eye cracking with lines of blood.

'G-go away,' he whimpered, his paws clutching handfuls of his hair as he whimpered. She took in a deep breath as she swiped for a handful of his fur on his forehead. He howled out angrily as she wrapped her arm around his neck. The beast stood up, throwing Dawn off her feet for a moment.

'Open your mouth!' Dawn pleaded as she pressed his hand into his jaw. She could feel the wounds that had been inflicted from the Crimson's wing. His jaw widened as she thrust her arm into his gaping mouth and pushed the pill onto his tongue. She withdrew her hand sharply as the beast's muzzle snapped shut. She pressed her weight against his nose as she forced it to the floor. The beast whined pathetically as its body rested on the mud. She felt his throat tense and heard the sound of saliva falling down his neck.

Dawn let go of the creature and took in a deep breath. His left eye continued to bleed. Was it was too late? The humans were bad enough being possessed by this disease. What would happen if a fully grown guardian was to fall to it as well? She looked across to the damaged woodlands. The Crimson had been truly fearful in that moment. He was scared of Donahue.

'Dawn… I… I'm so sorry…' he cried out. Dawn turned her attention back to the partial Barghest as it slowly rose to its feet. His eyes stared at Dawn, bloody tears welling in both. The left eye was unchanged but his right seemed to have subsided somewhat.

'I should have listened. I will make this up. I…' Donahue was panting, deep moans escaping his monstrous mouth.

'Donahue…' Dawn sympathised as she placed her hand on his shoulder. She now knew why he had become so rattled. Like the others it had made him aggressive. The medicine was only going to stall though. They really had to get to the city, to save him and the others.

'Forgive me, please forgive me!' He barked out as he shoved her out of the way, knocking her to the floor. As she looked up she watched as the beast stood on all fours, the full and menacing Barghest in bright daylight. Blood droplets fell to the road as he shook his body violently and fled down the road.

'Donahue, don't go!' Dawn screamed out in desperation. She scrambled to her feet and launched herself upright. As soon as she was on her feet, he was out of sight.

'Donahue!' She called out at the top of her lungs.

'It must have invaded,' Angelica spoke softly from where she stood, 'It does not invade through wind or spit. It must be ingested. It must mix with the acids of the stomach. Lady has been with Donahue, is there a way he could have taken it?' Dawn thought back to when they first encountered the bloodied people and the realisation hit her like a stone to the head.

'We were attacked and he protected me. I think he swallowed some of their blood.' Angelica nodded in understanding.

'Lady, when the people turn it is horrible. If Donny turns…' Angelica was interrupted. The two ladies listened at the howls of a deranged monster. More of them were coming, the ones that had fallen to this aliment.

'What in hell is happening?' Dawn spoke, staring up and down the road. For so long it had only been the crimson angel she had been running from. Now people with bloody eyes were coming directly after her.

'Their minds are controlled lady,' Angelica responded, 'It is like the war, oh the war the war that ended their race.' Angelica's clouded eye flickered, hints of purple and white trying to break through.

'We're going to the capital,' Dawn decided, 'We get the cure there and save as many as we can.' She picked up a stone from the side and threw it to the back of the truck's window. It shattered as she kicked in the remaining glass. She reached into the car and pulled out the bag that had held her and Mike's belongings. The strap fell over her shoulder. She pulled out another bag. She opened it and checked its content. This was Donahue's, filled with food and water. He had prepared as much as he could for the journey to the so called safe house. There was enough for two for a few days. Angelica crept up behind her and reached into the truck. Underneath the passenger side was a leather holster. It contained a gun.

Common sense stabbed the back of her mind sharply. She turned. A policeman stood before her, blood spots on his vest, his upper lip stained a deep red. Alarmed by how close he had managed to get to her, she nudged Angelica to move out of his reach.

'You are needed,' he gurgled out, 'Come with us.' His eyes were a deep red, blood welled down his cheeks. Dawn cast her hand forward and stared at him directly. She was too close to the truck. If she tried to blast him here she would destroy herself as well.

'If you come any closer I will force you back,' she spoke out. Either he did not hear her warning or ignored it as he lunged towards her, screeching as he did so. Dawn's common sense sparked and she ducked to the side before the man could touch her. Angelica ran her fingers through her straw-like hair as she diverted into the forest quickly, motioning Dawn to follow. Common sense was skittering in her mind as she approached the trees, keeping her gaze on the policeman who strode slowly towards her. As soon as they were clear of the road she cast her energy towards the toppled truck. The metal bent as the gas lit. With a thunderous bang the road was set alight. The possessed policeman was thrown to the ground from the impact, his head smacking against a solid redwood that rose tall into the sky. Dawn kept her eyes on the infected policeman who was pulling himself to his feet. A horrible burn was evident on his arm yet he seemed to not care for his own injury.

Dawn followed Angelica closely, strapping both bags securely to her back. As they stepped on the muddy ground, Dawn looked at the fallen trees. One of the trunks had a red stain that slid across the bark, shining in the winter light. Common sense was being unclear. Each time she stepped deeper into the forest, common sense faltered and sprang back. They both heard a fierce calling from the distance. More were coming.

'Angelica, we should go back to the road,' Dawn insisted. The woman shook her head, strapping the holster to her leg as she stopped in her tracks. Slowly the woman raised her hand and pointed directly in front of her. Through a gap in the trees, crimson eyes stared back coldly towards the two girls. One of his wings was trembling violently and no longer looked the deep fiery red it had been before. It was pale with blood running from deep white holes within it. Common sense sparked angrily at Dawn as she stepped back quickly.

'Stop!' he called out to her. She took another step back, feeling finger nails digging deeply into her arm. She screamed out, turning her head and being met by two bloody eyes of a different man. He was in his late twenties, his shirt torn from the various trees he had forced himself through.

'Come with us...' he snarled at her. She pushed her hand against his chest in fear. She tried to force her energy to come forth but it was scattered within her body. Her common sense heightened. The bloody tears never stopped weeping as he pulled her closer and began to drag her through the forest.

His expression suddenly fell cold. Dawn noticed the red slit across the man's throat, his hands loosened their grip. She pulled back in disgust and watched as he fell to his knees, then to his side. She could hear the crimson angel coughing violently, stumbling awkwardly to her side. Blood was running down his chest and his damaged wing. The infected policeman stepped through the forest, very close to the three of them. He roared out angrily and Dawn whimpered in fear. He charged forward, his hands stretched outward. He did not aim for Dawn though as his hands grabbed the angel's wing and bent it backwards. The crimson groaned as his good wing came into view.

'Whoever is controlling you...' he struggled to speak as his wing rose and pointed towards the man's neck, 'I will destroy them!' His wing slashed over Dawn's head and directly at the diseased man's neck. The stranger fell backwards, a clean slit across the skin. The crimson hid his wings from view as he fell to his hands and knees, grasping his chest. His eyes watered as he began to cry silently in pain.

Dawn glared at the crimson creature. In the far distance she could still hear them. She couldn't work out how far away they were, whether they were howling out at the tops of their lungs of if they were talking in scattered phrases. They were after her for some reason. She looked back at her creator whose bleeding was now starting to subside. The people being infected didn't seem to be his doing.

'Lady has a choice to make,' Angelica spoke coldly as she pulled a small revolver from the holster. The gun pointed at the top of his head.

'Father modified this gun. It is powerful and he knows it is,' Angelica smiled as she offered the gun to Dawn. The Crimson unsteadily tried to step back. Dawn hesitated as she saw the instrument being offered to her. The Crimson knew it was dangerous. It would either badly injure him or kill him.

'Lady, I understand your hate, I understand it. You can hear them though lady can't you?' Angelica tried to explain herself. Dawn had two choices. She could kill him on the spot and then move on. Without the protection of Donahue, how long would she be able to travel before being succumbed by the creatures out there?

'All you do is kill,' Dawn spoke directly to him, 'You burnt the children's home down with the children inside. You killed Ricky. You… you killed my only friend Mike!'

He finally spoke, 'I did kill those at the home. I did kill the Ricky boy that got in my way. I did not kill Mike.'

'Don't lie to me!' Dawn snapped, 'You wanted him dead the moment he stepped into your house.' She reached for the gun that was in Angelica's hand.

'If I wanted him dead, he would have been as soon as I opened the door,' he told her quickly. 'I wanted to terrify you. I needed one of you to buckle and to give in to my commands.' Dawn's hand hovered over the handgun in Angelica's hand.

'Angelica warns you to tell the truth,' the elderly woman spoke out.

'You're very lucky mongrel,' he gave a sinister grin; 'If I wasn't in such a bad state I could take that gun from you before you could pull the trigger.'

'Lucky mongrel,' she paraphrased. 'Tell lady the truth.'

'Mike was of use to me,' he told Dawn dully, 'Like an attachment to a pet I knew you wouldn't want to see him hurt. That is the truth but how can you prove me right or wrong?'

'You've lied to me before. You told me us two were the last angels,' Dawn continued. Angelica tightened her finger around the trigger, 'I cannot trust you if you've lied before.'

'As far as I know we are the last pure angels,' he glared at the barrel of the gun, 'There are hybrids, humans mixed with angel's blood. Even Donahue is not pure.' He turned to Angelica, staring at her directly, 'I know you are not mentally well, the wonders of being part human, but even you know Donahue is not an angel, not pure.'

'Lady, he tells the truth,' Angelica broke the silence. 'Lady, what do you want to do?' Dawn stared between the two. The cries were getting louder in the distance. She knew this disease wasn't his doing. He wouldn't risk her being hurt.

'Angelica has part of a cure for this outbreak. The army is after me, and if it is not yours, it's in your best interest and mine that it is stopped. Right?' she questioned.

'Wrong,' he scolded her, 'They have very little liking towards me. It would be easier to confine you out of their reach. However, you have a nasty tendency of consistently leaving my presence.'

'We cure everyone we can. Angelica had a vision a man can get the cure if we take this part there. People are in pain because they're after me and I don't want to burden them, not anymore. Help me free them and in return... I'll bring the angel's back.'

'Lady, that is not fair on you,' Angelica spoke out.

'It's not fair on them either,' Dawn spoke, 'I know how I was created. I wish I was never born because of it. I can't change that now but maybe

I could save them.' Dawn took her hand away from Angelica's and stared directly at the Crimson. He stared back at her, his expression stern. He was considering her proposition though. The silence chipped at her.

'And how do I know that you tell the truth, Sunshine?' he finally spoke.

'As much as I know you're telling the truth,' she argued, 'but in both of our interests, neither have much choice but to take the risk.'

'Very well,' he told her, 'I will take you to the city but you must do exactly as I say.'

CHAPTER 18

Dawn opened her eyes; the nightmare vanished as she returned to reality. The trees were dense and overhanging, casting shadows against the muddy road. She shook her head frantically, her fingers scratching against her scalp. The nightmares were no longer restricted to the night. For the past two days of travelling they had consistently hit her whether she was asleep or awake. Both the crimson angel and Angelica looked back at her.

'Does lady need to rest?' Angelica asked. Dawn shook her head, letting out a deep sigh. The three of them walked in silence, neither person wanting to speak to the other but all with the same goal. Reach the city and get the cure. Dawn's head was pounding; an irritation of false images and exhaustion was deeply affecting her state of mind. She wondered if Angelica's own insanity was like this, to be constantly fighting with your own thoughts.

She marched in line with Angelica, the crimson angel behind the two women. Angelica was taking in deep breaths, her arms hugging her sides, her eyes closed. Dawn was feeling the strain of travelling but it was really taking its toll on Angelica. Two rings clicked together that were threaded through a chain round Angelica's neck.

In the distance the trio could hear inhuman cries. Her common sense had not stopped emitting in her mind. She wished she could simply turn the switch off but it was too dangerous to do so. Dawn knew the last few were heading to the city, a city that has acting like a hive for them.

In that hive Dawn was sure they would get a cure for this but a sinister thought lingered at the back of her mind. Every hive has a queen. It was extremely likely the possessed subjects were collecting to be with their master.

Dawn's thoughts subsided as she heard ragged breaths to her side. The ageing woman curled her fingers around the golden treasures as her knees gave way and fell to the floor. The Crimson walked past the two.

'We need to stop,' Dawn insisted, lifting Angelica from the muddy floor, 'She needs to rest.' The Crimson stopped in his tracks and turned to stare at the two. Dawn stared back, knowing that he did not care for the quarter-blood. Dawn groaned as she lifted the heavy body from the floor and placed Angelica's arm around her shoulder. They held hands as Dawn aided her but the strain kept them to a slow walk. A loud scream was heard in the distance. Dawn's common sense heightened, warning her that they were closing in once more.

Angelica's features turned pale as she shook her head violently. From her coat pocket she pulled out the plastic container. Within it remained a single pill.

'Lady must take it,' Angelica spoke directly to Dawn.

'Can't you hold onto it?' Dawn asked, 'We're all going up together.' Angelica shook her head in response, pushing the vial into Dawn's hand shakily.

'He will protect you no matter the cost. He only allows Angelica because he knows you will protest if Angelica is left. If those creatures attack he will make a choice.'

'He'll choose me...' Dawn understood.

The Crimson approached the two. Before Dawn could say a word he lifted up Angelica and cradled her in his arms. He turned and set off down the road. Common sense backed. Relieved, Dawn followed closely.

'It is a strange day when one so proud holds one so dirty,' Angelica let out a light laugh.

'Do not misinterpret this as me aiding you,' he spoke coldly, glancing at Dawn as he spoke. Dawn nodded in understanding as the two angels continued to walk. He didn't want her slowing the journey and knew Dawn wouldn't leave her behind. His choice would always be to protect Dawn.

The Crimson's injuries had slowly been recovering although his body had not been that badly damaged, at least not compared to his wing. Dawn had not seen his wings since the incident as he chose to hide them. At times he would wince and circle his shoulder joint though. Dawn was anxious. Her protector was likely to reach his limit at some point. She needed to know more about these people. From the way that Donahue and Angelica had argued, it seemed this had happened before.

'Can you tell me about the war?' Dawn asked him, 'I want to know about my ancestors.' The Crimson peered back at her from the corner of his eye. It was the first time she had directly asked him about the angels. It was the first time she had spoken directly to him since asking for his protection.

'You want to know the ailment of these creatures that hunt you,' he corrected her.

'You can understand why, can't you?' Dawn told him. 'Angelica said these demons are like the ones in the war.'

'The ones of war were far more dangerous. This is a failed copycat using lesser creatures,' he informed her, 'Someone else has found a way to replicate it in humans... to an extent. They seem keen to have you regardless.'

'Like you...' Dawn mumbled under her breath. His eyes narrowed as she pointed this out. Alarmed, Dawn cast her gaze to the muddy floor.

'Do you realise that the path I take us is not a straight one?' he turned back to face the road as they walked. She looked back up at him. She hadn't noticed. She was tired and agitated. Whether they had taken a straight path or going round in circles was not something she had been keeping a track of.

'They try their luck when you white out or are sleeping. If I was on my own I would happily welcome them to their deaths but with you under my protection it is far better to take detours.' In the days they had travelled the creatures had come and gone in short waves. When they did the Crimson did as he promised, he drove them back if they were partially taken, killed if they were fully possessed. She'd watched in fear but each time he had managed to drive them off. Each time they had decided to attack their numbers had grown. Originally it had only been two that came for Dawn when she had entered a truce with the Crimson. In the early morning Dawn had been thrown awake by her common sense acting as an alarm clock. When she stood she had awoken to twenty bodies surrounding their camp and the crimson angel with bloody hands.

'As I said long ago, I am tired of chasing,' he concluded, 'If bringing a handful of human's back to sanity satisfies your wants to bring back our people, I am happy to oblige.'

'I did swear on it,' she muttered. Dawn had become tired of running. People had died because of her and she wanted it all to end. If she had a choice she would have saved these people and left. She knew he would never stop hunting her down and knew she did not have the heart to kill.

'So did you want to know about the war?' he spoke after the silence. It was a calm tone, one she had not heard him use towards her.

'Please,' she responded.

'The war was between two divisions. They were the united and the liberators. The united wanted to keep the traditions of the angel's and the liberators were controlled by only one mind.'

'The mad king?' Dawn guessed. The Crimson smiled as she spoke, an expression that was not held for long.

'This mongrel blood I am carrying is mad,' he spoke, 'He was intelligent and powerful. He referred to himself as a god. He would boast he could grant the deepest desires of others. That was why he was called the mad king, because of his ludicrous remarks. What angel possessed such power to grant miracles? But he wasn't one to give false statements. I did not hear of any angel or human that asked for something and did not receive it. There was a hefty price for it though. The most common would be that your mind became his and your body was no longer yours. This was an army that did not know to reserve their own lives or to love their families. They only knew to follow command. Angel's began joining his cause no longer for the promise of wishes but in fear of their own lives. The title mad king remained because of his ravenous appetite for power.'

'How was he stopped?' Dawn asked him.

'Only after hundreds of thousands had been killed was he captured and brought to trial. He had run out of tricks and his power dwindled as fewer angels were available to take over. He was sentenced to death but when death was announced,' he let out a long sigh and closed his eyes, 'He sentenced the others with him.'

'How did you survive then?' Dawn wondered. He hesitated in giving his answer.

'I was… missing in action,' he finally said. He hadn't given her a true answer and she doubted he would provide her with one.

'They're coming,' Angelica whispered. Dawn looked around her. Her common sense had delayed as the gears whirred in her mind, steam hissing angrily into her ears. He placed Angelica on her feet and stepped in front of them, his head turning slowly, looking back and forth across the road. Dawn expected to hear the forest roar with the cries of the bloodied but it began to grow silent. From the corner of her eye she noticed one of the possessed run from behind the trees. The Crimson noticed it too, charging towards it. Her vision began to blur as the road itself turned dark and red. There was a thin line between her sixth sense and the nightmare and she realised the nightmare was slipping past her.

'No, not now, no,' Dawn panicked as the red walls began to encroach her vision. The Crimson looked back and stared at her as she fell to her knees. The winter's wind was replaced by the heat of the machine, the lapping fire of the prison from the past. She watched as two more charged towards the red angel before her vision faded entirely.

'Why are you with him?' Sky's ghost called at Dawn as she stood in the red corridor. She watched in despair as his other victims walked around the corner and into the red fade.

'I don't have a choice,' Dawn replied frantically. Sky walked towards her. Her mother stood before her, her green eyes glaring at Dawn in anger.

'He killed us. He killed us all,' Sky cried out, a tear falling from her eye. Dawn shook her head violently, trying to shut her out of her head, turning and looking away.

'I didn't have a choice,' Sky shouted as tears ran down her cheeks, 'Right now you do. You have the choice to…'

'Well I've made my choice and I'm not stopping!' Dawn yelled out. As she did so her reality flooded back. Dawn was on her knees and hands and could feel tears under her eyes. In front of her was a human with open, bloody eyes. His hand was outstretched, as though reaching for her. Death had stopped him mid charge. Crimson had delivered it upon him.

She scrabbled to her feet and looked around, trying to spot the angel that was protecting her. She could not see him but heard the distant cries of the possessed. Deep within the trees she could see Angelica had left the road and now wondered into the thick of the forest.

'Angelica?' Dawn called out. The elderly woman did not turn to look at her. The trees enveloped around her as she strode further and further away from the road. Dawn charged after her. Angelica eventually stopped walking, her left hand held out in front of her, the right gripping the pistol. Dawn caught up and approached her from the side.

'Get back to the road. It's not safe…' Dawn's words trailed off as her eyes gazed towards the woman's hands. Zigzags of blood were on her palm. Dawn grabbed Angelica by the shoulder and turned her round to face the truth. Angelica's eyes had deep red veins appearing. A shed of a tear fell, only it wasn't a tear. It was blood.

'Lady, Angelica said a slight lie,' Angelica spoke calmly, 'Angelica did not foresee this disease. Angelica was infected. Angelica has worked night and day trying to cure it but in the end, she could only delay. She saw it wasn't her in the city. She saw only you and him in the city.' Dawn placed her hand against her face, the other on the hand holding the gun. She wiped her thumb against the old woman's cheek, smearing the blood across her skin. Dawn pried the gun away from Angelica in fear of her hurting herself.

'No, it's not too late. I can... I have the medication,' Dawn quickly tried to search in her pocket.

'Do not,' Angelica spoke sadly, 'It is the last. It only stalls. A cure is needed. The city will provide. A man will... he will know...'

'Then you'll make it, we'll get to the city, get the cure and cure you. You just need to fight it,' Dawn begged.

'My master...' Angelica's words were darker and more spaced out. Angelica twitched and trembled violently, the warm liquid oozing from her eye. It dribbled down Dawn's wrist and fell to the floor in small red droplets. There was no white or iris or pupil, only a deep crimson that ran from corner to corner.

'Please fight it Angelica,' Dawn begged, the gun shaking in her right hand.

'My master desires you!' Angelica's voice rose to a near shriek, grasping Dawn's wrists in fury. Her demonic eyes glared at the young angel and she began to laugh. Dawn froze in fear as her eternal eye cast doubt into her mind. Her common sense jiggered, not sure if this was danger, especially as the woman before her had been so close. The laughter was so inhuman that it sent chills down her spine. Angelica's grip tightened leaving marks on Dawn's wrists. Dawn pulled back as hard as she could, trying to shake her off. Angelica let go of her, stepping backwards, cackling and dribbling as she tried to push the disease out of her mind. Dawn held the gun out and pointed it at Angelica. The tool felt unnatural as her fingers coiled around the trigger, biting back tears.

'What have I forgotten lady?' Angelica wept, 'It was so beautiful and so sad. It hurts so much. My mind wonders... oh how my mind wonders away from me.' Dawn lowered the gun. She couldn't bring herself to kill Angelica.

'Angelica... Fight it... please...' Dawn whimpered. Angelica turned, glaring at Dawn in hatred. She was barely there, rambling and struggling with her words, her intelligence draining. Dawn couldn't bring herself to pull the trigger. She could only watch as Angelica mutated into the monster that the devil had turned her into. Angelica lunged towards her. Her power had become so immense Dawn couldn't breathe, thrown into the tree behind her, the entire forest trembling from the force. She heard the gun crash against the ground from dropping it. Dawn was overwhelmed in emotions. She couldn't control her energy. She couldn't bring herself to fight back.

'Let my master taste you!' Angelica cried out, spitting as she did so. There was a flash of light and a loud bang. Dawn whimpered as Angelica stared blankly at Dawn. The smell of burning flesh surrounded her as Angelica's forehead dripped with blood. Then the monster that had once been Angelica collapsed to the floor.

Dawn covered her mouth, trembling and concealing a scream. She bit back tears as she placed her hand on Angelica's cheek. She was still warm. She was still breathing. Slowly Angelica's human eye opened, staring blankly at Dawn, red tears still running. She tried to wipe away the red fluid as she felt Angelica's cheek grow cold to the touch. It didn't take long for her to pass.

The gun hurtled towards her, sliding across the parched dirt and touching her leg. Dawn placed her hand on the weapon, looking up in shock. The Crimson stood awkwardly, his eyes partially covered by his blonde hair. Immediately Dawn picked the gun up, her hands shaking as she pointed it at him.

'You didn't have to kill her,' Dawn yelled at him. She didn't care that there were monsters in the woods. The only monster she saw was the one in front of her.

'If I hadn't, what would have happened to you?' he asked her. She gulped back, anger welling in her. He could have saved her. They could have found a way to take her to the city, to get the cure and to cure her. She didn't have to die. Her fingers tightened around the trigger on the revolver, raising the barrel and pointing it to the angel's head as he had done to Angelica. He didn't deserve to live. He had killed so many. If she pulled the trigger, she could bring closure.

You have a choice. She felt the chill of Sky's words echo in her head. Of course she had a choice. Her hand trembled as she glared at the monster in front of her. He had killed the children at her home. He had killed Ricky and Mike. He had killed her mother and the other missing people. He had killed them all, all to satisfy his obsession with bringing back the angels.

Do what I couldn't. Sky pressed to her as Dawn felt the presence of her nightmare trying to enclose around her. The forest started to turn red, the Crimson in full view in front of her. He took a step forward, his expression contorted as he did so. In the distance the forest fell silent. They were still out there. They were still in pain, like she had been. They were still alive inside. She still needed to get to the city.

'You didn't need to kill her,' she whispered to him as she lowered the gun. He let out a hefty sigh. She didn't realise that he had been worried. Her eyes gazed towards Angelica. She could smell burning and noticed the skin had turned a strange colour. It was a sharp blue that edged across her head and began to creep around her body. These bullets were not normal. They were meant to kill things far greater than humans.

'Let me take the gun from…' the Crimson tried to reach for it.

'Your oath is to take me to the city and to get the cure to them. It is not to kill them.' She glared at him.

'You ask… an impossible thing,' he tried to reason; 'I know my oath and you know yours, sunshine. You cannot keep your side if you are dead though.' Dawn didn't respond, staring at what use to be Angelica. In her pocket she could feel the small capsule. It was the last bit of medicine, the only chance she had to free the others.

'I'm not leaving her out here, not out in the open. She didn't deserve this.' she said aloud. The Crimson gave a single nod, approaching a nearby tree, his healthy wing coming into full view. With a single strike he cracked the earth and shifted it. A deep crater opened within the trees roots. Dawn pulled Angelica's bag from her cold body, taking the last of the rations. As the straps lifted from her dead shoulders, Angelica's golden chain slipped from underneath her dress. The chain threaded through two rings. Curious, Dawn took the necklace off Angelica and held the rings in her hand. She stared at one of the two rings and read its encryption. *Eternally yours, Donahue.* Dawn stared at the two rings as the Crimson lifted Angelica's body and lowered it into the opened grave.

'Were the two married?' Dawn asked in shock. He kicked the surrounding dirt into the hole, burying Angelica beneath it.

'Engaged,' he told her, 'You can't take a maddening woman's hand in marriage.' Dawn stood next to the filled in grave. Angelica had forgotten that she had loved Donahue.

'Do you have any words to say?' he asked her. She stared at the grave. She was speechless. There was nothing she could say in that moment to amend things. Eventually she shook her head and followed behind the crimson angel as the two continued their journey.

CHAPTER 19

The winter wind gushed into their sides as the two continued to walk, the grave they left behind neither spoke of. It seemed to be getting colder and colder as time progressed. The woodlands were replaced with open fields of grass. To the far left was the main road where the odd isolated car appeared. They stepped on the frozen ground of the field to keep out of public sight.

'We are not far from the city sunshine. When we arrive I need you to do exactly as I say,' he told her. It was the first time he had spoken since they had buried Angelica.

'Stop calling me sunshine, that's not my name,' Dawn replied bitterly. She felt for the two chains that were round her neck. One was the gift that Lucy had given her, a silver chain with a silver heart. The other was golden, threaded on it the two rings of lost lovers.

'Very well then, Dawn,' he told her solemnly, 'So long as you call me by mine.' Dawn gazed up as him as he gazed down.

'I don't know your name,' she admitted. From the very beginning when she had been warned in her nightmares of the Crimson she had been calling him just that. But he had never introduced himself. Donahue had never put a name to the man. Angelica did not even speak to him by his name in the brief time they had met.

'What is your name?' she asked directly as she followed his heels.

'Antares,' he turned away from her and continued to walk. For the first time she had a name for the monster that had been hunting for her all of her life.

'I don't know anyone called that,' she replied. 'Does it have a meaning?'

'I'm named after a star,' he explained shortly. He didn't look back, his eyes set on the journey ahead. Dawn waited for him to talk some more, to start a conversation. The walk had been lonely as he provided very little company. After what felt like ages she knew he wasn't going to delve any further.

'Does Donahue have a meaning? Is he named after a star as well?' she pressed, wondering if mentioning the other angel would spark a discussion.

'Not after a star,' he told her. He still didn't look back at her. Again silence cut through the atmosphere. Dawn felt her strides becoming shorter in strength. Dawn stared at the frozen field as they walked. The frozen puddles glinted slightly at the golden light that emitted from her eyes

'Can all angels change their form like he does?' she tried once more.

'No,' he replied again. Dawn stared at him and folded her arms, another breeze drifting underneath her now long blonde hair. She tried to think back to the little studying she had done. Back then she resisted her education but as she was changing more and more, she regretted her decision. Perhaps it was only some kinds of angels that could transform, like the eyes determining what they were to be. Perhaps it was because, as it was quoted, Donahue wasn't a pure angel. Angelica was part human and part angel, maybe it was also possible for hybrids of animals too.

Her own path was quite clear now. Once the people were cured and the person who sought her had been stopped, both her and Antares, the last pure angels, were to bring them back. The nightmares, since Angelica's death, had been restricted to her sleep but Sky's words constantly plagued her mind. Dawn had a choice. Her mother did not.

Dawn had made an oath and so far he seemed to be keeping to his. She wondered how long it would be before she had to commit to her own.

'Antares, after all this and after we've cured the people and stopped this other person, what's going to happen to me?' she asked him. The thought before made her feel sick and scared but she was sure she would feel far worse if people were still suffering. It may have been normal for angels to conceive at this age. It may have been normal for courtships to be determined and not fallen into through love. Dawn had no idea.

'I mean, how it's all going to work…' she trailed off. He kept in front of her, his attention focused on the end goal. Through the past days it seemed his every intention was to cure the people as well. He had rarely spoken to her however, as though she didn't exist as a person, but rather a tool to his plan. Perhaps that was all she was to him.

'I'll keep my promise,' she told him, 'I'll help bring the angel's back. I just want to be prepared.' He didn't respond. She sprinted forward and ran ahead of him. She turned to face him as his head lifted and his red eyes widened. She held her arms out wide and he stood still.

'Say something to me!' Dawn begged, 'You want me to mother the next generation but you're not going to tell me anything?' He peered back at her, his crimson eyes looking dully at her. The fire that had once been behind those crimson eyes of his had seemed to fade. He pointed directly in front of him. Dawn peered behind and noticed the tops of buildings coming into view. They were not far at all. In disgust Dawn stormed off. If the angel did not want to speak to her she wasn't going to keep trying. She had to save the people. More importantly she wanted to save Donahue.

'Before we enter the city I must teach you how to disguise your eyes,' he explained to her. She did not look back as she continued to walk, seeing looming fences that had been put up in a hurry. This was the city that had been quarantined. Her tantrum was halted as he grabbed her chin and turned her attention back to him. His crimson eyes looked directly into hers and instinctively she wanted to run.

'You will struggle to hold this as you have had no practise but if we are to make contact with humans they will panic at the sight of your eyes. Their own brothers turn on them because their eyes are not normal. Although yours are not secreting blood they are still abnormal to them. They will panic and I reassure you Dawn, weapons will kill you. You must know to hide your eyes and you must do so now.'

'I think they'll panic at yours first,' she pointed out. He closed his eyes, took in a deep breath and opened them slowly. A pair of blue eyes peeked from underneath his eyelids. His black pupils held the gaze of her white ones.

'How do I change them?' she asked him in astonishment.

'You know how to bring your energy to a boil. I have felt it first-hand. I have seen you bring energy to your eyes to help see in the dark. You must reverse this. Rather than exert it you must retain it away from your eyes and push it deep within your soul. You must hold it there and not allow it to flow back to your eyes when you wish to hide them.' He told her with caution. She nodded and closed her eyes. The energy that flowed within she was getting a better understanding of. It was like waves of water that drifted from limb to organ. It could be heated up and exerted which meant it could be cooled and retracted as well. She felt for the energy behind her eyes and shifted it away. She felt the energy pour from the backs of her eyes and down her throat. It was like swallowing hot syrup and it protested as it was pushed away.

Her eyes opened as she looked up at him. Her stomach felt queasy as she kept her gaze. He held her chin tightly as he pressed his face closer to hers. She felt uneasy as her energy tried to bubble back up. The unease was forcing it to simmer and the more she felt unsteady the more it stewed.

'No matter what, do not stop practising,' he informed her as he took a pair of shades from his shirt and offered them to her. She shook her head, the energy rushing back to her eyes and flooding them with their golden light.

'Is this not good enough?' she asked.

'Your eyes water and your pupil flickers dully. It'll be enough to fool them short-term but not consistently. Keep those shades on as much as possible. If they ask to see your eyes you must hide them as I have taught you. With practice you'll eventually be able to hold them for days on end.'

'You couldn't have taught me this sooner?' Dawn asked.

'I needed it so you could not seek human help, at least before I did. Now we have an agreement it is no longer necessary. Am I wrong sun…' he stopped himself before smiling, 'Dawn?'

'You're not wrong, Antares,' she replied. She took the shades from his hands and pushed the frame up the bridge of her nose. They were tinted a dark black, hiding her eyes completely. They were his shades, the pair of glasses she had seen him with before.

'Speaking of which, is there a negotiation that can be made?' Antares asked her. Dawn looked up at him with unease. His blue eyes had not reverted back. Now she had become so use to his red eyes, the blue ones now seemed out of place to her.

'Leave them to their fate. If they do not find you, their controller will have no reason to continue the search, especially if we can masquerade a death.'

'Would you give up trying to find me, even if there was a chance I was dead? This person might not even want me alive.' Dawn considered. He nodded in agreement and took a step forward. Dawn followed closely.

'Hold onto my back and do not let go,' he told her. She nodded as she placed her hand on his shoulder and pulled herself up. Her arms wrapped around his neck. His wings spread out, the first time she had seen them both since the attack. His right wing was a deep red that ran like running flames of lava. His left wing however seemed like stained glass. Deep within the centre were white holes that left deeper cracks. They ranged backwards, showing the jaw of the dog that had inflicted it onto him. She couldn't tell if it had recovered at all of not. Antares stared at his own wing and for a moment his eyes dulled in self-pity.

'When your wings flourish, you will be able to fly with ease. For one with red eyes like me, we are gifted with immense strength. Our wings were not meant for flying like light bearers, but to be used as weapons. Not to say that I cannot fly a short distance… so long as my wings are in prime condition.'

'He's clipped you then,' Dawn said. He nodded in agreement.

'If your wings had come forth this would make things easier,' he explained solemnly, 'Still though I must try and so you must hold on tightly. This will not be easy.' Dawn hesitated. If he was going to struggle to fly then wouldn't it be easier to slash into the fence and step through it that way? Her eternal eye sparked up that attacking the fence was not a smart move. She thought of circling the fence when she realised with her own external eyes that it would be a shady option as well. She spotted an army truck stationed at a corner on either side. Antares had found a blind spot to them.

'I'm ready,' she whispered, holding onto his shoulders as tightly as she could. His wings stretched outwards. With a strong swooping motion they threw downwards, a gust of wind pushing behind them. In strong successions he raised and lowered his wings, his feet lifting from the ground. She held onto him tightly, staring into the city as he flew upwards. As her eyes met the barbed wiring at the top of the fence she heard Antares let out a hiss from between his teeth. She stared at his broken wing; the cracks were expanding and erasing the red from his feathers. She tensed as he pushed his wings harder, lifting his body over the fence. She heard the wires crackling underneath them, hearing the electricity that ran through them. With a sharp cry he allowed his wings to fall against the wind and his body fall to the floor on the other side. His feet touched the floor with a loud thump as Dawn lost her grip and fell onto the floor.

Dawn quickly rose to her feet. His left wing was worse than it had been as Antares gripped the floor, his blue eyes watering. The city was empty. Leaflets were scattered across the walls and floor. They signalled an emergency evacuation of the place. Cars had been abandoned on the roads. Dawn took a few steps forward. Skyscrapers towered towards the sky with no office workers within them. To think the evacuation had happened less than a week ago. The radio had broadcasted that the possessed people were all heading towards this city. Why? She looked across the running fence that had been put up quickly by the authorities, either to keep them in or out. In the far corner she could see a body lying close to the outside of the fence, dried blood underneath its red eyes.

'Do you know where to go now?' Antares spoke up. Dawn walked back to the Crimson and realised that she didn't. The partial cure was in her bag and Angelica had kept insisting to get to the city. There was a person it needed to be given to. She didn't have a clue who or where though.

'I don't... I assume that...' Dawn trailed off with uncertainty.

'We need to find a place of shelter then,' he informed her as he hid his wings from view. He began to walk forward and Dawn kept close. These people had accumulated here though and she did not know if he could fight them all off or not.

'If it turns out her vision is false, that is not my doing,' he pointed out to her. Dawn realised the implication he was insinuating.

'I'll still keep to my promise,' she gritted her teeth, 'but we leave no stone unturned.' They walked over what was a gridlock. The traffic lights were still on, signalling to cars that they could move forward. There were no people driving today. She wished she had asked for more information from Angelica. Where was the man? What was his name? What did he look like? Anything more would have helped.

Antares' stopped in his tracks. Dawn felt it too, a chill running down her spine as common sense began to pick up. Danger was coming. He looked back at her to grab her attention. He moved swiftly forward, taking long strides. Dawn followed as closely as she could, forced into a light jog every so often. As they stepped onto a footpath and past a shop her common sense jumped.

'Master requires...' a man crept out from the shop entrance. He stood behind the two, eyes bleeding onto what was once a formal suit.

'Get behind me Dawn,' Antares warned her. She nodded as she took a step away from the possessed man. As she gazed behind Antares, she saw the figures of men and women walking down the road. They were already swarming towards them, at least half a dozen.

'Listen carefully,' Antares spoke out to the office worker, 'I know your mind is controlled. Your controller wants the girl. The girl wants your controller to let these people go. Is there no proposition that can be made?' Dawn watched in confusion as the horde stopped moving, staring directly at Antares. Their controller must have been listening through them.

'The great warrior is weak...' the man chuckled.

'Weakened but not weak,' he spoke, 'Your bad attempt at recreating demons will turn back to bite you. You don't have the power to hold a hive of minds.'

'Please let them go,' Dawn begged, 'They haven't done anything to you.' Dawn felt him grab her hand as the crimson angel looked back at her and narrowed his eyes. He did not want her to speak.

'Master requires the girl... for that power,' the office worker struggled to form the sentence.

'Then I have heard enough,' he told the possessed man, 'I will not allow you to touch her.' The office worker began to laugh, closing his eyes as fresh red tears ran down his cheeks. The human's screeched out from behind the duo, running towards them. In one quick swipe, too quick for the eye to see, the office worker fell to the floor, a clean slit across his neck. The horde stopped in their tracks, hissing and snarling at the pair. Dawn felt her eternal eye perk up.

'We need to move, now!' Antares ordered her, anticipating the same danger that was about to come. The pair ran along the road. Dawn's eternal eye built up. Danger was coming closer. It seemed no matter where she looked there was no place that was safer than the next. They would have to break through.

The two passed under a bridge. On the other side a woman in broken high-heels glared at them with bloodied eyes. She howled in a beastly tongue. Yaps and cries echoed around them. Swarms of infected climbed over cars and came out of abandoned buildings. Dawn extended the palm of her hand and threw her energy out. Five humans were cast back, thrown into the surrounding buildings. She could smell their skin burning against the flames. As they fell against the brickwork, dazed from the outburst, another seven emerged and hissed at her. Antares strode forward, pushing back the group that was in front of them. She watched in horror as each body that fell, another two people replaced them. They were facing an ungodly army.

They scrambled through them as quickly as they could. The crimson warrior was beginning to slow, suffering from his wounds. Dawn did her best to cast them away but after three strong blows her energy was erratic and weak. Her legs trembled as she continued to run, knowing that she had over-exerted herself. The flames subsided and remained as flickering embers deep within her. More were coming. A flock of screaming demons clashed into her side. A man grabbed her throat, pushing her deeper into the demonic group. She struggled to pull the revolver from her holster. She kicked up sharply and his grip loosened as she pried away. Dawn was cut off from Antares. The horde continued to grow in numbers as they raced towards him. She held the gun up, trying to get a shot in. There were five bullets left. There was no way either was going to break through.

A racket of bullets echoed loudly as she covered her ears. The possessed surrounding her fell to the floor. Between the cracks of the demons she saw a man in his early twenties holding a gun in his right hand. His blonde hair was down to his shoulders, whipping back slightly as the strong winds gushed against him. Another stepped to his side, his greying hair cut short, a larger gun held in two hands.

'Get over here!' the younger one called out to her. Dawn stepped over the humans on the floor and rushed to their sides in a panic. She looked back into the mob and saw Antares was overwhelmed, the possessed acting far more violently towards him than they had to her.

'Grant, get her to the Library. Don't linger,' the older man spoke directly to the younger man. Grant took a step back with uncertainty, his gun held tightly.

'But Dave…' Grant replied. Dawn kept looking into the crowd. She'd lost sight of Antares. Her eyes intensified as she tried to spot him, to sense him, anything to let her know he was still at least alive.

'Go now!' Dave scolded him, turning back on the horde and firing at them. The young man grabbed Dawn by her wrist and stepped away from Dave. Dawn's common sense had overwhelmed her senses, with no idea whether these men were friends or foe. Anyone in this city could have been the controller and Dawn felt her heart pound against her ribcage as she realised the implication she was in.

'M-my friend…' Dawn's words struggled to form as Grant pulled at her wrist, insisting that she follow.

'Dave will get him. There's more coming, they're flocking this place,' Grant warned her. She made her decision there and then. She allowed Grant to drag her away from the chaos. A few other possessed humans charged towards them as they ran away. She was being led to a large building with large iron gates at the front. It was three stories high with a signpost out the front. An arrow directed visitors to differently named buildings but the arrow that pointed to the gate clearly signalled it was a Library.

'Open the gates, quickly!' Grant called out. A woman stepped into sight from behind the high walls, a set of keys in hand.

'Where's Dave?' she asked as she pushed a long silver key into the hole of the gate. Dawn peered behind her. She couldn't spot anyone.

'He's behind. He's trying to save the other one,' Grant told her as the two heard the gate click. Grant shoved the gates inwards, barely giving the lady a chance to step out of the way. Dawn was pulled in but as the lady tried to close it back, Grant pushed his foot in the way and shook his head.

'Don't close it Claire!' Grant snapped at her.

'They're charging straight for this place,' Dawn heard a voice from above. She gazed upwards, spotting a man in a long white coat on the roof of the three storey building. It was obscure seeing a man that way with a telescope meant for viewing the stars to be using it to see out into the city. That must have been how they had been spotted.

'We've got to close the gate,' Claire insisted. Grant snatched the keys from her before she could make a move.

'Bolt the library doors then, take her in with you. I won't let them on the campus grounds,' Grant commanded.

'I'm not going to be locked away,' Dawn heard herself shout out before she could stop herself. For the first time the two people stared directly at her. Her common sense was pounding against her brain, the intensity was almost suffocating. Either they were out there and closing in or she had handed herself to their controllers. Claire finally shook her head and placed her hand on the gate, her eyes narrowing towards Grant. In the distance they heard the inhuman voices calling out.

'We've got to close the gates,' Claire trembled as the screeching increased.

'I see them!' the man from the roof signalled to them, 'They're heading here but so are they.'

'Close the gates, you'll put us all in danger!' Claire shouted at Grant in distress. He kept his foot in the way, his hand holding firmly onto the bar. Dawn felt her common sense slap her violently in the head as she turned her gaze to the wall.

'There's one coming from that direction,' Dawn informed them. Neither of them questioned her as Grant pulled his gun up. A bloody-eyed boy charged from behind the wall and straight towards the gate. Grant fired the gun at him, sending him hurtling back.

'You lucky brat,' Claire hissed at her, 'Close the...'

'We're here, don't close it,' Dave yelled out. Dawn noticed the elderly man struggling to walk, limping badly as his leg was bleeding. Antares walked alongside him, using his own shoulder as support for Dave as the two began to hobble in. They entered the grounds and the gate was shut sharply. Grant thrust the key into the lock and turned it. Behind them they heard the library doors opening. Stood in the entrance was a tall man in the white coat.

'Quickly get inside,' he motioned to them. The group trailed in, the door closed behind them. Dawn felt her common sense shut off as soon as the doors closed. The room was bright, filled with artificial light that stretched from corner to corner. The bookcases were standing neatly from side to side, holding a vast amount of non-fiction literature. Signs pinpointed in several places various subjects of science, business, languages and much more. Advertisement spread from post to post reinstated that this was a college or university.

Dawn took an unsteady step into the heart of the building, ignoring the chatting that erupted from behind her. She knew her common sense was gone. It hadn't faded gradually to let her know that danger was still on the doorstep. It was gone. She looked back at Antares with uncertainty, wondering if he had blinded her eternal eye. Before she had a moment to think she felt her wrist being grabbed a second time as Grant pulled her close and looked down at her.

'Tell me who you are, right now!' He insisted, his gaze directly upon her.

CHAPTER 20

'What are you doing Grant?' Claire called out. The man that had rescued Dawn held her wrist so tightly it began to hurt. His focus was entirely on her. He reached out to grab her shades and instinctively she jerked backwards. His eyes narrowed, his suspicion rising. If any of them saw her eyes she did not know what would happen.

'Tell me who you are,' he insisted. Dawn felt eyes upon her from all directions. Antares edged his way forward, trying to get to her and about to intervene.

'Dawn?' she heard a familiar voice call out. Dawn peered over her shoulder and towards a staircase that circled round the building and up towards a second floor. Half way down the stairs stood a young lady with long red hair falling over her shoulders and down to her waist. There were deep bags under her hazel eyes, yet her eyes still glistened with life.

'Lucy?' Dawn recognised her. Before another word could be mentioned the woman raced down the stairs, her boots tapping against the marble as she threw her arms open and embraced Dawn. She clutched onto Dawn tightly, hugging her with an incredible strength. Dawn smiled as she hugged her back with her free arm, the other still being withheld by Grant's grip. She was glad to see a familiar face.

'Do you two know each other?' Claire asked Lucy directly.

'She and her friend stayed at mine for Christmas,' Lucy giggled. Dawn felt a pang of guilt hit her as Lucy brought back memories of Mike. 'It's so horrible you're caught up in all this.'

'It is for everyone,' Dawn replied. Lucy nodded in agreement, giving Dawn an extra big squeeze of a hug.

'I'm glad I could save you… No, I'm happy,' Grant mumbled as he let Dawn's wrist go, turning his back to the two females. Dawn gave him a puzzled look. This stranger had bounced all over the place and it put her on edge.

'Thank you Grant,' Dawn tried to bring peace to the room, 'I don't know what we would have done if you hadn't…' He walked out of vision and behind the bookcases before she could finish her sentence.

'You're both lucky. I thought we were the only ones that didn't leave.' Dave chuckled. Dawn slowly pulled away from the hug and turned to face him. He was now sat on a plastic chair, his hands kneading at his ankle awkwardly, indicating it was badly bruised or sprained.

'How did you know we were there then?' Antares asked him directly. Dawn picked up on his tone. He was suspicious of these people.

'Edward spotted you. We keep it in turns to look out from the science suite upstairs. Grant insisted we rescue you two,' he explained.

'Did he now…' Antares spoke deeply.

Claire continued, 'It's just a handful of people. There were more but… the military panicked when the infected ones tried to escape. Anything that tries to go near those fences gets shot at, whether in or out. We're kind of stuck until this blows over.'

'It seems those that haven't been killed had migrated here but that's okay. They can't get in.' Dave explained, 'This is a University campus so we are lucky there are fridges full of food and enough chairs we can push them together as temporary beds. There were not many people at this campus when the evacuation notice was issued. Edward was catching up on some paperwork and noticed us so let us in. He's a professor for biology, he's in the institute's lab and he thinks he knows how to cure everyone.'

"Where is the lab?" Dawn asked quickly. Claire placed her hand on Dawn's shoulder and shook her head once.

'He doesn't like to be disturbed when he is in the zone sweetie,' Claire explained, 'but he'll be down for some food with us in a moment. We'd love it if you joined us.'

'Thank you Claire, we could really do with some food,' Dawn smiled, 'But I don't suppose you have a bathroom or anything do you?'

'I can take you,' Dave piped in, slowly raising from the chair and applying pressure to his foot. He winced ever so slightly as it pressed against the ground. Dawn noticed Antares make a move to follow when Claire stepped in his way.

'Could you help me in the kitchen?' Claire asked him directly. Dawn followed Dave as he made his way up the stairs, looking back in fear. Antares hated humans. He had no interest in helping them and with his violent nature she was concerned. His eyes narrowed as he glared at her and instinctively she took a step away from him.

'I'll help you Claire,' Lucy smiled as she walked in between the two of them. Antares went to move but Lucy grabbed his hand, 'Can you help us get the flour down from the cupboards?' And with that Dawn was round the corner, now at the top of the stairs with Dave close to her side. He opened the door wide open for her. A brightly lit hallway stretched a few rooms down, each door clearly labelled. Near the end were signs for male and female restrooms and in between them stood two large doors that were brilliantly white. Above them was a white sign with black writing, letting people know it was the biology lab. Edward must have been there.

'I got to ask something lass, if you don't mind,' he started to talk.

'Yes Dave?' she asked.

'Why are you both out there?' he questioned her, 'If Lucy says you were with her this Christmas then why are you even in this city?' Dawn thought for a moment. She didn't want to lie to anyone but to tell the truth that she knew what the horde was and what they were after, she wasn't sure she could mention that either.

'There were originally three of us, not two,' Dawn started, 'and one of the people we were with was a scientist.' As she spoke she pulled the zip on her bag and slowly pulled out the plastic capsule. Within it was the final pill that Angelica had.

'What is that?' he asked.

'It's the start of a cure… no, not quite a cure yet. It delays it and we didn't know she was infected. A few days ago she insisted I take it and head to this city because this was where they were heading, to find a way to save them.' She paused as Dave stared at her for a moment. He was allowing the information to sink in and she hoped he would allow her to go to Edward. Dawn was now sure that if there was a man who could create the cure it would be him.

'I can take it straight to Edward, he can have a good look,' he finally spoke, reaching out to take the small vial. Dawn shoved it back into the bag and shook her head.

'I… I'd rather hand it directly,' Dawn insisted. Neither was trusting of the other. Dawn knew that anyone in this building could be the controller and as he had asked for it directly, she wondered if he intended to destroy it.

'You never needed to use the little ladies room, did you?' his voice deepened slightly. Dawn felt for her common sense and yet still it was vastly silent. He shook his head and hobbled down the hallway. Dawn followed, keeping an arm's length away from him as she did so. His hand rose and with a quick succession of three knocks he made Edward aware of their presence.

'Edward, there's someone here to see you,' Dave called through the door. When no one replied, Dave pushed one of the doors open. Dawn placed her hand against it.

'Be straight to the point with him,' he told her as he let go. She stepped into the lab and looked back to watch him leaving and heading back towards the others. Dawn pushed the large door inward. There were various tables and desks littered around the room. At the very front was a white board that stretched from floor to ceiling, corner to corner, writing covering virtually every inch in green, red and black. A young boy sat at one of the desks, his feet kicking back and forth with a crayon in his right hand and a piece of paper pressed against the surface with his left. As the doors shut he looked back and noticed her. She smiled softly at him and he gave a big smile back before going back to his drawing.

'I'm really sorry to disturb you,' Dawn spoke out quietly as she walked towards the white board. Behind a large screen a man stood over a desk. He didn't signal that he knew she was there, his eye set on the microscope and observing a glass slab. Dawn peeked over at the contents. It was a single droplet of red liquid and assumed it was blood. She stood to his side, trying to gain his attention.

'I need to talk to you,' she spoke a little louder; 'I was with a scientist who found a way to stall the outbreak. She believed there was a way to create a cure but...' He raised his head from the microscope and looked towards her.

'From what field?' he interrupted her.

'I... I wouldn't know,' Dawn explained.

'Then what was her full name?' he insisted.

'I never caught her full name. She's dead... was infected herself but she delayed it. I have the last of the pills that she made. Would it be of any use to you?' He pulled the glass slab from underneath the scope and placed it to one side.

'Do you have anything else?' he asked her briskly. She stared at him for a moment, trying to grasp what it was he was seeking from her.

'Any notes she wrote or what the ingredients are. Anything else besides the pill?' he continued.

'I'm sorry, this is all I have,' Dawn told him, pulling the vial out from the bag a second time and offering it to him. He took it from her, taking the cap off the plastic container and swiftly moving to the side of the room. Dawn followed him closely as he poured the last capsule into a Petri dish. He stood before a large machine connected to several computer servers, the cables aligned between the gaps of the metal structure that held the massive database in place.

'If you want me to check your theory, you'll need to give me some space,' he spoke aloud. Dawn stepped away from his view, looking back at the large doors. From below she could hear the voices of the few downstairs yet she did not hear Antares'. She wondered if it was a good omen of not.

'The distance my son is at least,' he insisted. She nodded as she stepped behind and walked towards the desk. The young boy didn't look up, his crayon scribbling furiously against the paper. Slowly she pulled out the chair underneath and sat close to him occasionally looking at the screen that blocked her view from Edward.

The young boy pushed pieces of paper into her hands without warning. Her eyes struggled to see the drawing as her shades blocked the light quite extensively. Slowly she went through them, noticing drawings of stick people on them. Eventually she came to the last sheet and paused for a moment.

'Were you drawing me?' she asked with uncertainty. He let out a single chuckle, pushing his thumb into his mouth and began to suckle on it. Her hair looked like long trails of spaghetti and her hands were larger than her face. He only appeared to be just old enough to start school.

'It's a very nice picture,' she told him. He was still smiling childishly as he dropped the crayon in his hand, reaching for a bright blue one and placed it against a new sheet of paper.

'What did you say your name was?' Edward suddenly was behind her. It surprised her, almost dropping the page. Anxiously she felt for her shades to make sure they were still on.

'It's Dawn,' she told him.

'I'm running the contents through tests now. I appreciate you offering this to me,' he told her.

'Thank you. I hope it helps,' she told him.

'If it's the breakthrough I've been after…'

'Edward?' Lucy announced herself to the room. The trio looked across to see the two large doors wide open, Lucy standing between them.

'Lucy, always a pleasure to see you,' he smiled at her. The young boy stood up from the desk, running behind Edward, hiding his face behind his legs.

'Awe, is Nathan still shy?' Lucy giggled towards the young boy, 'That's okay. I'm big and scary.' Edward smiled as he picked up the young boy, hugging onto him awkwardly.

'Claire's set out food if you wanted to go down and eat with us.' Lucy spoke directly to Edward.

'Thank you. If you hadn't reminded me I'd have forgotten to eat,' he replied, taking that as his cue to leave the room. Dawn went to follow but felt Lucy's hand on her sleeve. She looked back at the student.

'Hold on Dawn, we'll go in a moment. I wanted a girl on girl talk first,' Lucy proposed.

'Okay,' Dawn replied, taking a step back and standing in front of her.

'When you and your friend came to my home, you said you had to leave. I know I said I wouldn't pry but…' Lucy looked over at the door, her expression turned to that of concern, 'Honey, I've noticed the man your with you're not too comfortable with. Was he the reason that…'

'It's not…' Dawn cut her off quickly but could not finish her sentence. He was the reason she left Lucy's home. He was the reason… at least she thought he was the reason that Mike was dead. Lucy reached for Dawn's hand, holding it in between her two palms. The two stared at each other in a moment of silence.

'You can trust me Dawn,' Lucy gave the hand a gentle squeeze. Before Dawn had a moment to respond the doors swung open. Antares came into view, looking directly at the two women.

'You haven't eaten,' he spoke directly to Dawn. She pulled away from Lucy's soft grip and nodded towards him.

'I'm coming,' Dawn spoke.

'I'll catch up,' Lucy chuckled, running her fingers through her red hair and flicking it awkwardly to one side. She gave Dawn a smile and Dawn smiled back. Antares' hand pushed Dawn against her shoulder, persuading her to leave the room. The two large doors swung back into place as they stood onto the corridor.

'I gave it to Edward' Dawn finally whispered, 'He's running tests on it now.' She felt his hand grip the back of her jacket tightly, pulling her against the wall. Dawn looked up anxiously as the crimson angel's eyes came into full view.

'You are not to trust these things,' he spoke coldly to her, 'Do not leave my side again.'

She ushered under her breath, 'You're not in control of…'

'If you want my co-operation to save these vermin, you would do exactly as I say!' he snarled at her, 'Their controller knows I protect you. That is why they attacked me. There is no madness as to why they left you alone to come to this building. Their controller is more than likely one of these guests. Trust absolutely no one but me.' He let her go and threw the doors open as he stepped into the hallway. Dawn followed him closely and wondered why he simply did not target the one that was controlling them. Surely his eternal eye could sense which one was dangerous. That was when Dawn realised why the tyrant was so on edge.

'Are you blind?' Dawn asked quietly. His stride slowed as she asked this. Slowly he looked back, his eyes now casting the illusion of human blue eyes. Not a single word left his lips as his head lowered slightly, turning back and making his way to the stairs. His silence spoke for him. He was as blind as she was.

The small group were sat around the table and had been discussing at great volume until they noticed the duos presence. The people fell quiet as Dawn looked between them.

'How come your shades are still on?' Dave asked, shoving a microwaved kebab for one into his mouth. Dawn placed her fingertip to the frames. She could feel the intense light under her eyes, revealing that she was not human.

'Her eyes are sensitive to the light,' Antares cut in as he escorted her to one of the empty seats. He applied pressure to her shoulders, forcing

Dawn to sit. On the plate was another microwaved ready meal kebab for one.

'Can the young lass not speak?' Claire butted in. She finished her plate and glared at Antares. He paid no attention to her as he sat next to Dawn. He looked at the microwaved food with unease.

'It's fine Claire. Do you mind if I keep my glasses on?' Dawn motioned.

'I'd rather see your eyes, just to be sure,' Grant spoke up. Dawn looked over at the man through her shades. If she removed her shades, would she be able to hold them long enough? Her energy trembled within her; it was difficult to guide the waves.

'I know we're all uneasy but I have faith she's not one of the monsters,' Edward spoke out on her defence, 'One of the early signs is aggression. I haven't seen any sign of that.'

'What colour are her eyes then?' Grant continued, 'How do we know that she isn't turning?' Before Dawn could defend herself, a hand grabbed Dawn from behind. Lucy had now joined the group and spun Dawn's chair to face her. Her shades her taken off in a quick motion as Lucy looked directly at her. Dawn gazed directly at Lucy, Dawn's hand gripping the fork tightly, trying to find some reassurance. She forced her energy deep inside as quickly as she could. It was thrown down her throat and into her stomach. She wanted to hurl at the sudden heat thrown in her belly. She could feel her own eyes watering. Lucy stared deeply into them. Dawn felt suffocated, wondering if she had spotted that they were abnormal. Lucy's hands rose to either side of Dawn's head, slowly turning her to meet the group.

'See, it's fine, they're green,' Lucy explained, giving the group a moment to stare at them. With that she placed the shades back on for Dawn and let her go. Dawn ducked her head, letting out a quiet sigh as she let the energy flow back into their rightful place. Lucy pulled a chair out from close to Edward and sat herself down, pulling a plate close to her and wrinkled her nose at the food.

'We're sorry Dawn, it's just those things are terrifying,' Claire spoke. The group nodded in succession.

'I-it's okay,' Dawn mumbled, cutting into the microwaved meal and taking a bite. The group didn't return to talking between themselves, only to eat in silence. Plastic forks clicking against plastic plates as overly processed food was consumed. Dawn finished her meal and drank the water that was in front of her. Antares pushed his plate to the centre of the table after deciding that he would prefer to be hungry.

The silence was interrupted as a beeping sound chirped from Edward's pocket. He pushed his hand into his lab coat and fished out an electronic tablet.

'Dawn's actually done us a great favour,' Edward stood up from the table.

'How come?' Dave asked curiously, 'Hey, was that meds stuff useful to you?' Antares raised the arch of his eyebrow towards Dawn and with his inciting gaze she lowered hers. He wasn't amused that she had shown more than one person.

'It appears so,' he smiled directly at her, 'Dawn gave me the last piece of the jigsaw. Once I can establish it correctly, if I test it on one of the people outside and know it works…'

'You could save the lost souls?' Lucy exclaimed, 'That's so wonderful!'

'Look at these two, little gifts from heaven.' Claire hummed cheerfully.

CHAPTER 21

Dawn's body crashed to the floor of her temporary bedroom after her fight with the nightmare. She groaned, opening her eyes and staring at the ground. She hated the ghosts of her past, of Sky and Mike, telling her over and over to leave this place, to not trust the Crimson. Awake, she sighed angrily, pulling herself to her knees and nursing her arm.

Antares had insisted Dawn be kept in a room on her own and that his was next to hers. It had been difficult to sleep through as the cries of the infected constantly howled out into the night. Eventually she did sleep but apparently her nightmare would make sure she never slept well.

As she looked up, she noticed the door was open. Hurriedly, she clambered to it and shut it tight. She was sure she had closed it last night. She let out a sigh, glad that no one was peering into her room when she woke. She walked to the bedside and stared at her reflection. Her golden eyes shone back. If they knew what she was, would they welcome her or shun her? She didn't want to discover the result. If she kept practising, she could hold normal human eyes; perhaps, live a human life. Angrily, she gripped the furniture, her eyes glaring back at her. There was no human life for her at the end of this. She had made a promise to Antares and for the entire journey he had kept his promise. She was scared of what would happen if she went against him after all this.

As she stared, she noticed a figure behind her. A young boy stood next to her bed. She had been too obsessed with her own image to check the room. In a panic, she grabbed the shades and placed them over her eyes. It was too late; he had seen her for what she was. The young boy didn't say a word as she charged towards him, falling to her knees and grabbing him by his arms. His expression changed, one of curiosity to one of fear. He whimpered, trying to pull himself away from her grip.

'Shhh...' Dawn desperately tried to calm him. She realised her fingers were digging into his fragile arms. She let go, placing her hands instead on his shoulders, trying to comfort him. Her golden eyes were glowing behind the lenses, her white pupils staring at Edward's son.

'Please don't tell the others,' she whispered to him in fear, 'they might worry.' He edged back, shivering and hiccupping. He was scared of her. She was scared of him.

'Please Nathan, please don't tell. I'm not one of the monsters outside, I promise,' she pleaded to the young boy that didn't reply. He rubbed his hand against his eyes, looking away from her. He didn't say a word to her.

'Dawn?' she heard Grant's voice calling from outside of her room. Dawn looked over her shoulder. This was it. If he wanted to tell them, there was nothing she could do.

'There you are Nathan. Your daddy's been wondering where you are,' Grant had already entered the room, picking the young boy up. Dawn felt sick, clutching onto her arm as she lifted herself from the floor.

'Did you disturb Dawn?' Grant pouted to Nathan, pressing his index finger against boy's chest. Nathan whined, turning away and holding onto Grant. He chuckled as he hugged onto Nathan.

'No, not at all,' she spoke quickly, her fingers to her shades to make sure they were on. Grant stared at her and a chill ran down her neck. He'd been acting strange around her from the very beginning. He'd been following her closely and staring at her relentlessly since she'd arrived.

'We're heading down for breakfast. You coming?' he asked her. She nodded, smiling sweetly at him. He didn't return the smile, turning and leaving the room. She waited for him to leave the room before letting out a relieved sigh. She pulled her bag over her shoulder, stepping out of the room and slamming the door. As she approached the stairs, she peered towards the lab. Antares stood with Edward. The two seemed to be conversing. She was glad to see that nothing bad had happened during the night.

'What's the matter Lucy?' Dawn heard Dave ask from the main library. Dawn made her way down the stairs one step at a time. She could see that toast had been laid out across the table. Grant sat next to Nathan, talking to the young boy. Dawn felt a pang of anxiety. She had no idea if Nathan was going to speak or not.

'You can't tell me you didn't hear the noises,' Lucy insisted to Dave, pacing back and forth in front of the door. Lucy's hair was out of place, deep bags under her eyes. It appeared she hadn't slept well, if at all.

'We hear them every night,' Dave sighed, 'but they can't get in. We made sure.'

'Not them!' Lucy snapped, 'There's something else out there. Don't you hear that it's completely different in tone to them?' Dave took a step back as Lucy let out a defeated groan. She looked up the stairs and noticed Dawn, mustering a weak smile.

'We're doing another scout after we've eaten,' Grant looked back from the table, 'Edward said we need to get one thing. Once we've got it, he's certain we could cure everyone out there.'

'What's the missing ingredient?' Dawn asked as she approached the table. Nathan whimpered as he grabbed Grant's arm and hid his face into the man's sleeve. Dawn stopped in her tracks. Grant dismissed the young boy's strange behaviour towards her.

'A fresh sample of blood from one of them,' Grant continued.

'You can't risk going out again,' Claire spoke out, 'We've got blood here already.'

'No we don't,' Edward walked into the Library, Antares close by, 'The sample I had has been misplaced.'

'I second that we don't go back out,' Lucy chipped in, sitting down at the table and shakily picking up a piece of toast.

'Only one of us needs to go out, after all, they are on our doorstep,' Dave chuckled.

'They're not on your doorstep,' Antares cut in, 'None of you notice how silent it is?' The group went quiet and listened intensely. There was no sound. Dawn approached the glass window and peered outside. Although the surrounding walls enclosed her vision, she saw no one at the metal gates.

'Are they gone for good?' Claire asked rhetorically. The room was quiet. The outside was quiet. Dawn's sixth sense was quiet. The crimson angel stood close to her, bending slightly so their eyes were inline.

'Do you understand what you've done?' Antares whispered harshly into Dawn's ear, 'Because the whole group knows that you've brought a breakthrough, their controller has sent them away. You must do exactly as I say from this point on.'

'Yes Antares,' Dawn whispered back to him. She was scared and knew she had made a horrible mistake. She should have given the cure to Antares for him to deliver. Now she had put them in danger, the people that had been possessed and the people that were barricaded in this building.

'You can't just go out,' Claire called out. Dawn glanced towards the door and noticed Antares as he approached the door.

'If you need a sample, I will bring you back a sample!' Antares snapped at her. Dawn could see both the determination and the anxiety in his expression. He wanted this to be over quickly.

'Don't yell at her that way,' Dave scolded him, 'You may have saved my life but you have no right to talk down to us. We're all in the same shit.'

'I'll lock Nathan in his room and we'll all go out together,' Edward decided for the group.

'We're safer in numbers,' Grant understood, 'We just got to get one sample and we'll be back.'

'Dawn should stay with Nathan,' Antares tried to persuade the group, 'You only need one person to keep an eye on the boy.' He didn't want her leaving the building and Dawn appreciated it. She looked over at Nathan who looked back up at her with uncertainty. He hadn't said a word. Whether he was shy, scared or mute she had no idea. He knew her secret though. It made sense for her and him to stay in the building. Bury the secrets and stay out of harm's way.

'If anyone should stay, it's Dave,' Claire insisted. 'Can't do much with a twisted ankle and Nathan may not trust strangers too easily.' The group turned to look at the aging man as he swallowed the last of his toast.

'Dave, can you keep an eye on us while we're out?' Edward asked him directly.

'If that's what you all want,' he agreed hesitantly as he took Nathan from Grant's clutch. The remaining group was uneasy as they all stepped outdoors. Dawn watched as Claire pushed the key into the gate and turned it, locking it in place after they had stepped out. The group was shook up. Grant clicked the magazine in place of his gun.

'Everyone got a weapon?' he asked the group. Dawn felt the holster on her leg and looked down at the pistol she had taken from Angelica. She wished she had something more but knew the group was limited on weapons. Claire and Edward were each wielding butcher's blades. Antares' had refused to take anything and Lucy held a very small handgun. Dawn gazed up at the Libraries roof and spotted Dave holding the shotgun, Nathan stood close to him.

'Keep noises to a minimum. I would rather find only one and not have it call out to the others,' Edward insisted. The group walked away from the sanctuary and into the heart of the city. Edward had been adamant that they needed a fresh sample and had been sure they would come across a fresh enough body. The plan was to head in the direction Dawn had fled from the day before. As they walked only the group's footsteps made a noise. No one dared to talk.

Dawn felt her hand reach for the back of her left shoulder and scratch in between the blade. Her walking pace was slowing. The group continued on their travels. The world was silent save for a few pigeons that pecked at the ground and fluttered upwards when the group disturbed them. Her sixth sense was still blind. Antares constantly scanned the surroundings like the rest of them did. There were no bodies on the floor—no sign of the possessed. If they were to come, surely they would come because of her. It seemed as though they were hiding.

Dawn stopped in her tracks as the group continued on, taking in a deep breath through her nose. Slowly, she exhaled, placing her hand against her left shoulder again. She felt a burning sensation tingling against her fingertips. Hesitantly, she applied pressure and let out a gasp as she felt them burning. She moved her hand away quickly, taking in another deep and laboured breath. There was now a distinct pressure that was pushing from underneath her shoulder blades. Like a person enduring the pain of wisdom teeth pushing through gums, she too felt her skin smouldering from underneath as her energy pushed against it. Her wings were trying to break through.

'Are you okay?' Grant parted from the group and approached her. She nodded, taking in another deep breath and exhaling.

'Stubbed my toe,' she lied to him as she forced herself to move forward. She needed Antares. She needed to know how long it would be before her wings broke free from underneath her shoulder blades and pierced her skin. She only just learned how to hide her eyes. She had no knowledge of how to handle her wings sprouting.

'Did you know me before this?' Grant whispered. Dawn looked up at him, completely puzzled.

'Not till yesterday when you saved me,' she told him. She took in another deep breath as the pain slowly faded. She was sure there would be another episode in time. She started her walk back to the group. Grant followed closely, their bodies almost touching.

'You look a lot like... never mind,' he trailed off, looking back towards the group. They were a good distance from the flock and Antares was keeping close to Edward. He did not know she had strayed from the group.

'Who do I look like?' she asked curiously.

'Like my sister,' he whispered. Dawn stopped walking and so did he.

'Your sister?' she questioned.

'I was very young she went missing,' he explained, 'We were at a fun fair that had come into town and I kept riding on this one carousel while she kept an eye on me, like a big sister does. She was watching me from the crowd and I was on one of the horses. It circled round and round and I kept waving to her and she kept waving back. But when the ride finished and I got off she was gone. I never saw her again.'

'Do you know what happened to her?' Dawn asked timidly.

'That's the thing,' he said, 'When I saw you, I was sure you were my sister. Even now the resemblance is uncanny. I know it sounds stupid, but is there any chance that you are Sky Moore?' Dawn felt herself cringe at the sound of her mother's name. He noticed and stepped towards her. Frightened, she took steps away from him.

'You are Sky!' he insisted. He sped towards her in an attempt to embrace her. He was stopped as her hands held his arms and pushed him back, preventing him from touching her heated shoulders.

'N-no, I'm not Sky,' Dawn struggled to speak, 'I'm Dawn. I'm only twelve Grant. How old would Sky be today?' There was a long pause between them. She stared at his blonde hair and his green eyes, realising how similar they were.

'She'd be in her mid-twenties,' he realised as he let out a deep sigh.

'Is that why you saved me?' Dawn asked. She felt sick with guilt as her human relative slowly looked back up to her. His eyes welled with tears as he pulled his arms away sharply.

'I was so sure,' he spoke, 'You look virtually identical. I needed to know if–'

'Guys, you need to come and see this,' Claire called back to them. The two hesitated staring at each other with disbelief. Dawn made the first move and re-joined the group. Grant stepped in line with her and gazed across the road. On the floor lay several bodies, people with bloody eyes that were now dead. Dawn gasped in horror.

'So they've started turning on each other?' Grant asked. Edward shook his head, pushing his foot against one of the bodies. It rolled on the floor, its open eyes staring up at the sky. In the centre of its chest was a gaping hole within its ribcage and a deep scaring trailed to the side of it.

'Their hearts are gone.' Edward made his diagnosis, 'See? There are teeth marks around the opening.' Dawn looked back at Antares but he was paying no attention to the bodies. His eyes were narrow, scanning his surroundings slowly. Something was on his mind. Did he know what this meant?

'Eaten?' Lucy cried out, gripping onto the scientists arm and hiding behind him.

'Are they eating each other's organs?' Claire whimpered. Grant raised his gun in anticipation.

'No,' Edward spoke. He pulled away from the body, a syringe filled with blood, 'Those are not human marks.' Dawn stared at the marks that were around it. The cuts that dragged through the skin could only be one creature. The Barghest.

'We have what we need, right?' Lucy spoke out. Edward nodded, signalling that they should leave. Dawn's ears picked up on a single pebble fall from above her. She looked upwards, her eyes gazing at the road that ran over the one he stood on. On the bridge above them, a set of cracked bloody eyes looked down upon the road. His paws bent over the structure, a tail tucked tightly between black legs and ears flat against a big and heavy skull. He panted awkwardly as he stared directly at the group.

'Donahue!' Dawn gasped in surprise. Antares picked up on the name and turned to see the beast that had clipped his wing. Donahue was in the city like the rest of the possessed. He looked down at her, recognising her through his injured eyes. The group noticed Dawn's attention had drifted elsewhere and looked up at the dog. His true Barghest form did not show and appeared to them as a mongrel dog.

'The animals can catch this too?' Grant spoke aloud. Antares grabbed Dawn and pushed her behind him as he glared at the guardian. The dog's tongue lolled out, blood dripping from its white canines and spotting on the gravel below. The dog clambered over the bridges wall and landed on the road in front of them. Lucy's gun rose and pointed at the dog. Edward took a small step back.

'This is the first case I have seen in an animal. The structure of the illness . . . this doesn't make sense,' Edward spoke as he lifted the blade and tried to usher the group closer together. Donahue kept his eyes on Dawn, his head lowering and twitching slightly. He was fighting with himself. She could not see the tell-tale signs that he had fully transformed.

'Please stay back,' Dawn whispered towards him. His ears perked upwards as he heard her voice. In the distance the group heard the cries of the other possessed. They were coming and in great number. Donahue heard them too, turning his head and gazing behind him, snarling as he overheard them approaching.

'Get back to the library, now!' Antares yelled at the group. Lucy kept her gun pointed at the dog as the group made their way to leave. Dawn ran to the front of the group and spotted two people running towards them at full charge, their bloody eyes on show.

'Run!' Claire cried out. Lucy snapped out of her trance as she ran back to the group. Donahue paid no attention to them as the group fled from the scene of scattered bodies. The possessed were closing in and quickly. Grant pointed the gun at one of the people's legs and fired. It fell to the floor, hissing out as the group ran past them. More were coming from within the buildings. Dawn peered back behind her to see Donahue. He had gone missing. Dawn felt her common sense flood back to her. It screamed and rattled in her mind frantically. She was no longer blind. It screamed out to her as she peered to the left hand side. A man in construction uniform latched onto her arm.

'Come with—' the man started but was cut short. A deep red slit appeared over his neck as his grip loosened on Dawn. Antares shadowed over her and ushered her to keep moving.

'No matter what do not stop,' he huffed out as the group continued to run. The sound of guns firing and the possessed screaming intruded within her mind. She heard Edward wail out. Dawn stopped running and turned to see a possessed woman grabbing him by his arm, throwing him to the ground. Dawn ran back towards him, hearing Antares' protest to not go back. The woman turned to face her, red tears smeared across her face. Dawn cast her hand forward and threw her light into her. The possessed was cast aside from Edward, howling out as the light burned into her face.

'Get up,' Dawn tempted Edward, holding her hand out for him. His eyes were wide open. He had seen light come bursting forth from her hand. Dawn's common sense rattled erratically in her head. More were coming.

'Now!' she yelled at him in fear. She grabbed his hand and pulled him to his feet. She ran forward, holding onto the scientist's hand tightly as she did so. After a few moments of his feet being dragged forward, he pulled his hand away and ran for himself. The place was flooded with the possessed. They clambered from behind cars, from buildings and from the shadows between them. The group was forced into an uneven circle as the possessed came charging from all sides.

A surreal darkness leapt in front of the group, the light draining from their surroundings. The dog stood with his back to them, his tail straight up high and its ears alert. Donahue charged forward and roared loudly. It was a sound unlike anything she had heard before. It carried across the entire city, a mixture of the roaring winter winds, the shriek of a human and the howl of a wolf. The possessed scrambled backwards, trembling and cowering at the sound the beast emitted. The beast took two steps towards them and howled once more. The group was forced to cover their ears from the immense sound that came from the dog's throat. The possessed recoiled and fled from the scene. Dawn's common sense flittered out of her mind as they scarpered.

The dog turned to face the group, its cracked eyes and white pupils on display. Claire let a whimper escape as she took several steps back. Lucy was knelt on the floor, her hands covering her ears and trembling. Edward's head was turning between the stray and the girl that had cast light from her hands. Grant kept his focus on the dog, the gun trained on the beast. Antares stepped in front of Dawn to separate her and the dog.

'Let us pass,' Dawn spoke directly to him, 'We can cure—' her speech was cut short as his head lowered, blood dripping from his jaw and a deep growl coming forth from his throat. His silver eyes dimmed and glowed from behind the web of red cracks. His paw lifted and clawed at the side of his head in frustration. Dawn held her hands out in front of her, preparing for the worse. Perhaps the disease did have a hold on him.

The dog roared loudly towards the group like he had done with the possessed. Dawn's common sense flickered, struggling to grasp the location of the danger that was imminent. She felt a force trying to close her eternal eye. She fought against it, feeling her own energy lashing at the invisible toxins in her head, trying to keep her senses open. Donahue sped forward and leapt into the air, his jaws wide open. Antares stepped back and abruptly pushed Dawn to one side. She was pushed to the floor and watched as her world became brighter. The deep red of Antares' wing came into full view, slashing into the side of the beast. Blood spilled over him and the floor as the group jolted and kept a distance from him. Donahue was forced to the ground and Antares lifted his wing once more, ready to strike him again. The dog did not give him a chance as he darted past them and ran between the buildings and out of sight.

Claire screamed out, pointing at Antares in disbelief, 'The devil. He's the devil!' Dawn heard guns click and point at her creator.

'Don't hurt him. He's not—' Dawn cried out in desperation. They turned their attention to her instead, each member as wide eyed as the first. She moved her fingers up her cheeks and to the bridge of her nose to check her shades. They were gone, knocked off in that brief moment. She heard her shades shattering underneath Grant's shoes. They knew. They all knew they weren't human.

'Please let me explain,' she tried to reason with them. Grant stood forward, raising his gun. She noticed his eyes welling with tears as he did so. She scrambled to her feet, peering at Edward, hoping that he would defend her as she had defended him. He was gobsmacked though, as gobsmacked as the rest of them. All except Grant, a man whose hands were trembling as the gun pointed at her, his finger to the trigger.

'What have you done to my sister!' Grant bellowed out in anger. Her common sense sparked. He wasn't waiting for an answer from her. She forced herself into a run, fleeing down the neighbouring street. Her common sense erupted in time for her to duck, the bullet casting over her head and pinging against the steel structure around her. She heard Antares yell out for her. She peered back to see he had been shot at by the group, blood welling from his back. She fled round the corner, her boots striking the ground furiously as she ran for her life.

CHAPTER 22

Dawn eventually slowed, hugging her chest and taking in frantic breaths. To them, she was a monster like the possessed. Grant had assumed the worst, that she was a monster that had stolen his sister. She felt guilt knotting her heart at the thought of this. Wasn't that the truth?

She peered back, hoping that Antares would be close behind her. He was nowhere in sight. Was it possible for him to be killed by normal bullets? He was already badly injured. It may have been enough to drive him over deaths edge.

A red trail caught her attention. It made a pathway towards the side. Slowly, she straightened herself and anxiously approached it. Spots of blood were dotted across the abandoned road. Fresh blood. It was possible it was Donahue's open wound that had created this trail. Donahue hadn't seemed possessed, at least not like the others. He had aimed for the group but felt he had not aimed for her. Common sense itself had been uncertain. Dawn did not have a chance to figure out who he had targeted. He was subjected to this disease, whether fully or not. He would know which of them was controlling the group.

She followed the trail carefully. Her hand reached for the revolver and pulled it from its holster. Her fingers applied pressure to the barrel, opening the compartment that held the bullets. There were five bullets inside. There was no spare ammo. She clicked it back into place, looking at the entrance of the abandoned parking lot. The trail of blood led into it. The building had several floors to it; cars parked from floor to floor. The buildings lights were gone. If she had to, she would have to use the gun.

She stepped into the entrance. The building was dark, the natural light struggling to seep in. Cars were parked in their bays. Some had been pulled out; deep punctures in their side created by the Barghest that had thrown them from their positions. She heard her own heels click against the concrete floor as she ventured deep into the building. She approached the broken neon sign, signalling the stairways. She had no idea if he was on this floor or as high as the rooftop. Her fingers tightened on the gun in her right hand.

'Donahue?' Dawn called out shakily. Her voice bounced around the building, lifted upstairs, and jumped from the walls. She gazed at the floor, trying to find the blood trail. There were deep stains in the gravel of crimson blood in patches, a single slither of bright red shining in her light showed that some of the blood was fresh. It snaked up the ramp that led to the next floor. She cautiously followed it.

As she reached the second floor, she saw a body of one of the possessed lying next to a car. His hand was reaching for the handle, as though he had tried to get to the safety of the vehicles confinement. The light in her eyes intensified. His chest had been clawed like the others had been. In disgust, she approached and studied it. She could clearly see the ribcage shattered and mangled with the muscles that surrounded it. She looked in, seeing the lungs and various veins running through it. His heart was missing.

A car alarm blurted out from above and Dawn jumped, looking directly at the ceiling. The sound of metal crunching racketed along the walls as the alarm whined out pitifully before it was silenced. He was on the next floor. She approached the second ramp and began to climb. She raised and pointed the barrel at the shadowy figure in front of her. Darkness enveloped the creature in front of her as the sound of crunching drifted to her ears. She noticed fresh blood colouring his canines, a human heart within its jaws. With a slow motion, his jaws concealed the organ, tilting his head back and swallowing it whole. She took in a deep breath, trying to steady herself.

It was hard to tell in the blackness whether he was angel or Barghest. Only his silver eyes showed, white pupils staring at her, red cracks darting back and forth on his irises like naked tree branches in the winter.

'The cure is almost finished,' Dawn mumbled quickly, 'We'll be able to get it out and...' An inhuman chuckle left the guardian angel's lips, the light continuing to fade around him. The red liquid could no longer be seen, only his injured eyes.

'You cannot save them,' he scorned her as he crawled along the floor towards her. Dawn coiled her finger around the trigger, stepping backwards as she stared at him. His eyes were getting closer and closer as he stalked towards her. She intensified the energy behind her eyes, desperately trying to see. Donahue's face illuminated slowly in front of her, his features were human in appearance. His hand rose slowly towards her, his nails were dirty with blood.

'Keep back, I don't want to kill you Donahue,' Dawn plead as she felt her back touching the concrete walls. Her shoulders began to burn again as she swallowed hard, trying to ignore the pain.

'I cannot die,' Donahue replied coldly. His fingers reached upwards. Dawn trembled, constantly pointing the gun to him. He wasn't reaching for the gun though, instead his hand clutched onto the golden necklace around her neck. The rings were tightly held against his palm. Dawn brought her left hand to the back of her neck, undoing the clasp and allowing the chain to be free from her. Donahue snatched it as soon as he heard the catch come undone. He stared at the two wedding rings, turning his body away from her.

'It's true then,' Donahue mumbled, 'Angelica is no longer with the living.' Dawn kept the gun aimed at his head, the light constantly slipping. The Barghest was eliminating the light. She struggled to keep her sight on him.

'I'm sorry,' Dawn whispered, 'She'd been infected.' The man crawled away from her, his eyes narrowing and staring at the floor. She saw a tear fall from his eye. Clear. He had still not turned, not completely. Dawn let out a sigh of relief.

'There is no hope for me anymore,' Donahue began to sob, letting his body fall flat to the floor and started to cry like a lost child.

'The cure's almost done. I can get the cure to you and...'

'It's not this disease that is taking me,' Donahue wailed. He walked away from her awkwardly, the shadowy curtain containing him and hiding him completely from her. Her eyes burned as she tried to pierce the darkness away.

'My darling fiancée found a way to stop it before . . .' Donahue spoke to no one, 'He must have known.'

'Who knows?' Dawn asked.

'He wants you,' his silver eyes were directly in front of her. The hurting angel was standing only inches away from her. 'He can smell it through me. Your wings are breaking through and that is when . . . Don't let him take you. Don't make the same mistake I did!' His eyes shined directly in front of her. She felt his palm pressing against her left shoulder, long claws gripping into her skin.

'Dawn?' she heard Lucy call out. She gazed towards the direction of the voice; her vision blocked by the intense gloom. Lucy had managed to find her. She wondered what had happened to the group, if they had been murdered, and prayed they had not been. Dawn looked back in front of her, wondering what Donahue would do. His eyes were no longer glowing in the darkness. Her hand quickly felt for her shoulder where he had pinned her. There was nothing pushing against her.

'It freaked me out a little, but you're still my friend. Please get down here. The place is giving me the heebie-jeebies.' Lucy's voice sounded urgent. Dawn stepped away from the wall, holding her hands out in front of her. The blackness was so strong that she could not see her own hands, despite her eyes burning as brightly as she could get them to shine. The Barghest was somewhere in the room. Dawn heard footsteps rushing up the ramp.

'What a relief,' Lucy let out a sigh as she grabbed Dawn's hand. 'This place is creepy. Let's back to the others. I'm sure you can explain properly then.' Dawn nodded as her golden eyes staring into Lucy's hazel ones.

'Where are the others?' Dawn asked. Lucy pulled her down the ramp in a hurry, the small handgun held in her left hand. The ground floor cast long shadows from the sunlight that entered through the entrance.

'They're all back at the library and safe. I snuck out to find you. Those things are still out there after all.' She bowed her head. 'And your friend managed to convince them that you and he aren't diseased. I don't trust him though. He has red eyes and those poor souls have red eyes too. It's a bit too coincidental, don't you think?' The two were interrupted by a low growl. The Barghest stood in the way of the exit. His cracked bloody eyes narrowed on the duo as the great beast snarled at them. Lucy took a trembling step back, raising the small gun and firing quickly at the dog. The bullets penetrated his body, revealing small red wounds of blood. He stood on his four paws, his head lowering and his teeth bearing.

'Help!' Lucy screamed out in fear, tears welling as she covered her head with her hands. He threw himself towards them. His jaws were wide open revealing white shining canines dyed with blood. Dawn brought her gun forward in a panic. She pulled the trigger. A loud ringing sound drummed into her ears. All other sound was obsolete as the bullet sunk into the Barghest's skull. The canine was thrown off course, its jaws snapping a mere few centimetres away from Lucy's head. Its body collided into the pillar.

Donahue gasped out as his body fell to the floor. Dawn's hands trembled, the revolver dropping to the floor from within her fingers. She had come here to save the people and Donahue. She didn't mean for this to happen. She ran to his side and hugged him awkwardly through his fur. His eyes remained open, the silver dulling as light poured back into the parking lot. He took in a deep breath, his eyes slowly closed, and let out one long exhale.

Dawn turned back to face Lucy, still shaken from the ordeal. Lucy's eyes were fixed on the fallen angel, but it wasn't the eyes Dawn was used to seeing. They were a vivid magenta in tone, a cross between purple and red. Her white pupils turned to Dawn, staring at her intensely. The young light bearer wheezed as she felt her hands slipping from the great beast. Lucy's eyes burned brightly. An intense pressure pushed against her mind and forced her to keel over.

Dawn was thrown under the current of her nightmare, reality's light disappearing rapidly. Her body was flung to the floor angrily. The corridor's walls cracked, deep red light piercing through it and surrounding her. She looked up the faces of Antares' victims staring at her, judging her. The missing people who had been killed for his sick experiments, Mike who had been murdered in cold blood, and Sky who was her non-consenting mother. Stood between them was Lucy.

Dawn now understood the meaning of these reoccurring dreams. Her energy boiled angrily, extending her arm upwards and throwing out her inner strength. The ghosts shielded their faces as the intense light banished them. The corridor fell apart like stained glass and fell through the floor. A deep scar etched into the wall, a faded pink light burst forth. It was a door, a portal similar to how she escaped the corridor and into Antares' embrace before. She sprinted forward as the nightmare fell apart around her.

Dawn burst through the light and into another world. She was stood in Lucy's bungalow, morning light casting through the windows and into the lounge. Lucy was covered by a dressing robe, bed-haired and sleepy hazel eyes looking towards a teen boy.

'I have to go after her,' Mike protested as he threw the front door open. Dawn felt the snap of the winter air enter the room. Her body trembled in grievance, desperately wanting to cling to him and never let go. This was only a vision though, a sight into a past she was not a part of.

'She'll be back soon. Give her some space Mike,' Lucy reassured him, placing her hand on his shoulder and turning him towards her. Her fingers pressed against his cheek. He turned to face her. His eyes dulled slightly. From the corner of his left eye, a deep red formed. He closed his eyes as a red teardrop dribbled down his cheek.

'Give her some… space…' he repeated her words in a hypnotic trance. She smiled as she leaned forward, grasping for the door handle. He shook his head hard, his eyes no longer dulled but the blood remained. He knew. He knew something was not right.

'No! He yelled out, pushing the door open and out her hands reach. 'I can't leave her. What's wrong with me?'

'Nothing is wrong. Oh dear, you're letting all the cold in,' she huffed out as she tried to push Mike back into the house. Her hand made contact with his cheek. Blood stained her fingertips. He stared in fear as he felt for his own cheek, the blood slipping over his fingers. He stared at his hand in confusion and looked back at her.

'What have you done to me?' he demanded. She stood still, her head lowering. Dawn trembled as she stared. Mike had been infected like the others.

'Let me out, right now!' he demanded, pushing into her side. She glared at him, her magenta eyes showing. He gasped in surprise. She thrust her hand forward, launching him into the bookcase. His forehead struck the corner as his body fell to the floor. He let out a groan, fresh blood forming on his forehead where it had been cut. Lucy walked towards him, wiping the blood from her fingertips onto her trousers.

'Like you ever had a chance of protecting her,' Lucy laughed. 'She has to die, Mike. A human child could never understand the path she must fall down.' She picked up one of the fallen books from the floor. Mike looked up at her groggily. His expression was not full of fear but full of determination. He vowed he would protect Dawn no matter what. He grasped the side of the bookcase with his fingers, his feet kicked against the back wall. Lucy looked up as the bookcase tumbled down on her. The wood splintered under the weight as it crashed into her, pinning her to the floor. The teen scrambled to his feet, leapt over the scattered books and ran out the bungalow.

'Mike!' Dawn screamed out in a panic. He could not hear her. Lucy's past self slowly got up from the floor, splinters of wood falling to the carpet. The angel ran out the door to follow Mike. Dawn chased after her. Lucy ran from street to street in frustration, trying to find Mike. He knew too much. He was going to warn Dawn of Lucy's intent.

Lucy ran to a warehouse, a large lorry parked just outside the steel gates. She glared across the road. Mike was running towards the road. Dawn saw herself at the other side. Lucy's eyes came into full view. From her back wings came into form, burning intensely with an undying flame. She turned her focus on the parked lorry. She cast forward an intense fire. The lorry was pushed off of the road. The tank caught fire. The explosion catapulted into Mike's direction.

'Run!' Dawn heard Mike call out. The lorry collided into his body. Dawn screamed out, turning and glaring at Lucy. She thrust her open palm forward to strike her. A chain wrapped around her wrist and pulled it back. She brought forth her other hand and again, it was restrained. Red chains snaked towards her, latching onto her limbs and her neck. She was thrown backwards, the past shattering in front of her. Around her stood the clouds of nothingness, left behind from the shattered mirage. Dawn's eyes were glowing intensely as she stared in front of her. In the stillness, the villain stood before her, the one who invaded her mind.

'You killed him!' Dawn yelled at her in anger and grief.

'I had no choice,' Sky replied, 'He was about to tell everything. I couldn't risk it. Besides, I hoped if you thought the Crimson had killed your friend, and that would be enough to keep far away.' Dawn's eyes filled with tears and screamed out in hatred and guilt. Lucy had kept them within her home, pretended to care for them. Dawn tried desperately to strike Lucy with her energy. A blast of light sparked abruptly, taking the breath out of Dawn as she took in shaken breaths.

'Don't you understand the monster he is?' the red haired angel questioned Dawn. Lucy had been untouched. Dawn had no power in this realm for it was Lucy's manifestation. The images of Sky and Mike stood behind Lucy, puppets she had created to manipulate Dawn's emotions.

'You're the monster! You control the army, don't you?' Dawn took in staggered breaths as she recovered from her outcry.

'Yes Dawn,' Lucy chirped, 'I turned the people and spread it out. Perhaps, I was naïve to awaken them so early, but when you left, I needed a way to get you back.'

'Why do you need me?' Dawn asked with uncertainty.

'The day you were born was the day I died,' she spoke bitterly. 'You have no idea the pain you go through when fire takes you. I only live because he answered my prayers. I begged to live and he granted it.'

'Who granted your wish?' Dawn questioned.

'The one both Antares and Donahue have spoken to you about. The one that claimed an army of possessed angels and drove our race to near extinction. He lives Dawn, his body a prisoner in hell. He reached out to me and boasted that only a god could have such power to bring me back to life. I asked for him to do so.' Dawn was taken aback. She could only think of one possible person that could grant desires. She'd assumed he was dead. But then none of the angels had said he was dead, only that he was sentenced.

'I refuse to grant his bidding,' Lucy spoke coldly, 'That's why I needed an army. That's why I need you. Dawn. I need the power that he possesses, and I know exactly how he became so powerful. On the day an angel fledges, their power pulls into their heart. He used to consume the hearts of angel's whose wings had recently fledged to gain that power. That is exactly what I plan to do.'

'You're mad!' Dawn responded.

CHAPTER 23

'Perhaps I am mad,' Lucy whispered softly. Dawn was curled on the floor of the car park, her head tossing and turning as Lucy kept her captive within her nightmare. Slowly, she strode towards her, placing her hand on the shivering girls back. Lucy curled her fingers gently underneath Dawn's shoulder blades and could feel a pressure pushing back. It would be less than an hour before her wings came through. Lucy picked up the pistol Dawn had dropped onto the floor and removed the holster from the girl's leg, strapping it to her own.

'I'm sorry it had to be this way,' Lucy whispered to her, stroking the girl's blonde hair back and slowly lifting her body up. She cradled the teen in her arms and slowly stepped out of the dark building. Lucy's wings burned brightly out in the winter's sun, glad that she no longer needed to suppress her true form. The others would be too busy with the Crimson and was certain one would kill the other. She had seen through her minion's eyes that all had fled into the library. She had forced the possessed to swarm that building, to keep them in. Only the crimson angel would be bold enough to try and break through, and she would make sure that they killed him on sight.

Lucy's mind was cluttered. A barrage of migraines and insomnia had been seeping at her consciousness and eating away at her soul. It was a struggle to control both the possessed, and the dream she kept Dawn captivated in. There was another danger approaching, one her eternal eye pinpointed.

'I'm surprised you managed to get past them,' she commended, not needing to look back at Grant. He kept a gun trained to her head, his finger curled tightly at the trigger but not firing. He showed no fear in his expression or body language. Her wings burned from behind her back, fire flickering in the wind as the winter nipped into their sides.

'Put her down and step away from her.' He motioned with his gun. She smiled sweetly at him; her eternal eye straining desperately. There was no way the boy had slipped out of the building. It was plausible that he never entered with the rest. Her eyes had only been looking for the crimson angel, the only creature that could stop her.

'Do you still believe she is your sister?' Lucy asked curiously. He shook his head once. There were too many signs pointing that she wasn't.

'Your sister was killed,' Lucy explained as she turned to face him, 'That man with the red eyes tortured and killed her. He did it to create Dawn. She's an inhumane experiment of his, a desperate act from a desperate animal. He wanted to bring back his species from the dead by any means necessary.'

'Are you one of his creations too?' he asked her.

'I am Grant,' she told him the truth, 'That's how I knew Sky was killed. I witnessed it. He killed her Grant.' Her eternal eye was struggling to keep up with her situation as she bowed her head. Dawn groaned within her arms, fighting the nightmare that contained her consciousness. Lucy stared at the barrel of the gun, keeping as calm as she could. It was too much of a threat to try and seize him as well. Already her minions were difficult to control as she had forced them all to the libraries doors. As far as she could tell, no one had left the building.

'He's evil,' Grant mumbled under his breath.

'Precisely'. Lucy smiled. 'And I did everything I could to stop Dawn being with him. She wouldn't listen though.' He bit his lip; the gun never wavered from her. He was taking the information in, but something else was on his mind. She looked through the eyes of the possessed, flickers of walls and doors entering her mind. They howled out in anguish as they tried to break in but she could see no one.

'Are the others at the library?' she asked him softly and he nodded in response. 'Is he with them too?'

'He's a prisoner of ours. We suspect he's responsible for this army,' Grant told her. Lucy's eyes strained, focusing on Grant. She picked up on the deceit in his tone. He was lying. She held Dawn tighter to herself, the young teen whimpering as she did so. His eyes narrowed, focusing his vision on her. She focused her vision on the possessed, letting Dawn's nightmare weaken. The possessed howled out and struck at the wall. A crack edged downward, and the walls split into several parts yet stood. They weren't at the wall. They had been striking large mirrors. She had been deceived by them.

'You're in sight. It's now or never!' Edward's voice crackled through the man's pocket. Lucy lost her concentration; her ears strained towards the voice. They planned on taking away her army. Her eternal eye flickered and lost focus in that moment. Blindness swept over her eternal eye. Her wings flared out, the fire burning wildly, clinging to Dawn as she drew her wings downwards. A pair of hands pushed past her flames and thrust her wing to the floor. She looked back at the crimson eyes that glared at her. Grant fired, the bullet shooting and hitting her in the head. Lucy's arms dropped; Dawn fell to the floor as they did so. She covered her face with the palm of her hand; the blood dribbled gently down her forehead. Dawn's fingers grasped the floor as her eyes opened. The nightmare obliterated in that moment. She felt tears to her eyes as she scrambled to her feet. She could feel her skin itching terribly from underneath her shoulder blades.

Lucy screamed out hysterically, losing her calm. In the distance, the small group heard the army cry out in anguish. Their emotions entwined with their masters. Dawn peered through the gaps between the buildings and could see the possessed charging straight towards her and Antares. Lucy's wings burned intensely, his hands smouldering from within them. He switched his grip to her arm instead. Lucy immediately cast her wings downwards, forcing both the angels into the air. The Crimson held on tightly as the angels flew higher and higher into the sky. The two watched the spectacle as Antares eventually let go of her. His remaining healthy wing spread outwards, a strange vial held within its feathers. Grant turned his gun upwards and fired directly for it. The bullet drove into both the vial and his wing. They combined and shattered into a brilliant crimson.

Dawn watched as the sky was filled with the red colour as droplets began to fall. The possessed stopped in their charge and stared up at the falling rain. The crimson droplets cast over the city and fell to their faces. The blood washed over their cheeks and away from their eyes. One by one, the people collapsed to the floor from exhaustion, their eyes clear of their redness.

'Grant, I . . .' Dawn began to speak.

'Nathan convinced us,' Grant explained, 'Said that Lucy was the bad one and that you were just scared. Guess he'd seen her for what she was. He kept saying she would turn him into a monster if he told anyone.' The two turned their attention to the sky as Lucy screamed out. Her wings blazed as she struck the mighty crimson angel. Antares' grip was forced away from her arm as he crashed to the floor. Dawn ran to Antares' side and placed her hand on his shoulder. He pulled himself up from the ground, blood dribbling from his mouth. Antares' shattered fragments of his wings came into view. The remaining stubs were pale and cracks run zigzagged across them like a broken mirror.

'Your wings!' Dawn reached her hand out to them. He ignored her plight as he knelt on the road, taking in relieved breaths. People lay on the floor around them as the rain continued to fall. The blood from their eyes formed puddles on the ground. Some people were conscious and dazed while others were sleeping.

'It was a success team,' Grant pulled the walkie-talkie from his pocket and spoke into it.

'We can see. You three need to get back to the Library as quickly as possible.' Edward's crackled voice came through. Lucy landed in front of the duo. Her magenta eyes flickered as hot tears welled within them.

'You don't know what you have done,' she said. Grant raised the gun quickly. Lucy thrust her hand forward. A blaze of blue fire struck the gun, knocking it out of his hands. The barrel melted into the tarmac of the road as Grant shrieked; his hands torched as well. Antares awkwardly pushed Dawn behind him, pulling himself to his feet. His wings were destroyed, and his arms were badly burnt, yet he was still adamant on protecting his creation.

'You'! she snapped at him, 'Your deranged experiment created us and destroyed us. I was burnt alive when your wretched machine malfunctioned. You stared at me through the flames as my body was set on fire. I tried to reach for you, but you left me there to perish. You left us all to perish. Why was she the only one that survived?' Dawn ran from him and knelt to Grant's side. He was crying, the skin burning on his palms.

Tears welled in Lucy's eyes as she yelled, 'I was saved though. He approached me at the gates of death and asked what my desire was and that it would be granted. I wanted to live.' Dawn looked back at the angels. A chill ran down the back of her spine as it did with Antares.

'Do you understand what you've done?' his eyes widened. Dawn watched with uncertainty.

'You never taught me of him. I know now who I made my contract with.' She spat.

'Contract?' Dawn questioned with uncertainty. Lucy turned her attention to Dawn. Grant kicked against the gravel and tried to lift himself in fear.

'He wants me to deliver you Dawn,' Lucy spoke directly to the girl, 'In exchange for my life I am to present yours.'

'If you bring her to him you will give him the strength to break free of his prison. He will turn Earth into hell itself!' Antares yelled at her. Grant pulled himself to his feet as Dawn offered aid. She used her shoulder as a brace for him.

'He's in hell!' she snapped. 'Without my help he'll never be able to get out. I know how to stop him. He became powerful by eating the hearts of the young. That's why I need you Dawn. With that power, nothing could stop me.'

'You cannot deny him without retribution,' Antares spoke, 'I have seen it happen far too many times. You must trust me.'

'No. You had witnessed it many times during the war in the times where he was not a prisoner. I plan to reach hell itself and kill him there!' She yelled at him. She pulled a chain from her pocket, a small black token jingling towards their direction as she spoke.

'That's the key to hell? How did you get that?' Antares questioned fearfully.

'It was part of his plan. I was to bring her to him directly in hell, but he knew I created an army with the intent of destroying him. I'll now have to rely solely on the strength in Dawn,' she said.

'Grant, get back to the others,' Dawn whispered quickly into the man's ear. Grant took a step back, staring directly into Dawn's golden eyes.

'I won't leave you,' he protested. His eyes filled with tears. For years, he had wondered what had happened to his sister. He had lost her once before, and he didn't want to lose her again.

'I'm not your sister.' Dawn chocked slightly on her words. 'I'm not your family. I couldn't be any more grateful for you saving me, but you need to protect your family, back there.' She pointed towards the library. Grant looked towards the building. They were waiting for him.

'It hurts that your sister's blood is on my hands. Please don't allow it to be yours as well,' Dawn begged him. Grant looked between the angels and then back at Dawn. He took in a deep breath. He knew his sister was never coming back. He had hoped desperately that Dawn would be her, but his illusions were shattered. He turned and ran towards the library, knowing that he needed to protect the others. Dawn watched as he left.

'Because he knew my intent he didn't disclose where hells gate it. That is one thing I need from you,' Lucy continued to speak to Antares, interrupting Dawn's thoughts, 'The lock to hell's gate. Where is it?'

'I will die with its location,' Antares spoke coldly.

'Then I have no use for you,' she declared, pulling her arm from behind her back and revealing the gun that Dawn had dropped. Both angels felt the rush of fear pelt their eternal eyes. The gun shot. The overwhelming noise was so close to Dawn's ears it sent a shrill ringing sound through her head. Her mind howled out that she was dead. Her eyes told a different story as she watched the crimson angel's eyes close, and his body slump to the floor.

CHAPTER 24

Dawn pulled back, and her fingers clenched into fists. Lucy stepped in front of Dawn. Her wings outstretched in a mesmerising fire of blue and purple. The two angels held their ground. Lucy's true eyes shone deeply, an aura that seemed to hold the gazers attention and draw them towards her.

'There is no one left to protect you now,' Lucy told her sternly, her wings lifting and filling her surroundings with an intense flame. Dawn felt a heated pain underneath her shoulders, growing more and more in intensity. Her golden eyes shone brightly as she stared at her supposed sister, one created from blood like she had been. She had killed the people that had tried to protect her and had caused pain for hundreds if not thousands of people. Now the people that had once been her army lay on the floor.

'There is no one left to protect you either,' Dawn motioned to the idea of her army. Lucy gave a knowing smirk as her wings drew downwards sharply, lifting the angel into the air. Common sense sparked and Dawn darted to the side in response. An avalanche of blue fire rained down upon her. Dawn swept her energy around her body, creating a brilliant light that engulfed Lucy's barrage. Her energy boiled within her as she tried to out speed her sister. Dawn's eternal eye picked up as she sprinted towards a tall building, turned off neon lights indicated great end of Christmas sales. Her common sense lifted once more as she charged into the front doors. She slammed the doors behind her as an intense heat swept behind her.

Both angels knew when the other was going to attack, so long as both could see with their eternal eye. Dawn concentrated as hard as she could. She knew where her eternal eye lay within her. Carefully she cupped it and closed its vision. Her common sense was now shut off. Dawn was now blind to danger, but at least it meant Lucy would not be able to sense her anymore.

Dawn walked quickly through the shopping mall she had entered. She was facing a fully-fledged angel, an angel that held an angel killing gun. The only chance Dawn had would be to get the gun back and to fire it at Lucy. She sped past toy stores and coffee shops, watching the windows carefully. The ceiling was nothing but glass, and above she could see the fiery winged angel circling overhead. Dawn kept herself in the cover of the shop doors, hiding her position from Lucy.

Dawn looked up the stairs. They led to a large window and through it showed a car park that stood as its neighbour, the same car park that Dawn had confronted Donahue in. Perhaps he had something on his person that would protect her. She didn't like the idea of taking from a body, but it was a desperate situation.

Her boots clicked loudly against the mall's floors as she sped through the building. Shadows cast through as Lucy encircled it. The angel had spotted Dawn and followed her movement swiftly. Dawn's eyes glowed intensely as she ran up the stairs. The window came into sight. The distance between the mall and the car park was a larger gap than Dawn had anticipated. Lucy came into view; her fiery wings held out wide. Dawn threw her energy outwards. The light burst forth, shattering the glass. It struck Lucy in several places as she covered her face with her hands. Dawn jumped through the opening; her arms stretched out. Her shoulders were burning intensely, and so she hoped her wings would burst forth.

Her fingers clasped onto the opposing buildings window ledge. The jagged bricks cut into her skin as her feet kicked frantically at the wall for footing. Dawn's wings refused to push through, and so she pulled upwards with her arms and over the wall. Lucy came into view. Her white pupils were staring intensely at her. Dawn threw out her energy sharply, a brilliant shine of light glaring towards Lucy. The fiery wings encircled Lucy, protecting her from the heat, but her sight was temporarily blinded.

Dawn's eyes glowed intensely as she ran down the ramp of the building quickly. Donahue's body would be on the ground flood. That was where he had fallen. Antares held no tools, but Donahue may have had something on him, something to at least fight off the crimson angel. Her eyes darted between the vehicles. The light filtered in from the entrance of the car park, revealing the colour of their paintwork. Next to a strong and sturdy pillar was a smeared stain of red. Donahue was missing. The young angel circled the pillar and checked between the cars. His body was nowhere in sight.

The shadows in the building changed direction. Dawn opened her eternal eye. Her common sense was forced back into action and screamed at her. She knew she could not run from the danger that was about to come. The only way out of the building was through the entrance, and she had cornered herself. Against the protest of her mind, Dawn sprinted forward, trying to hold her energy tightly. She stepped out into the light and looked above her to see Lucy descended upon her. Dawn's arms reached up towards her, casting the full strength of her energy to Lucy.

Lucy fell sharply through the light. She had felt the pain of fire first hand, and Dawn's third outburst was nothing to her. Her hands gripped Dawn's wrists as she lifted the young teen and threw her across the gravel. Dawn scraped across the tarmac road, the small rocks chipping at her skin. Dawn cried out as Lucy pinned her to the floor, her shoe pressed against the girl's torso. The fledged angel pulled out the butcher's knife and held it close to Dawn's chest. Her golden eyes looked up in fear. She heard a distinct sizzling sound coming from behind her. The tarmac was heating from underneath her shoulders.

The wind howled loudly around them as the world took a sinister turn. There was a distinct scent in the air, and Dawn knew it wasn't her mind playing tricks. The scent of salt and water began to increase. Dawn felt water lapping at her fingertips. Small waves shifted underneath Dawn's arms. Lucy's attention left Dawn, instead staring at the water. The fiery wings were shaking, embers flickering from them. The city was not close enough to the sea for these smells to be so intense. Lucy's expression changed to one of disgust and anxiety as she gripped Dawn's shirt tightly. The blade was pressing against Dawn's skin. It wasn't sinking though; the metal was trembling against her skin.

The water rose around them, encircling the two girls. Lucy lifted Dawn to a sitting position. The blade was now to her throat and looking out at where the waves were coming from. Dawn surveyed her surroundings and noticed who had sent Lucy into a panic.

'You're too late!' Lucy spoke boldly towards a shadowy figure. The man stood in front of the girls was dripping yet. His dark black hair was straight as water dripped from the bangs, and water trickled from the sides of his blue lips. It was Donahue seemingly back from the dead. Only his eyes showed that it was not as it seemed. His eyes were fiercely bright and gold, light casting a surreal glow, demanding that he be awed. Lucy was frozen in fear. Her hands struggled to hold onto the blade. Dawn made her move, striking the fledged angel's hand with a weak spark of her energy. The blade was knocked out of her fingers. Lucy was shaken from her state and dropped Dawn, running for the knife.

Donahue marched forward, water flowing off his back and limbs. Dawn shuffled back as Lucy managed to retrieve the knife. Donahue's boot stomped sharply onto her hand. Her fingers, with a knife beneath it, clamped to the floor. She looked up at him, awkwardly bowing before him.

'I'm very disappointed in you, child,' Donahue shook his head at her. Lucy's free hand felt for the holster, the gun she had stolen from Dawn. Her fingers fumbled for the gun, drawing it forward, and her fingers coiled around the trigger as she wept loudly.

'Die in hell!' She screamed out at him in desperation. The barrel lifted and pointed directly at his head. He gave a knowing smile as she trembled violently on the spot. She didn't pull the trigger. She couldn't pull the trigger. Slowly his hand rose and pointed at her. Her eyes widened as she turned the gun on herself, pressing the barrel to the side of her head. He coiled his own index finger in tightly. Lucy shrieked out hysterically as her own finger copied the motion. Lucy fell to the floor; the bullet passed through and clattered on the ground beyond her.

Dawn panicked as she rose to her feet. She was already exhausted from fighting Lucy, and now the pain pressing against her shoulders were becoming more and more unbearable. Donahue turned his attention to her. His golden eyes were burning brightly, far more brightly than her own could.

'You're not Donahue.' She gasped in fear.

'Then let me introduce myself formally. I was previously Gyan Lycenia, fourth of his name but a name many refuse to call me by. I took on the name Lucifer when I was king to those that have now passed,' he told her proudly.

'You're the mad king,' she spoke aloud.

'They called me that too.' He smiled seemingly not insulted by the nickname he had been given as he turned his attention to Lucy. 'Such a shame'. Dawn couldn't help but look at the young woman as well. Her red locks had fallen over her torso and her features. Her magenta eyes remained open but not looking. Lucy had done all of this to defy her gods demand.

'You want my heart . . .' Dawn gulped. 'You brought her back, so she could deliver me to you.'

'You are missing the greater picture,' he didn't deny her claim as he held his arms out at his sides, 'Understand that I could do so much for you in return. For the cost of your life, I could bring back those you've loved. I could give Mike back to this world, the children who suffered at Antares' hands, and even bestow Grant his sister. For one life I could do that, but I would need the strength of your heart to do that.' She trembled as she stood awkwardly to her feet. The forsaken angel approached her slowly. She could not bring herself to move away. She was frozen in place by her emotions. If she gave herself up, they would all live. The people that had been hurt, all because of her, could be given a second chance.

'I know that you are a selfless person.' He placed his hand on her head. 'Everything that you have lost, you don't need to weep and blame yourself. Surely, you know that none of it is your fault. What you can do, Dawn, is set things right. Rectify what these mislead lambs have caused.'

'You could bring back Mike and the children?' Dawn asked. Her breathing was more laboured now; the pain shrill and sharp at her skin.

'You can, Dawn,' he reassured her. 'The loss of your life is a very burdening thought, but yes, for the cost of your life I could grant all that for you.' Dawn wanted the pain to stop, both physical and mental. She had before wished she hadn't been born, not in the wicked way that it had been. She had the choice to bring them back, to bring everyone back.

She opened her mouth, about to give her answer but retracted from her thought as she witnessed black cracks appearing over Donahue's body. He writhed on the spot. He blinked once; the eyes were silver. The lips parted, trying to speak to her. She took a step back in fear as the white pupils flickered. He let out a strangled cry in frustration. He blinked again, and they returned to the bold golden eyes they were. The black cracks subsided. A low chuckle came softly from his throat, hushing gently.

'Now, Donahue, my sweet and naïve child, it's time for you to stay asleep,' the king whispered reassuringly to himself. Dawn trembled where she stood. Donahue was trapped, a puppet with strings being pulled by the king. Donahue had tried to regain his body. He had tried to tell her something but had been suppressed.

'Before I decide, I have one question,' she spoke. She hoped that Lucifer would tell her what Donahue had tried to tell her.

'What is your question child?' he asked.

'Donahue . . . Did he ask for his desire to come true?' she questioned him. His smile disappeared. He gave a single nod. Dawn realised why Donahue was not a pure angel. He was a demon, converted by the granted wish. With the implications of bringing back the others, she wondered if they would be themselves if she did take on his offer.

'I won't make a deal with you,' Dawn told him sternly. She was afraid that they too would be converted to puppets. She understood too little of how such power worked, that only the few angels she had spoken to knew of his deceit.

'Your own conspiracy is of a higher priority than those that have lost their lives in the pursuit for you?' he asked. She peered down at Lucy's body. The gun was still held tightly in her cold fingers.

'Yes,' she told him. She had been told the horrors of making a contract with him and seen the nightmare it bestowed upon them. She could not bring herself to risk it. He shook his head slowly, sighing in regret as he did so.

'Such a shame,' he said. His hands rose. The people that had been cured suddenly screamed in pain. The army, standing tall, lifted from the ground. Their eyes were bloody and were staring directly at her. They weren't a mess of feral creatures. They were organised and completely loyal to the king's gestures. He motioned towards her, and the group charged. Hundreds of committed soldiers came for her, and there was nowhere to run to.

The heat underneath her shoulder blades intensified sharply. She shrieked as she felt a molten fluid crack through her skin, a brilliant light forming from behind her back. Her eyes intensified as she stared upwards. Her wings were strings of golden light, flowing from her back and peeking towards the sky. The possessed were within a hands reach of her. She lifted her new wings high and swept them down sharply. Her body lifted into the sky abruptly and awkwardly as the army met in the centre and looked up at her. Frantically, she beat her new wings, trying to work out how to fly properly.

The king forced Donahue's lips into a smile. He clicked his fingers, and the people below twitched erratically. One of them bowed forward; their arms wrapped tightly around their stomach. Their back ripped from behind their shoulder blades as bloody wings formed from behind. Dawn pushed an intense heat through her wings, heating the air around her and suspending her in the air. One by one the possessed were reformed, gaining wings that solidified with their own strings of blood.

'I will break free from my prison. It was your choice to deny the power I offered,' he told her as the demons underneath her howled towards her in unison. Their wings flapped; their bodies rose towards her. She forced herself higher into the sky. The possessed followed her. Their wings were flapping awkwardly as blood dotted on the floor. She flew as high as she could, but the possessed followed, with each beat of their wings they became stronger. Each time she avoided one, others came close behind her. They were soon above her as she was forced to descend, being pushed closer and closer to the mad king.

Dawn flew down swiftly and crashed next to Lucy's body. The possessed were charging towards her. In desperation, she grabbed the gun from Lucy's palm, knowing that only two bullets remained. Lucy's other hand was held tightly shut, a chain on show from her fingers. Dawn pried the fingers open and noticed a strange and black object. It was the key Lucy had boasted about before, a key to hell itself. She pulled the small object from her hand and flew upwards once more. The possessed flew up to meet her. She cast her light out as fast as she could. They seemed to not care for the pain she put them in as they continued towards her. They grappled for her arms, lashed out for her wings and groped for her body. Frantically, she weaved in and out of them.

She raised the gun, pointing it at Donahue when she noticed him on the ground. Her eternal eye opened sharply. The golden eyes saw a new image before her. The key trembled within her palm with anticipation. A dark aura cast over Donahue's body. Images of chains straggling from unknown forces seemed to linger around him. If she shot at Donahue, she realised she would only be shooting a dead body. She had to target the source.

The possessed were closing in behind her, and she could not outrun them forever. She flew sharply forward, flying straight for the mad king. He stared up at her in amusement. She screamed out, feeling the key grow cold in her hand as she forced herself directly into the king. Her palm opened; her fingers entangled in the chain. The key's temperature plummeted as hers eyes shined brightly, and her body was thrown through his.

CHAPTER 25

Dawn's body collided into steel as she took in deep breaths. The world was pitch black. Her eyes glowed as she knelt on the cold floor and peered behind her. A white crack suspended in the air. A warmer breeze than in there filtered in. She heard footsteps thundering towards her. The possessed were racing towards the portal. The key was on display in the palm of her hand. She closed her hand tightly around the small tool, and the crack vanished from sight. She opened her hands slowly, and the crack reappeared. Lucy had mentioned how she had gained the key to hell—a way to unlock the gate. Dawn had that power in the palm of her hand. She nestled the key deep into pocket and closed the gate with it. She shakily stood up.

Dawn cast the light from her wings sharply, and her surroundings took form. She was enclosed by the deep sea that tunnelled around her. The tunnel itself was a dark and icy monument. A strange fish swam swiftly away from her. Its scales looked slimy, and its head was filled with nothing but sharp teeth. She glanced upwards and then down, trying to catch sight of the sun or the moon. She was too deep to gaze upon them. Her feet were resting on a strong steel chain. Water had frozen around the links. Sharp icicle shards point in various directions. They were sparkling white against her own light; the salt trapped with them catching it like glitter. There were chains overhead in the seawater itself, held taunt and trailing over her. There were chains below her to her sides and some protruding slightly into the trap of air that Dawn stood in. They all seemed to collate to a point far ahead of her.

She was at hell's gate, and hell had frozen over. She had always envisioned hell to be full of fire and death, but it appeared that she was wrong. Her skin formed goose bumps from the intense cold as he folded her wings in tightly, trying to keep herself warm. The strong light pressed against her like a heater. Even with her energy, the cold was only just bearable.

Dawn squinted as she saw a flicker in front of her. It was very small and very dim. Two small spheres peered out in her direction. The light belonged to the king. Dawn clutched onto the revolver as tightly as she could. Dawn understood Lucy's plight that she herself planned to step into hell with her army and overthrow him. It was now up to Dawn to stop him. There was no army for her to back her up.

Dawn peered down at her jean pockets. She could go back. She could leave hell and never come back, leaving the forsaken angel within his prison. He still had influence on the world above. He had to be stopped once and for all.

She trod along the metal chains. The ice crunched from underneath her boots. Her hands clutched tightly to the gun, terrified of dropping it. It was the only thing she had to defend herself. The only tool she knew would work against angels. The light in front of her continued to stare at her. He could see her and her gun. She stretched her wings out briefly and pulled them in tightly again, a constant fight between needing more light to see and needing more warmth to stop herself from freezing.

Dawn's ears picked up. A droning sound rumbled through the sea's depths like thunder. She kept taking steps forward, keeping at the same pace, trying to see where the sound had come from. Her wings extended. She saw nothing but the black sea and the metal chains. She pulled her wings in, the cold snapping at her skin. The thunderous sounds rolled back in. Dawn didn't want to run; the chains were slippery underfoot. If she fell off, she would fall to the ice that circled below her. If she broke through, she feared the sea would kill her.

Common sense sparked within her mind. She took in a deep breath, exerting her wings sharply outwards. The surrounding tunnel hissed as the heat reached out to it. The chains were moving. The chains lifted in the sea and came crashing into the underside of the tunnel. Dawn darted upwards, pushing her wings down to force her body into the air. The metal chain missed her feet by an inch. The sea began to flood the tunnel; the black liquid seeped inwards. Her foot touched back onto the chain below her as she sprinted forward. Her common sense sparked. She ducked low, hearing the metal chain crashing into the ice tunnel above her. Splinters of ice rained down on her as she covered her body with her wings and continued to race forward. The sea lapped over her feet. The freezing temperature snapped at her. She lifted herself as the sea above flowed into the tunnel. The water was coming in quickly. She spread her wings out and flew down the tunnel. She twisted and turned, avoiding the crashing ice the chains forced upon her.

Her common sense screamed out to her as she peered upwards. A chain crashed directly down upon her. She went to scream out, but the water filled her mouth. Her right wing was pinched between two heavy chains, pulling her under the water. Dawn tried desperately to pull her wing from the metal links. She was pinned down in hell. The water was forced down her throat, unpleasant and thick. Her eyes opened. A set of golden eyes were a mere feet away from her own—the outcast king.

'Shh, child, you can breathe this water,' he whispered serenely to her. Dawn pulled frantically at the chains, struggling to understand. She took in frantic gulps of water; her head felt light from the feeling. She felt her hand reach for her pocket, but her common sense drilled into her mind sharply. Reaching for the key was the worst thing she could do. The trapped wing prevented her from leaving, but bringing the key out in display would open the lock. Her hand groped for the chain. Her lungs were expanding and retracting. They were filled with the salty sea, yet the sea she swallowed was dense with oxygen. She stared back at him in fear. He was floating in the water with chains clipped to his arms and legs. He breathed in the water like the air above. His wings were stretched out from corner to corner. Single strands of hair that seemed to have lost their glow, each connected and strung back to the thick chains that kept him in hell. The chains sprouted from unknown depths of the sea, each clinging to their prisoner.

Dawn peered down at her hands. Although the key was still secure on her, the gun was missing. She peered to her left and saw it resting on one of the thick chains close by. She tried to reach out for it with her hand. It was too far away for her to reclaim. The king watched her patiently as she struggled against the bonds that held her in place. She looked directly at him. Her wings glowed against his features. His skin had wrinkled and turned blue from the years of being under the sea.

'It appears we are at a stalemate child,' he spoke calmly. 'I cannot reach your heart at this distance. If I were to lift the chain, you'll reclaim that gun of yours. It's not a risk I am willing to take. We're at quite a predicament, don't you agree?' Dawn swam back, her wing keeping her from swimming any further away from him. Even if the chains were not secured to his arms, she was able to keep a distance between them of more than an arms-length. She stared at the various ties in his body. Bolts had been driven into his limbs, securing the chains to him. His left arm was behind his back, chains trailing from it as well. A heavy collar was secured tightly around his neck, chains extending from it also.

'It's quite lonely being here in the dark,' he continued, 'I could have you stay here with me. Having your wonderful wings brings a comforting light to me. Decades have rolled by without me seeing the faintest of natural light.' Dawn stared at him in horror. The cold clung to her like shards of ice. Breathing in water was torture in itself; her brain constantly telling her she was drowning, and her lungs now ballooned with the sea. She had made a grave mistake coming here, but in her panic, she did not know what to do. His army was above, but they could not enter hell without the key she held. She could not leave hell with herself being pinned. Opening the lock would only tempt fate with his escape.

'Please do not cry child.' He motioned towards her. Dawn pulled her free wing inwards, realising that she had been sobbing in a panic. Her wing glowed intensely, trying to keep herself warm, trying to keep herself calm.

'What do you plan to do to me?' she finally spoke to him.

'As I said, we are at a stalemate. What would you propose young child?' he asked her. She looked between her own wing and the gun that lay on the chain. She extended out her free wing, trying to grab the gun that way. It was out of reach though. Her trapped wing kept her in place. There was no way she could kill him and free the army that way. There was another option though. To sever the link he had to the world above.

'Free Donahue,' Dawn answered. 'Relieve him from his contract. If you did, you would lose your contact with the world above. No one has to die.' He looked upwards. His smile left his features as he did so. She shivered as the silence dwelled on. It wasn't what he wanted to hear. She had no idea how long ago the great war was, whether it was decades, centenaries, or millennia. The angel had within his steel fingertips a girl that held the key to his salvation, a girl that could kill him also if given the chance.

'I and he are eternally bonded. Our souls are entwined, our souls shall always live on. If it was possible for me to free him, then all three of us would die,' he told her. She thought back the to the last time she had spoken to Donahue, how he had cried out that he could not be saved, that he could not be killed. This is what he meant by it. When Dawn had killed him, his master was able to take control of his body as a feat to keep his other half alive. His smile returned as he noticed the gears turning in her mind, putting the pieces together.

'I have grown to like you Dawn, whether you have faith in my words or not.' He grinned. 'I could still bring back those that you have lost. You know the sacrifice that would be required.'

'No.' Dawn shivered. 'I can't trust you. Not after seeing Donahue. Not after seeing Lucy. Even if I were dead, you would have control over them. I would not want to impose that on them.'

'There is no such thing as true freedom but liberation. I can certainly offer that to them,' he spoke softly.

'I won't have you manipulating the people I love,' she kept defiant to her word.

'I suggest a negotiation then,' he continued, 'Instead of your heart, may I ask for a feather?'

'What does a feather do?' she asked in fear.

'As much as a torch would. It would give me light in this barren darkness. A small luxury for my prison,' he gestured. He reached his arm forward, the chains rumbling through the sea as he did so. He opened the palm of his hand and grinned at her. She kept her free arm curled tightly around her, unsure if he were telling the truth or not.

She began to question, 'If I do give you a feather, what will you do with me?'

'I'll let you slip out of hell,' he answered her. 'These chains may hold me here, but I am not truly a monster. I would not wish this upon another.' Dawn was confused at his approach. Above, he had thrown an army towards her in desperation. Down in hell, he had been calm and sincere with her. The conflict of language unnerved her. Her common sense had become increasingly quiet some time ago. Even her eternal eye could not tell if this was dangerous. She could sense no blindness.

'Those that I knew said you thought of yourself as a god. If you are that powerful, why do you offer me things in return?' she questioned further.

'I will not lie to you Dawn; I am incredibly fond of you. Perhaps, it is the loneliness of being isolated or that you wish to speak to me as a person rather than a fiend. Let me put it to you that when a human offers a service to another, it is always for a selfish reason. Even those acts they proclaim to be unselfish will still be beneficial to them in the future. I follow that philosophy that anything I offer is an offer that I myself will benefit from. I will benefit from your light, young child, and I would benefit from you being on the world above. You are incredibly special, a link between humans and angels like no other before. You mother was human and yet you are purely one of us. I would benefit more from taking your heart, but perhaps my own heart is no longer in it. I take a great risk child that after taking your feather and releasing you that you do not take that gun and strike me down with it. With me being so fatigued, I do not trust that either I or he will survive the blast.'

'Okay,' Dawn timidly replied, 'A single feather.'

'Extend your free wing to me, and I will pluck a feather,' he explained to her. Dawn extended her left wing. He reached out further. The chains groaned as he did so.

'I cannot reach you. You must come closer,' he beckoned her. She pushed herself as far as she could through the cold water. She felt her skin aching as her trapped wing was stretched. Very gently, he pressed his thumb and index finger to a strand of gold within her wing. The two stared at each other. Both were uncertain of each other. She looked back at her trapped wing briefly. A flickering thought of the gun came to mind. If things went wrong, she needed the gun. She knew where it was. As soon as he let her go, she felt compelled to grab it.

The mad king gripped her wing tightly, pulling her towards him, 'Your thoughts betray you!' Dawn panicked, rushing her energy through her wings. They flashed brilliantly, and heat rushed to the ends of her feathers as she tried to scald him. She watched in horror as his hand turned a deep red in colour. She was burning him, but his determination ignored the pain that was being inflicted onto his palm. He raised his bloodied left hand; his left arm was not tied by chains. He had managed to pull them out of his bones. The salt water had never allowed his wounds to close. In his left hand, he held a dense shard of ice, hooked and sharpened. Dawn pulled at her wing frantically, trying to free it from the heavy chain. The revolver stared at her from the ledge. The hook touched the skin of her chest. She screamed out as she threw her energy into the metal links. Her body was propelled, ripping her own wing, blood circling in the water. She swam sharply to the left; her hand clasped the gun and pointed it towards him. She felt the cold instrument digging into her chest. She pulled the trigger. A flash of light flooded her as the blast from the gun echoed loudly around them.

The city was alive with the sound of sirens. A helicopter flew over the surroundings, a light casting down into the twilight from the dipping sun. The innocents lay on the floor. Their cheeks were stained with blood, but their eyes were clear. Their backs of their clothes revealed where their temporary wings had been. Some of their chests lifted slowly up and down as they took in shallow breaths. The cure had been a success, and they had been freed. They were no longer possessed and no longer ill. Some had not made it. Some were slowly regaining consciousness. Whether they would remember how their minds had been controlled, it was uncertain at this point.

The sun was setting on them as the chopper flared up the front light and cast it over the buildings. The university library was lit up with a handful of silhouettes peering up at the flying machine. The light cast along the road and made its way to the centre. The floor shined slightly from the water on the ground. Part of the road glistened against a white light. At first, the pilot simply thought it was a streetlight that had regained its power. Then it became apparent that something else was casting the glow. The pilot stared as an alien creature stood there, magnificent wings of light cast from its back. On closer inspection, the right wing was torn and revealed a V shape. Long blonde hair fell over the person's features, her sight on one of the bodies on the floor.

Dawn knew the humans were watching. She could still feel the pangs of the cold nipping at her wet skin and the pain drilling into her wing she had wounded on purpose to be free. Her chest was cut almost in the centre. The blade had broken past her skin, and she knew it would scar her for life. She held the chain that looped through hell's key at a distance from herself in her left hand. In her right, she held an unusual gun.

The man on the floor was trembling violently, fighting for his life and taking in deep breaths. The light bearer held out the pistol that could kill angels, a single bullet remained in the chamber. She clutched the gun in both hands, and the key jingled as it was rocked forward on its chain. The man was curled tightly on the floor. His eyes opened slowly and looked up at her. His mind didn't register the danger he was in. His body was fighting away the death that had claimed him. All he saw was the girl he had stolen over a decade ago, a girl whom he had swept from the burning building and ran away with her. His lips curved upwards, joy overwhelming him.

'I'm so glad you're safe,' he smiled weakly at her. His silver eyes were dim, and the whites of his pupil had lost their shine. She did not smile back at him. Dawn had waited on purpose, waited to see if Donahue came back from the dead. Because as Lucifer had stated in hell, they were tied together. So long as one of them was alive, the other could be brought back. She couldn't risk the devil reviving in hell. His eyes widened as he realised what she was about to do. She held her eternal eye shut, blinding him in response. Her finger closed around the trigger. His mouth opened to speak, but no words came out. A loud bang echoed around him. His eyes shut sharply, screaming out as fear overwhelmed him.

For a long time he heard the shrill ringing in his ears and was certain death had taken him once more. Eventually, the sharp light left his vision. He whimpered as his eyes squinted. Dawn was no longer in front of him, vanished from sight.

From the corner of his eye, he could see the single dented bullet close to his head. Beneath it was a single fragment of a shattered and ancient symbol. His fingers groped for the small black object, staring at the symbol engraved on it. The ancient language had been cut short, but he knew what it belonged to.

Dawn could not bring herself to kill. Instead, she had destroyed the key to the mad king's confinements. Without a key, the mad king would never be able to unlock his cage.

Lightning Source UK Ltd.
Milton Keynes UK
UKOW02n0009230316

270669UK00003B/41/P